I0549276

Bone Dust

Other Books by
Bette Golden Lamb & J. J. Lamb

Books in the Gina Mazzio RN Medical Series:
Bone Dry
Sin & Bone
Bone Pit
Bone of Contention
Bone Dust
Bone Crack
Bone Slice

Other novels by Bette Golden Lamb & J. J. Lamb:
Sisters in Silence
Heir Today...
The Killing Vote

By Bette Golden Lamb:
The Organ Harvesters
The Organ Harvesters-Book II

By J. J. Lamb (Zachariah Tobias Rolfe III P.I. Series):
A Nickel Jackpot
The Chinese Straight
Losers Take All
No Pat Hands

Bone Dust

By
Bette Golden Lamb
&
J. J. Lamb

TWO BLACK SHEEP PRODUCTIONS
NOVATO, CALIFORNIA

Bette Golden Lamb & J. J. Lamb

Bone Dust

ISBN-13: 978-0-9851986-6-4
ISBN-10: 0-9851986-64

Cover Design: Chelsea Erica Lamb
www.behance.net/chelsealambcreative

Bone Dust

Dedication

To Shelley Singer and Polly Podolsky
two creative minds;
two loving friends.
&
To Margaret Lucke, who always
goes that one step beyond.

Acknowledgments

As always, our gratitude, thanks, and love to what
has to be the world's greatest critique group —
Margaret Lucke, Shelley Singer,
Nicola Trwst & Judith Yamamoto

Bone Dust

Prologue

Russell Thorpe stood naked, stared at the straight edge razor, open on the rim of the wash basin.

He was very still so his heart would stop racing, took deep, even breaths, tightened his gut.

Pull yourself together, Russell.

He willed his body to stop the tremors that always threatened to shatter his courage.

He needed to feel the edge of the blade on his skin.

Push down, his brain screamed.

Cut.

The blood oozed, leaving a lightning jolt of pleasure zigzagging through his groin.

He turned up the volume on his iPod. Music filled the room. The sound pierced his brain, banged out a beat that made him vibrate.

Blood boomed in his veins.

Blood ran down his arm.

Blood made him sing.

"Ah ah-ah ah. Ah ... ah-ah."

He danced from one end of the room to the other waggling his butt, letting it flop loose so he could feel his cheeks jiggle.

Bette Golden Lamb & J. J. Lamb

Bone Dust

Chapter 1

Gina Mazzio set her fiancé's picture back on the desk.

Harry, what have I done?

You've been gone for six weeks and I've missed you every day.

Her computer keyboard was glistening with her tears. She yanked hard at her curls. "Stop it!" But she continued to cry, complain to the walls. "Why is it so quiet?"

Her rescue cat, Tuva, heard her, left the safety of her hiding place under the bed, and came running into the room meowing like a banshee.

Another voice heard from.

The cat jumped into her lap; Gina stroked its fur. "Oh, I'm sorry I upset you."

The phone did its beep-beep-beep thing just to show how wrong she could be about things being quiet.

For one wild second she thought it was Harry. When she read the window on the cell, she was crushed.

"Hi, Vinnie."

"How's my big sister doing?"

"Oh, you know. Sort of shutting down, getting ready to hop into bed."

"Nicely said, tough girl. Now, come on, tell me, how's it really going?"

Hell, Vinnie, I don't need you sticking in your two cents' worth.

Her throat clogged with anxiety. This had to stop, she needed to bring herself under control. Whenever she thought everything was back in place, she'd start bawling again.

Vinnie waited, finally said, "Life goes on, Gina."

"Must you always end up being a brat? That little homily of yours only states the obvious." Bile was running wild in her

3

throat, rising higher and higher to accompany her anger. "Is that *all* you've gotten from your therapy, Vinnie? Well, hurrah for you!"

"Yeah, that and the will to keep on living, if you're making a pie chart. But it's still a day by day battle with this PTSD therapy. Not much different than when we lived in the Bronx. So just calm yourself, Gina Mazzio, and we'll both get through all our shit."

"I know, I know, Vinnie. I'm just feeling sorry for myself."

"I'm always here for you. Doesn't that count for something?"

"Yeah, yeah ... it does. Sorry."

"Why won't you marry that man? He walks around with his heart flapping in the breeze, just waiting for you to snatch it and give it a new home."

"I know he loves me ... and I love him. But marriage? Been there, done that. I don't believe in that arrangement anymore. And he knows it."

"You've been with the guy for four years, Gina. You're being way too stubborn. Why?"

"Do I really have to answer that?" She grabbed a tissue, dabbed at her eyes and blotted the keyboard of the computer. "Let me refresh your memory: my ex. That's why. And you already know that. You're not exactly a fan of Dominick Colletti yourself. Get it now?"

"Dominick? That's really, really old news. And I thought I was the fucked-up one." He gave a humorless laugh. "That's over and done with. A long time over and done with."

"It wasn't so long ago that Dominick broke parole ... a year ... and now nobody can find him. That's a big part of why I don't want to marry Harry. This thing with Dominick is never going to be finished ... not until he's dead or I'm dead. I can't have Harry in the middle of it."

Gina pressed the phone tighter to her ear, walked to the couch and plopped down.

Bone Dust

"Maybe you should come to one of my group therapy sessions. Have you ever thought about that?"

"No. It's something Harry and I have to work out together and the last thing I need is to sit around and spill my guts to strangers."

Gina knew this conversation had landed her into dangerous territory. The thought of her brother almost committing suicide was still too real, too raw.

"Okay. If you change your mind, let me know. I'm here for you, Gina."

"I know."

* * *

Harry was settled in a room in a brand-new Tucson housing unit built on hospital grounds especially designed to accommodate "On 24/7" travel nurses and laboratory personnel, along with patients' relatives or any other short-term visitors.

The hospital was on the northern far edge of Tucson, in an area of primarily gated retirement and senior citizen communities—people from the East, tired of winter snows, and people from the West, mostly Californians who had sold their expensive homes and set themselves up for luxurious, carefree living in less costly Arizona.

Harry's corner room looked out across mesquite, tumble-weed, and cactus-strewn desert, but chemical odors wafting through the room from recently laid carpeting forced him to open the windows, allowing hot air to blow through the room.

He'd opted for this arrangement over an apartment—it was dirt cheap and his only other need was the car he rented – a red Porsche Boxster, with radar, that chewed up the highways and helped him forget about Gina. At least when he was behind the wheel.

Maybe I should have stayed in San Francisco.

No! He couldn't take one more minute of hearing that bastard Dominick's name.

That man seems to be the excuse for everything and anything negative in our lives, and especially Gina's refusing to marry me.

And the craziness of her still thinking Dominick was in San Francisco. That was just off the wall.

Harry flung himself onto the bed. At least it was a full-sized mattress instead of a twin. He'd planned to drive around for a while and sightsee before he had to go to work. But thinking about Gina brought him down. Now he was tired.

Well, at least he didn't have to report to ICU for another couple of hours. He'd signed on for the swing shift, his least favorite hours, but the thought of spending evenings alone moping over Gina pushed him into it. He was about to pick up a book when there was a gentle tapping on his door.

He sprang up and opened it. A pretty, dark-haired gal he'd seen when he first arrived was smiling up at him.

"Hi. You moved in quite a while ago and I decided it was way past time to come over and introduce myself since we're neighbors."

Harry took her hand. "That's nice of you. I'm Harry, Harry Lucke."

"Abigail Singer, but call me Abby. Everybody does."

"Where are you from?"

"A little town about thirty miles north of the Golden Gate Bridge. A place called Novato."

"Shoot, Abby, I'm from San Francisco. I know where Novato is." She had bright eyes, and a nice smile. Before he could think it through, he blurted, "How about we do some sightseeing in my little Porsche? Do you work the swing shift, too?"

"Yup. Those are my hours." There was an awkward moment before she said, "So, that's your Porsche. I saw that pretty baby parked outside. I drool on it every time I pass by."

"Up for a ride?"

"Are you kidding me? I'd love to go."

Bone Dust

"It's a rental, but I'm already thinking about what it would be like to own one of those babies."

"Let's drive with the top down," she said. "We'll probably fry, but I want to feel the air on my face."

"You got it!" Harry said. "Not a lot of time until work so we can't wander too far."

She gave him a big smile.

* * *

The sun was menacing. Dominick was digging into hard pack trying to plant cactus. Always cactus of one kind or another. His hands had been stabbed at every job. It didn't seem to bother the Mexican crew he worked with. They just did their work planting, cleaning up, and smiling.

When Dominick squinted through his sunglasses, the world was so hot and bright, it left him breathless.

Man, this is killing me.

Standing hunched over, he leaned on his spade handle; had trouble even moving today. He was sweating out last night's blow-out with the guys—mostly his kind of people: laborers, road workers, landscape specialists, and yeah, they were Mexicans.

That's damn funny. Mexican specialists? More like grunts.

He liked to drink at El Peso, a local joint where most of the wetbacks frequented. He'd seen what happened when one of them poked his head into the other places. They ended up face first on the sidewalk.

Dominick eyed the others in his garden crew.

Sick of them. If they'd stay on their side of the border, I might make a decent wage. But they work for nothing and I'm stuck in the same spot. Get whatever they get.

"Hey, hombre," said the head man. "Get your ass back to work!"

"Yeah, yeah. Just catching my breath."

"Well, fuck that. Get back to diggin' those holes like I told ya to dig twenty minutes ago. Those cactus got to get planted today."

Work for dogshit and I have to put up with this dude. Well, at least he speaks American, not like all the others. Even says he was born here in Tucson, but I don't buy it.

Dominick ambled over to the spot where he'd been told to plant some funny looking cactus. Still couldn't keep the different names of them in his head.

Crap, they're all one thing to me–shit with fuckin' thorns that hurt like hell.

After he started digging, it didn't take long before he hit *caliche*. He grabbed a pickax and put his back into fracturing the white stuff. It seemed to be everywhere, at least in everyplace he had to dig. If he didn't break it up it was a sure bet whatever he planted would die. Not that he gave a damn. But if word got around that what he planted died, no one would hire him.

Even after a year, with each stroke, it was still Gina's face he was smashing.

A whole year since he'd broken parole, run away from New York to Frisco, and almost nailed Gina's ass. Stupid drinking, gambling, running out of money. All because of Gina Mazzio.

Yeah, my ex is still walking around while I'm here busting my balls to stay below the radar.

Thinking of Frisco and the woman he'd strangled there made his stomach flip-flop.

Don't even know if she died.

Once the tough layer of caliche was shattered, he dug out a generous hole for the plant and carefully set it inside trying to avoid the painful barbs poking out of its tough flesh.

One of these days soon when I finally have enough money stashed I'm going back to San Francisco and nail that bitch Gina once and for all. After that I'll get lost in Canada and start to have a real life.

Chapter 2

Gina's Fiat wouldn't start ... again.

"Come on, you she-devil," she mumbled. "It's first thing in the morning. Too early to give me this crap." She looked at her watch and hopped out to the street and popped open the hood. After a few minutes she saw the problem.

Damn distributor cap is packed with crap again.

She lifted a smock and her tool kit from behind the seat and started cleaning out the accumulated crud. Ten minutes later she was back in the car and hurrying to make up time as she headed to work. She rubbed the dashboard. "You little monster ... keep this up and you're gone, gone, gone! Hear me?"

The car purred back at her without skipping a beat.

After parking, she flew down the side streets to the hospital, slipped inside one of the back exits, and rushed to the elevator.

Jenni Webb looked up at her as she stepped onto the Internal Medicine Unit. Gina already knew what she was going to say, but Gina let her get it off her chest.

"The car, huh?"

"Yes, and don't tell me to get rid of it again, 'cause it's not going to happen." Gina pulled her keys out and shoved her large purse in the lock-up cabinet in the nurse's station. "Sorry I missed report."

Jenni raised an eyebrow.

"I know, I know, and that after two days off. All right already, give me the essentials."

Jenni scrolled through their patient list on the computer screen. "Mostly, what we have is the growing numbers of complications from the flu—elevated temps, severe headaches, chills, pneumonia. But all of these symptoms are in high gear ... really severe."

Jenni pointed to the computer. "You can scroll through the notes and see what I mean."

9

She continued, "Just to add more to the mix of URIs, last night's admissions added four unexplained GI problems. And another woman has nonstop diarrhea and vomiting in combo with pneumonia."

"I don't get it. We're barely into the influenza season," Gina said. "What's with all the flu complications already?"

Jenni shrugged. "I just work for the good of humanity, the same as you. As you can see, we're flooding them with fluids and antibiotics."

"Are the meds starting to work?" Gina asked, sitting and logging into another computer.

"The GIs are only getting Pepto Bismol until the lab work is in. I wish I had stock in that company; I'd be one rich woman. And while I'm at it, I'd also like a piece of the Tylenol action ... even the generic companies. One thing's for sure, every last one of these patients, URI or GI, is pretty damn sick."

Jenni looked up at the ceiling.

That always puzzled Gina who wondered what she saw up there that helped her think. "You know, I don't get why we're getting more and more of these patients with pneumonia."

"Yeah," Gina said. "I've been on this unit for close to a year now and I've seen a bundle of flu complications and an equal number of treatment failures. It doesn't seem to matter what the basic problem is, they're not getting better. Even treating some of them blindly with shotgun antibiotics ought to do something."

"I don't know. I, for one, wish they hadn't stopped doing that," Jenni said, keying again into her computer. "No more antibiotics without confirming blood work or cultures. Although if you ask me, this whole antibiotic resistance business lays right in the lap of the food industry pumping antibiotics into animals."

Gina went silent. Jenni stared at her. "Now don't you worry, I haven't been mouthing off about this to anyone who counts."

"What's that's supposed to mean, Jenni?"

"You know what I mean. I don't want to get a bad reputation like you, Gina Mazzio."

Gina turned her nose up to Jenni. "You mean like I used to have, smartass."

"Well, anyway, the team's out there finishing vitals. We can dish out breakfast for those that can keep it down as soon as you tell me if you heard from Harry."

"No, I haven't heard from him." Gina turned away. "I think he finally got the message once and for all that I don't want to get married."

"He's been gone about a month, hasn't he?"

One of the nurses' assistants gave Jenni a piece of paper. She immediately tapped into her computer. "I don't get it." She pointed at the screen and Gina moved in to see it.

"This is one of the overnight admissions. Diagnosis: Gastroenteritis, dehydration. And that mug of hers is as red as a Valentine heart."

"Interesting analogy," Gina said. "It's probably food poisoning." She looked at the screen. "I see they're running the gamut on her. Stool cultures, blood cultures ... all pending ... CBC says she doesn't have a systemic infection. But her temp's going through the ceiling."

Jenni looked at the lab screen. "Yeah, that's true. Look at her white cells ... right in normal range, and so is her sed rate."

"That doesn't even make sense. Has she done any traveling outside the US?" Gina sat down next to Jenni and read the notes. "Oh, it's Doctor Good-Looking's patient."

"Yeah," Jenni said. "Brad Rizzo's patient. The best catch around and he only has eyes for you."

Gina could feel her face reddening. "Oh, come on."

"I tell you ... it's not only that killer New York accent of yours, but you're Italian, just like him. What a deadly combo." Jenni tapped in a few keys and the computer brought up the patient's history. "To get back to your question, Emma Tyson hasn't been anywhere out of the country or even traveling around the US.

"Why was she admitted?"

"Duh!" Jenni said. "Emma is old, dehydrated, and it looks like she's getting a URI, too ... coughing her head off. Do we need more?"

One of the lab guys set his tray loaded with multicolored specimen tubes, tourniquets, needles, on the counter. "Good morning."

"Hi, Russ." Jenni barely looked at him, but she was tucking in a smile that was going to burst free at any second.

Gina had seen this phlebotomist a few times but had never really had much to say to him. She watched his eyes turn to gray stone. "My name is Russell, Ms. Webb. And you know I hate to be called Russ."

"I'm so sorry, Russ. I keep forgetting."

Russell grabbed his tray and hurried away.

"What's up with him?" Gina said. "I thought he worked nights."

"Not anymore."

"What's the deal?" Gina asked.

"He hit on me for a while, even went out with him. That was a really big mistake, but now I won't give the jerk the time of day and he's been really weird ever since."

"He seems nice enough," Gina said. "Not bad-looking with that brown wavy hair, although I like them a little taller." Jenni stood and went into the adjoining meds room. "Shoot, he just doesn't want you to call him Russ."

Jenni started pulling out her patient meds from the cabinet.

"What I'd like to call him is nut job."

"Why?"

"He owns a cabin in the woods and he took me out to teach me how to use a bow and arrow."

"What's wrong with that?"

Jenni turned away. "I don't want to talk about it."

12

Bone Dust

Russell heard what Jenni said to Gina as he walked away.

If that bitch knew my full name was Russell Owen Thorpe, she'd have a field day. Probably call me ROT, just like his foster sister did.

He was still fuming, but tried to push the nurse out of his head.

She'll pay someday and it won't be too long.

His mood lightened at that thought and he was smiling when he walked into the first room on his order sheet. The patient's name had a question mark next to it lightly penciled in.

Yeah. He'd drained her yesterday. She was pretty sick.

It was a private room with her bed near the window. Looking out you could see a spread of the city outside, that is if you were standing. She wasn't seeing much of it. All she could do was lie there and softly moan. Her pain made Russell's stomach churn.

Not only that, the woman was already looking like death warmed over. Her skin was as pale as the white of an egg with a criss-cross of tiny blue veins that covered the delicate skin of her closed eyelids.

There wasn't much time. Not only would the breakfast trays be handed out soon, he needed every minute to do what had to be done.

The draining was his big thing, there was also the thrill, the danger of possibly getting caught. But he'd been blood-letting like this for a year now and they still hadn't caught onto him.

He set his tray on the patient's stand, hurried into her bathroom, and grabbed the cardboard hat on the toilet the nurses used to collect and measure her output of urine. He ran back, set it on the floor next to the bed.

His movements were starting to wake her, so he quickly pulled out a 60cc syringe, an alcohol swab, tourniquet, and a lavender-topped specimen tube, all of which he put next to her on the bed. When he wrapped the rubber tubing around her arm, she opened her eyes and turned to him.

Her voice quavered. "Hello, Russell. Come to drain me dry again."

He gave her a fleeting smile. "Yeah, 'fraid so, Mrs. Tyson. Why don't you go on back to sleep? This won't take long."

She turned her head away. Like most patients, she didn't want to see him jab a needle into her arm. Russell tightened the tourniquet, readied the syringe, wiped her arm with the alcohol sponge.

Not bad. At least she has a vein that hasn't given out yet.

He shot a glance at his watch, knew he had at the most five minutes to do what he had to do.

She was dozing off as he pierced her vein without any trouble and drew out a 60 cc syringe full of her blood.

He kept the needle in place but he emptied the full syringe into the measuring hat on the floor. Repeated it until he had taken 240 ccs. In the last two days he'd taken a pint of blood from her.

He then took a small amount of blood and added it into the lavender-topped collection tube and put it into the tray.

He was breathing really hard now, feeling less sure that he would get away with it this time.

This could be the day I get caught.

His heart was galloping, climbing up into his throat as he withdrew the needle from her vein and planted the syringe in the sharps container.

Russell placed a cotton ball and elastic tape on her arm where the needle had been and turned his attention to the collected blood.

He carried it into the bathroom and tossed it into the toilet, covering the bowl with a thick film of blood. He washed out the hat, dried it with paper towels and flushed the toilet several times before the residue finally washed away.

Bone Dust

He was breathing hard as he straightened everything and had just put his equipment tray together when Gina walked into the room with the patient's breakfast.

Russell patted the woman's head. "Now you rest easy."

The woman's eyes fluttered open when Gina said, "Good morning."

"I'm not ... very hungry, nurse."

When Russell left the room, he heard the patient say, "Why don't you leave it there. I'll just close my eyes for a minute, then I'll eat."

"Let me help you get ready."

"Maybe in a little bit. I'm really tired."

Russell would have to hurry along now to make up for lost time, but he whistled as he went down the hall to the next patient.

Chapter 3

Gina rolled a tray stand closer to Emma Tyson's bed.

"Let me help you sit up, Emma?" she said to the patient's back. She pulled a tea bag from its wrapper, dropped it into the cup, and poured hot water over it. "Tea time, Emma."

This time when the patient didn't answer, Gina hurried around to the other side of the bed so she could see her face.

Oh, my God!

The woman was chalk white. She looked as though every drop of blood had been drained from her body.

"Ms. Tyson?" Gina gently shook her arm. No response. Her skin felt moist and cool. The patient was definitely nonresponsive. Gina tried to take a radial pulse.

Nothing.

She hit the patient's call button and yelled into the speaker after Jenni answered: "Call a Code! Tyson's vitals have dived—she's in shock."

Gina turned the patient on her back, grabbed an extra blanket from a bedside chair, and covered and elevated Emma's feet. The patient's carotid pulse was weak and thready.

A calm voice on the hospital PA system announced the Code, gave the location. Gina immediately began CPR.

It seemed like an eternity before the emergency team wheeled the crash cart into the room.

Gina stepped out of the way as they pushed a board under Emma's mattress.

One of the team started CPR again; the patient was tubed, bagged, and padded.

A scary strip of ventricular fib rolled across the EKG screen.

"Let's get those meds going," the leader ordered. Another team member pushed meds into the IV line; another keyed into the computer for Emma's lab work. "She sure as hell can't be hypovolemic. She has a better crit than mine."

"Maybe," one of the others piped in. "But she's whiter than the sheet she's lying on and her B/P is almost gone."

"Damn it, she's flat-lining," the leader said. "Come on, guys, get the defibrillator going. Start at 200."

The hum of the machine seemed deafening to Gina. The attending physician arrived and stood at the doorway to the room.

Paddles were ready.

"Clear."

All hands were removed from the patient and the bed. The old woman's back arched with the jolt.

All eyes were on the EKG screen. A flat line raced across the screen.

"Turn it up to 400."

"Clear."

The patient's back arched again, but there was still no cardiac rhythm.

Gina stood at the back of the room, out of the way. She felt helpless. Tears filled her eyes. The voices were just a blur of sound; she concentrated on the noise of the machines that might save Emma Tyson's life.

"Hit it at 600," the team leader said.

Everyone was silent after the last electrical surge.

Nothing.

"Call it," the attending said.

Gina looked at all their solemn faces.

"Time of death, 0800."

For most people the day was just beginning.

* * *

Later that morning, Gina sat down in the nurses' station—it always depressed her to lose a patient. She tried to remember anything special about Emma Tyson. She'd been admitted when Gina was off and they'd barely gotten to know each other. There'd been no time to establish that special nurse-patient

18

relationship. All that stood out in the short time she knew the woman was that she was in a lot of pain, or as nurses like to say ... uncomfortable.

Some obit: Emma Tyson, born in 1929, who gave no one any problems or was ever rude... or ... well... comfortable.

Is that what life is supposed to be about? Slip in and slip out, never make any waves so everyone can say how nice you were?

She pictured her own obit. It would read: *A loud, troublemaker from the Bronx.*

Her thoughts were interrupted by a hand resting on her shoulder. "I heard you were with Emma Tyson when she died." Brad Rizzo pulled a chair up next to her.

Gina looked into the MD's green eyes. They were filled with concern. "I don't know why I feel so terrible. I hardly knew her."

"You would have liked her."

Gina leaned forward. "What makes you say that?"

"She was a lot like you."

He gave her one of the sweetest smiles she'd ever seen on a man's face, and to top it off, a dimple appeared in each cheek.

"Kind of outspoken and pushy when it comes to making sure people get what they need," he said.

Gina took in the rest of his six-foot-two frame and didn't like the way her heart sped up. "I don't know whether I'm being slammed or if I've gotten some kind of left-handed compliment."

He gave her that smile again. "Why don't I pick you up for dinner and we'll discuss it further."

She was caught off guard. She took in a deep breath and tried to relax. "Look, Brad, you know I'm already deeply involved in a relationship."

"Sure. I know about Harry. He's a great guy, but that doesn't mean we can't have dinner together." He took her hand. "It's just dinner, Gina. I'm not asking you to marry me."

"That's sure as hell not a word I'm fond of."

"What's wrong with the word, dinner?"

"No! Marry! That's the word I'm thinking of."

"Why don't I pick you up at six? I promise I won't propose."

Chapter 4

Russell was walking into the lab when the Code was announced. He knew it was for Emma Tyson because of the room number.

No more pain, old girl.

He looked around the lab—no one was paying one bit of attention to the announcement.

The call was repeated: "Dr. Gray, will you please go to room one-twelve."

Dr. Gray. The Code Blue guy. Doctor Death.

The lack of reaction irritated him. It wasn't as if the staff didn't know it meant someone could be into their final moments.

Everyone at Ridgewood, medical or nonmedical, had gone through the emergency drill endless times. They all knew the euphemism for a Code Blue emergency.

Some of the idiot women were still gossiping, like nothing special was going on. It always amazed him how they could yak away, keep on doing their job at the same time. Russell had to concentrate really hard on everything he did, while those idiots could work, talk about celebrities and clothes as though they were the only things that mattered.

The manager came out of his niche and eyed Russell. It was time for him to start drawing blood in the front area now that he was finished on the units.

The out-patients were lined up to have their blood drawn for testing. As soon as he stashed his tray and supplies, he'd have to go out and meet and greet the hordes that came through the lab every single day of the week.

Actually, he didn't mind jabbing people in the arm. It wasn't that he liked hurting them; pain was always the enemy. What turned him on was the challenge of finding their veins and taking their blood.

A private joke: it was rare that he didn't hit the nail on the head. Every time he thought of that, he chuckled. The minute he

21

touched someone's arm he could almost sense where those skinny, blue things were hiding, even the ones that were buried deep under the skin—it was like being a Inspector searching for clues.

The Vein Caper.

He laughed at his own joke, but not loud enough for anyone to hear him.

The lab was his safe haven. Blood spinning, blood analysis machines humming, technicians looking in microscopes, all the special tests, the on and off ringing of hospital telephones, the constant sound of fingernails tapping on computer key- boards. And it wasn't only the machines, there was the hum of voices— patients, lab techs, lab assistants, all working, talking, consulting, moving in and out of the place, like the never-ending tide. And sometimes the constant buzz would escalate to a blast of sound that was almost deafening

Never a dull moment. Busy, busy, busy.

For Russell, it was the perfect place to not only hide in, but to work anonymously. Here he could be submerged in a viscous, burgundy delight. He could watch blood flow into tubes, spin into a dance. Watch blood, the healer or the destroyer, perform its magic.

Here, he was a worker ant moving anonymously in the stream.

Here, no one noticed *him*, noticing *them*.

Russell looked around again. It appeared he was the only one who wasn't involved in some task. It was like this world kept moving, while he watched from another dimension.

Sometimes he wondered who was real, them or him?

Well, that was stupid. He was certainly real enough.

Maybe they didn't pay a lot of attention to him, but everyone appreciated his skills with a needle. And they didn't make fun of him like Jenni did in Internal Medicine.

Bone Dust

Ever since I took her out to the cabin, she looks at me like I'm dirt. Should never have taken her there. Never. Well, I've got my eye on her. She better keep her mouth shut.

The manager walked in again, gave him an angry leer this time. Russell knew he'd better get moving.

He removed Emma Tyson's hidden lavender-topped tube from his tray and tossed it into the disposal bin for contaminated products.

He'd been secretly testing her hemoglobin and watching it dive for the last three days. Although Emma's blood test was reported normal, he knew her real blood values—she'd gone downhill after he started draining her, increasing the number of milliliters each day.

Was he sorry for her? No. Did he feel something watching her fade away? No.

She'd been in pain. Real pain. He'd put her out of her misery. She didn't need to suffer. No one did.

And someone always has to go.

* * *

Gina was scrolling through Emma Tyson's computer record. The woman had been admitted when Gina was off. But she felt compelled to carefully read through all the nurses' and doctors' notes; she could see nothing that stood out.

Emma had been admitted with a whole bunch of URI symptoms, the same thing that seemed to be making the rounds with this rapidly spreading flu infection. Older people seemed especially susceptible to it.

One look at the woman's color this morning and Gina knew that she was anemic. It was puzzling. How could her hematology have been even close to normal?

Too late now. Still, it doesn't make sense. Jenni is usually very observant. It's surprising she didn't pick up on the patient's condition and bring it to Brad Rizzo's attention.

Thinking of Dr. Brad, which is what his patients called him, tweaked her memory. She remembered their first interaction a year ago, and it was anything but pleasant.

* * *

"You what?" Brad Rizzo had screamed at her.

Gina wasn't used to being put down for her nursing skills and this jerk, who'd only come on staff a month ago, was making her feel like a fool.

"I DC'd her IV ... she was leaving in less than an hour."

"Did you have an order? Because I sure as hell didn't write one."

He was pacing back and forth in the nurses' station and it was just Gina's luck that four or five docs, plus most of the floor nurses, were there to witness her being read the riot act.

"Am I actually allowed to think?" Gina said, her hands on her hips. "The woman is leaving." But Gina knew she'd screwed up. She should have had the order before removing the IV.

"I planned on medicating her one more time before she left ... not that I have to explain anything to you."

He moved to the medicine cabinet. "Now open that damn narcotic box and get me 50 milligrams of Meperidine. *I* wanted to spare the woman another injection because during her stay here she'd been turned into a pin cushion."

Gina pulled out the medication and as she drew it up, she could feel her face burning with embarrassment.

He was right: she *had* screwed up. But she still wanted to deck the over six-foot bastard in the worst way. And no less, the guy was an Italian from New York. Talk about bad karma.

With my luck his family and my family are probably buddies from the old country—they seemed to have a million of those buddies. I'll become the brunt of jokes from both families for the next century.

That put her back to thinking about Dominick, her ex-husband, and the friendship of their two families which had been nothing but trouble for her.

Bone Dust

By the time she'd finished getting the med ready, she felt like her five-foot-ten frame had melted down to the size of a Munchkin.

* * *

Jenni wandered into the station and looked over Gina's shoulder.

"Poor woman," Jenni said. "You would have liked her."

"You're the second person to say that to me."

"Who was the first?" Jenni grabbed an alcohol cotton ball and began swabbing down the counter.

"Dr. Brad." Gina turned away from the computer and looked at Jenni. "So why would I have liked this particular woman?"

"She was cheeky ... and a royal pain in the ass. Doesn't that sound like you?" Jenni was joking, but Gina could tell there was something wrong.

"Hey, what's up, Jenni?"

"Oh, it's nothing."

Gina squeezed her arm. "Come on, something's wrong."

"It's that guy from the lab."

"Russell?"

"I don't know." Jenni pulled up a chair and dropped into it. "There's something seriously wrong with that guy."

"Maybe if you'd stop teasing him about his name you'd get along better."

Jenni looked at Gina and all her bravado slipped away. She looked really frightened. "He's been following me home for the past week."

Chapter 5

Russell followed Jenni from work again. He parked and waited outside in his fast-food-trash-filled Ford Ranger pickup and thought about his mother while Jenni went into the grocery store.

Yes, that bitch looks like my mother, with her dark hair and dark eyes. Even has the same nasty mouth when she doesn't like what I'm doing, and has that cloying sweetness when she wants something from me.

Well, the roll of the dice took care of Mommy when some drunken teenager ran her over, dumping him into foster care. Fourteen years old and fucked.

And where was Daddy? Daddy was unidentified, or missing in action. One or the other. His mother wouldn't tell him. And did it really matter?

Jenni was back with her groceries, packing them in through the hatchback of her red VW Golf.

He followed three cars behind her. Not that he didn't know where she was going. The most important thing he'd found out in the month that he'd tailed her—she wasn't dating anyone. It looked like there was no one else in her life.

No one to get in the way ... bitch!

* * *

After work, Vinnie, Helen, and Gina arrived at her apartment at the same time. Gina knew she'd stolen a parking place right from under her brother's nose. The little Fiat just slipped in before he could even beep. As he drove up alongside, he flipped her a birdie. With both hands she returned the gesture, then shrugged and waved him on.

Gina made sure iced tea was sitting on the table for him and Helen when they finally did grab a parking place.

"You little rat," Vinnie said. "We had to circle the block three times."

"You're younger, and as you always say, smarter, so how'd you get aced out, little brother?"

"One of these days—"

"Oh, will you two cut it out," Helen said. "Can't you ever get together without fighting?"

"Baby, I keep telling you, this isn't fighting." He slipped an arm around Helen's waist. "This is a Bronx hello."

"What are you doing here anyway?" Gina could tell Vinnie was definitely uncomfortable and would like nothing better than to head out the door.

"Harry called," he said.

"Why is he calling you?"

Helen piped in, "Gina, I've been your best friend for years. Harry called me because you won't return his calls."

"What's the matter with you anyway?" Her brother was getting worked up and his hands were flying everywhere.

"Give the sucker a break ... answer his calls." Vinnie took several gulps of his iced tea. "You know he's nuts about you ... which makes me think he's just plain nuts. But he took the job in Tucson so he'd be closer to you, even though he had a great opportunity in Chicago ... jerk turned it down." Vinnie began pacing back and forth. "And I thought my PTSD was a problem."

Gina's heart started racing. Her eyes found Helen's.

"Don't worry about him, Gina. Your baby brother is getting better all the time. The nightmares are still happening, but less and less." Helen laughed. "I don't have to clue you in about his job status at Ridgewood because you call his team leader practically every day."

"She's a friend."

"Not for long," Helen said, "if you keep bugging her."

"Listen, you two. I haven't answered Harry's calls because all he wants to talk about is getting married and as long as Dominick is on the loose, that's not going to happen. I can't let that maniac kill both of us."

"Harry's a big boy," Vinnie said, now talking softly. He reached for his sister's hand and squeezed it. "He can take care of himself."

"I'm not so sure ... not against Dominick. He almost beat me to death. The man's a killer."

"Well, at least talk to Harry."

"I can't talk to him right now," Gina said. "But I will soon."

"Let's forget about this," Helen said. "Come on over for dinner. I'll make a huge salad."

"Thanks. But not tonight."

"Why not," Helen asked.

"I have other plans."

* * *

The downstairs doorbell rang on the stroke of seven. Gina had been pacing back and forth in the living room for the past five minutes wondering why she'd agreed to have dinner with Brad Rizzo.

She could still see the questioning expressions on Helen and Vinnie's faces. They'd been dying to ask her where she was going. She couldn't say it. Couldn't tell them she was going out with another man.

Hey, I'm a big girl. I don't have to answer to them or anyone else.

Besides, Harry had been gone for six weeks—she was lonely, and all she wanted was some company and a night out. But she couldn't help it—she felt guilty about seeing someone other than Harry, no matter what she told herself.

The bell rang again. She ran her fingers through her dark curls, still not used to having longer hair. She straightened her blouse, tugged at her skirt, and spoke into the speaker.

29

"Is that you?"

"None other than."

Gina pushed the release for the apartment house entrance and met him at her door.

She offered to shake his hand while his green eyes took in all of her in one sweep. Lifting her hand to his lips, he kissed her palm lightly.

She turned away and walked into the living room, more to hide her burning face than anything else; his gesture had been gallant enough to make her head spin.

Gina offered him a seat. "Would you like some wine?"

"I'd love some, but we have a reservation at Rizzo's. We don't dare be late or my uncle will never speak to me again."

"That Rizzo's is your uncle's restaurant?"

"Yup. Best Italian food on the West Coast, right from my father's brother's hand."

"I thought you were from New York."

"And you think you know me," Brad said, laughing.

"Shall we?" He said, looking at his watch.

"Far be it from me to cause a family rift."

* * *

She didn't know what she'd expected, but a run-down MGA wasn't it. She couldn't imagine his long, lean body squeezing into the small English roadster. As she looked closer, she could see the car was apparently in the process of being restored. The dull, flat grey primer paint was a good indication it was ready for a new paint job.

"Sorry, the seats are kind of grubby, but I was waiting for it to get its turquoise coat before I reupholstered them."

After getting her settled, he came back around and slipped into the driver's seat. "Buckle up."

"I wouldn't have pegged you for an old car person," she said. "What year is it? Fifty-seven?"

"I like to call it a classic, which is what it is. But you're pretty close. It's a fifty-six. My parents left it to me."

"Left it to you?" She was silent for a moment. "Are your parents dead?"

"Italians are supposed to have large families, but my uncle is all I have left."

When they arrived at the restaurant, a valet held the car door open and helped her out of the MGA as though they had arrived in a Ferrari.

"Hi, Andy," Brad said.

"Brad! Haven't seen you around for awhile."

"You know, a lot of night work." Brad looked earnestly at the valet. "How's your mom doing?"

"It's slow. But she's getter better."

Brad took Gina's arm. "Tell her I'm thinking about her ... send her my best." He steered Gina into the restaurant.

They had no sooner walked inside when a bear of a man grabbed Brad and hugged him tightly. "How's my favorite nephew?"

"You mean your *only* nephew." Brad pounded on his back and laughed. "Hey, Uncle Carlo, I want you to meet a friend, Gina Mazzio."

"Hi, Carlo."

"Mazzio, Mazzio, Mazzio. Hm-m-m-m. A good two-z Italian name, but not one I'm familiar with. I thought I knew all the Zs in San Francisco."

"All my family is in the Bronx."

"Ah, ha! I thought I could hear a strange accent," he said. "Come, come. I've saved the best table in the house for you."

He led them through a crowded, candlelit room. The restaurant had a large dining room, but it still felt intimate and elegant with its crisp white tablecloths and perfectly aligned silverware. The server smiled at them and seated Gina. Brad pulled his chair close to hers.

"Enjoy, enjoy!" Carlo said as he walked away.

"What a charming man," Gina said, getting comfortable and sniffing a flawless lavender rose in a cut crystal vase.

"Unless he loses his temper." Brad laid a hand right next to hers on the table. Although they weren't touching she could feel the heat from his body.

Gina laughed. "Why would anyone ever lose their temper with you?"

"Oh, no! You're not talking about that day I was an idiot and yelled at you, are you?"

He placed an arm on the back of her chair, leaned in close, and spoke softly in her ear. "I did apologize. And that was a year ago."

She could feel the hairs at the nape of her neck moving with his every breath. "Some things are hard to forget." Her words sounded low and husky, and she had to force herself not to grind her hips into the chair.

The server appeared, stood next to the table, and did a half-serious bow. "Dr. Brad, would you like to order some wine now?

Oh my god! Saved by the bell.

Chapter 6

The room was velvety black except for the soft glow of light from a waning moon.

It seemed natural the way they moved into each other's arms. The first kiss was tentative and exploring, but with each passing moment, Gina was caught up, lost in his warmth, enraptured by the taste of him. Her fingers explored, moved across his body. She felt the hardness of his flesh.

I can't do this. This is so wrong.

She tried to move out of his arms, but a swell of pleasure sent spikes of heat undulating deep in her groin.

"Stop," she murmured, but held onto him even tighter, refusing to let go, molding her body into his while his hands slid down to her inner thigh, rubbing back and forth, moving, moving inward.

Gina sat up. She looked around, confused. Her body was still caught in the dream and the throes of pleasure. But she was home, alone in bed.

She'd never seen the face of her lover in the dream, but she knew how her evening with Brad had ended. Their kiss goodnight had awakened a passion she hadn't felt for some time.

It had been a beautiful evening of sexual innuendos, sparkling conversation, and just plain fun, something she and Harry had somehow lost along the way.

Harry wanted her to marry him, but she refused to do that as long as Dominick was on the loose. She wouldn't give in no matter how much he pressed her. As a result, almost every intimate conversation deteriorated into a fight. Some of what had been said on both of their parts would not easily be forgotten.

Their relationship had been damaged. Badly.

Now he was in Arizona, gone for more than a month, and she was here, alone. Dangling. Not really knowing what to do. This wasn't like their usual temporary travel nurse assignment separations, this was a serious rift. Gina wasn't sure they could mend this one, or that she even wanted to.

For her, marriage had been a disaster, and now her ex-husband wanted to kill her. Harry wasn't that kind of man. He wasn't a killer or a wife beater, and she doubted he would or could ever do those things. But why would she want to chance being in that mess again?

* * *

It was a beautiful evening, the Arizona sky alive with a brilliant glitter of stars. It took Harry's breath away.

He pressed down hard on the accelerator until the Porsche was flying through the night. Abby's hair blew straight up from the rush of wind that attacked them.

"Yahoo!" she screamed, her eyes closed, chin tilted up. "This is fantastic!" She raised her arms and spread her fingers. "Hey, man, can't you go any faster?"

Harry hit the pedal harder and watched the speedometer jump to 90 m.p.h. He checked the rearview mirror, but all he saw behind him was the dark night without a sign of the law or anyone else.

"Aren't these the best hours to work?" he said. When you finish a swing shift, the night still feels young."

"Yeah, and the roads are really empty on Monday night." She again screamed, "Yahoo!" and half raised up in her seat. "Look at this, Harry. This is our own universe. Man, I could stay up until sunrise. I don't ever want to go to sleep."

Harry's voice cut through the rushing wind. "I'm getting spoiled, used to sleeping in until late morning."

"I've always loved the swing shift." She ran her fingers through her hair, trying to untangle it. "You get the best of everything."

He reached for her hand and squeezed it. "Thanks, Abby. It's been tough being here alone. Just talking to you has really helped me through a rough patch."

Abby smiled. The green light from the radio was a soft glow on her face.

"We've been having a lot of fun together. I'm glad I met you." She scooted closer and laid her head on his shoulder.

It was the first time Harry felt like himself in a long time.

* * *

Dominick was back at The Peso, into the same routine every night after work—get drunk, go home either alone or with a new pickup. Seldom the same woman twice.

A girl had come into the bar and was hitting on him. He'd been buying her beers all night and it was late; he was thinking about ending the night with her in the sack.

She wasn't half-bad. A little too much lard around the middle, but her boobs were big and he liked that.

"Hey, Machado, who's the pretty woman?"

Dominick barely nodded at the dude. Someone he'd worked with a couple of weeks ago.

He still wasn't used to being called by that phony name he'd chosen. But his driver's license, even the false birth certificate, had been forged under the name of Dominick Machado.

Just another wetback now.

People thought he was Mexican anyway, with his sun-brown complexion even though he'd had to grease his hair flat to finish the disguise. His Italian waves didn't quite match his new name.

Shit! Even learning to speak some Mexican.

Now a year out of jail, he'd begun to relax. It looked like skipping parole in New York wasn't going to catch up with him.

Arizona suited him fine, and California was a hop, skip, and jump away for that time when he was ready to deal with Gina.

Sure, the Yankees and Mets were back home, but he could see them now and then when they came to play the West Coast teams. Mainly, he no longer had to put up with New York's freezing winters.

The people out here were pretty nuts, though. Always mouthing off like their opinions were the only ones that counted.

What he saw were mostly old people living in fancy houses. At least that's who his crew usually worked for.

"Hey, Dommi, how about we blow this place? We can go to my pad and get comfortable." She winked, looked at him with flirting eyes.

"Naw, not yet. I'm just starting to get a heat on."

"I'll heat you up like you've never been heated before." She accented her words with a wiggle of her hips.

"Yeah?"

She ran her wet tongue across her lips, back and forth, back and forth, then planted a hand on his knee and leaned into him.

He didn't know why, but he was irritated by the way she bumped up against him. Made him think of the woman he'd strangled. Like maybe this one was lying too. Or something.

Was she trying to pull a fast one like that Frisco broad— shilling for some back-alley card game, making him lose almost all his money?

He shoved her away and she almost went down on the floor.

The bartender said, "Cut that out, buddy, or we'll eighty-six you."

Dominick jerked to his feet, his stool flew out from under him. "Fuck you," he said as he walked out.

Chapter 7

The little Fiat monster purred its way through traffic without a hiccup. Gina arrived on time for work and was prompt for the morning report.

I see you finally made it to work on time," the night- shift team leader said.

Gina bit her lip and nodded.

"Oh, yeah," said another nurse. "I couldn't believe my eyes. I'd almost forgotten what you look like." Gina held back a sharp retort as several others gave enthusiastic nods.

Jenni gave her a look that said, suck it up, don't take the bait.

According to the report, the census had increased sharply and beds on the unit were close to being filled with more influenza complications. Nurses, and others on the staff, were starting to call in sick with the flu, and the hospital was now officially short staffed.

Another patient, in her mid-40s, had died during the night, from the same flu bug that seemed to be killing most of the senior patients.

Secondary bacterial infections were hitting older people the hardest—pneumonia was by far the worst offender. IVs just couldn't replace lost fluids and infuse antibiotics fast enough without causing another whole cascade of problems. Just a rotten fact, old people, with their weakened immune systems, weren't able to fight back.

It was that time of day when doctors began popping in to check up on their patients. Brad walked up to her as she was keying notes into the desk computer. He whispered, "What a great evening. I was sorry when it ended."

She looked up at him, smiled. "It *was* fun. And that's the first time I've been to Rizzo's. It really lives up to its reputation for good food and an intimate atmosphere. Thanks again."

That really sounded stupid—like a dumb, unsophisticated boob. How lame can I get? Four years with one guy and I've lost all my pizzazz.

She could see her attempt at being easy-going and cool wasn't fooling him for a single moment, but his eyes were probing for some kind of real reaction. Something honest instead of some meaningless line.

Can't deal with this man right now. It's too soon.

"Are you off this weekend?" Brad said.

"Well ... as a matter of fact, I am."

"How about we do a reprise."

She hesitated a beat. "Whoa, I don't know, Brad. Let me think about it."

He smiled, his dimples dimpled, and she remembered him sitting close to her during their dinner together. It left her feeling breathless and conflicted.

"No pressure. Think about it." He gently touched her shoulder and walked away. Her skin burned under her scrubs where his fingertips had rested briefly.

* * *

Taking care of routine patient tasks—breakfast, meds, assessment—took up most of the morning. More and more of their patients were succumbing to infections and turning critical.

Gina grabbed a moment to slip into the work room for some needed supplies. Jenni was in a corner weeping.

"Hey, girl, what's the matter? Is there anything I can do to help?"

"God, I'm such a wuss." Jenni dabbed at her eyes with a tissue. "It's really nothing, nothing I can't handle." Then she began to cry again.

Gina wrapped an arm around her shoulder. "Tell me. Maybe talking about it will at least make you feel better."

It all spilled out in a rush. "That guy Russ is still following me after work."

"No! Are you kidding me? *Still* following you? You mean in his car?"

Jenni nodded, blew her nose, and tried to compose herself.

"Have you gone to the police? Maybe they can help."

Jennie shook her head.

"I don't know ... this is getting pretty serious," Gina said. "If the guy's really stalking you ... I mean, are you really sure? He looks all right, like an average Joe."

"Yeah, he looks all right, but there's nothing average about him. At first I thought it was my imagination, but yesterday I caught him again. He was following me to my apartment."

"Maybe you need to stay with someone. You're not originally from this area, are you?

"No. I'm from the Midwest. Indiana."

"Do you know anyone you can room with for a while?"

"No. That's one of the reasons I chose San Francisco—lots of employment opportunities and I could get away from family. But mainly, back home there's a guy who not only dumped me, but married my best friend."

"That's pretty awful."

Jenni started crying again. "I had to leave. Everyone was driving me crazy with constant questions, consoling comments. All that kind of shit. I had to leave, get a fresh start."

"We could be talking about me," Gina said. "It seems we're in the same corner, needing to get away from old haunts. I definitely know the feeling." Stray thoughts of Dominick and Harry floated through her mind like unwanted chaff.

"What am I going to do?"

Think there's a chance that if you're nicer to Russell he might leave you alone? Most of these guys just want to be noticed."

Of course, it never worked for me.

"Listen, I'll never be nice to that creep again," Jenni said. "I don't want to talk about it; I can barely stand to be around him. That's why I mess with his name—I know he hates it, and I probably shouldn't do it, but it's the only way I can get back at him."

"Hey, Jen, come stay with me for awhile. I've got an extra bedroom and I could use the company, what with Harry gone—"

"But isn't he due back soon?"

"No. I think he might have signed on for an extended stay," Gina said. "Even if Harry were here, he would understand. It would be okay with him, no matter what."

Jenni gave her a tentative smile. "Well, if you really don't mind, it might help me get a decent night's sleep."

"Tell you what, go to your place after work, pick up some of your stuff and come on over."

"Thanks, Gina."

* * *

Gina snatched a table in a remote area of the cafeteria, propped two chairs against the table to save a spot for Vinnie and Helen. The three of them hadn't gotten together for a week and she particularly missed seeing her brother.

She breezed through the line, which was never crowded during the early lunch hour. She chose a large bowl of roasted pepper soup—her favorite—and placed it on the tray next to an extra-large chunk of sourdough bread. A dessert of diet raspberry Jell-O jiggled next to a large cup of black coffee.

She was halfway through her soup when Vinnie and Helen eased into the seats she'd saved for them.

"Hi, you two." Gina put her spoon down and took a mammoth bite of bread.

Vinnie started hammering at her right away: "What's this I hear about you going out on a date?"

"Oh, leave the poor thing alone," Helen said, picking up her meatball sandwich.

"How did you hear about that?"

Helen gave her one of her cynical leers. "You're not forgetting about the Ridgewood grapevine, are you?"

Bone Dust

She was really in for it. Vinnie hadn't even started his cheeseburger or the ever present French fries smothered in catsup.

"Have you permanently broken up with Harry, Sis? 'Cause if you have, you sure haven't said a word to me about it."

"You keep forgetting you're my *younger* brother ... I don't have to tell you squat."

"Now before you turn me into a referee, you two stop it!" Helen said, her mouth full of sandwich.

Gina and Vinnie glared at each other; Gina was the first to look away. She finally said, "Brad Rizzo is a really a nice guy and it was just an evening out. That's all."

Helen placed a hand on Gina's. "What's going on with you and Harry?"

Gina took another spoonful of her soup, stalling for time. She didn't know what was going on. "We're taking a break from each other, I guess. That's all."

"Do you still love the guy?" Vinnie asked softly.

"I don't know how I feel, Vin. It's gotten so all he ever talks about is the same thing—getting married. You know where I am about that. I only want to be with him ... I don't want to get married. That's obviously not working for him."

"But, dear girl, dating? That puts a whole new crimp in the situation," Helen said. "It's like you've given up on him."

"Look, it was just a night out. I needed to get away from my routine, needed some company. Brad was really fun to be with."

Helen whistled. "And quite the looker."

Gina laughed. "Would you feel better if he was homely?"

She got two answers at once:

Helen said, "No."

Vinnie said, "Yes."

Chapter 8

Russell was in his trash-filled Ford Ranger pickup, parked down the block from Jenni's VW. He was thinking about his mother while he waited for Jenni to get off work.

There were moments when he missed his mother, who'd had a cruel, nasty mouth ... unless she wanted something. She'd always been mean to him, especially when she'd been drinking.

Which was always.

Her being struck down by some dumb kid and dying was her final act of abandonment. It forced him to live with Todd, his foster father.

Russell looked at Jenni's little red car. It made him restless to remember how he'd been so attracted to her; she was the center piece of so many of his fantasies. He even took her out to Todd's cabin because he desperately wanted her to like him.

He snapped out his reverie as soon as Jenni arrived and drove away from the curb. He followed to her first stop, a dry cleaners.

She wasn't inside very long and came out carrying plastic-wrapped clothes on hangers. She was hanging them on hooks in the back of her VW when something flashed in his peripheral vision. It was like someone had stood up close to the car and was staring in at him before disappearing.

Someone was watching *him*. Again.

He got out of the car and took a lap around it. No one was there, but when he looked up, Jenni had closed the rear door of her car and was staring hard at him.

Guess I blew it.

It didn't matter that she knew. He still continued to follow her from three cars back.

Maybe a little worry will make her call me Russell. Treat me like a man instead of some loser.

He stared at the plaque on his dashboard: Russell Owen Thorpe. He'd installed it there not only to declare ownership of his pickup, but to remind himself who he was. A person with a name, not just any name, but a good solid one.

Yeah!

He finally got tired of following Jenni and, pulled off the main thoroughfare, left her behind where she was still crawling along in traffic.

He hit the side streets to Carlin's Mortuary. He had a 5:30 appointment with his old high school buddy, Eddy, who worked as a mortuary tech. Eddy said Carlin's was one of the most popular establishments in the business.

Must be true because Eddy never had any trouble getting what Russell needed.

Always plenty of dead bodies passing through Carlin's.

He checked his watch again. He was going to be right on time.

* * *

His friend was waiting at the back door where they took in the stiffs. He had on his grubby one-piece coveralls under a chest-to-knee apron, and rubber boots

"Hey, man. How's it goin'?"

Russell nodded, got out of the pickup and approached Eddy. The closer he got, the more the chemical odors made his nose itch. He looked at the package the tech was holding and frowned. He felt a blast of anger surge.

"That doesn't look like my order, Eddy."

"Yeah, well, I'm kinda busy. You'll have to trim it down to size yourself. Besides, the boss man cornered me, started asking a lot of questions."

"What'd you tell him?"

"Said I was giving it to a high school biology lab for study." Russell could see Eddy didn't like holding the package, tossed it back and forth between hands like a hot potato. "I usually have no trouble sneaking in your order, but after today ... well, I don't know. It's getting too risky."

Russell laughed, reached into his pocket. "Sounds like you did okay and it's an easy two hundred bucks."

"We'll see." Eddy took the bills from Russell and slipped them into a pocket under his apron. "It's getting harder and harder to find stiffs that haven't had hip replacements." He let out a snort. "Too bad you don't want titanium replacements. Got bags full of that crap from the crematorium, although the boss loves getting them."

Russell was getting light-headed, ready to puke from the fumes radiating off his high school buddy. "Can't make bone handles out of titanium," Russell said.

"Gotta get moving." Eddy placed the bundle in Russell's arms.

"Got it!" Russell said, grasping the package. "See you around."

Eddy stepped back inside the building, Russell hurried to the Ford Ranger and drove to his favorite drive-in. He ordered a Big Mac and a double order of French fries. In the parking lot he unwrapped the burger, crumpled the paper and threw it into the back seat of the SuperCab, onto the pile of wrappers from previous meals. He downed the food, taking huge bites, barely chewing any of it, swallowing large pieces of meat in large gulps. He washed it down with a sixteen-ounce Coke.

He kept looking at the package.

* * *

At his kitchen table, Russell put on his latex gloves. He carefully unwrapped the outer butcher paper and then removed the plastic that Eddy had used to wrap the entire femur.

The leg bone shone a skeletal white and he shook his head, annoyed that Eddy hadn't cut off the head of the femur the way he usually did. That was the part he didn't want. Now Russell would have to deal with it.

He turned his IPod up loud, put in his ear buds so the neighbors wouldn't bug him, and took a deep breath. Then he poured a glass full of vodka, downed it in two gulps, and wailed at the ceiling

"Yeah man!"

The crashing beat of the heavy metal music raged through him. He picked up a fine-toothed saw and cut the head off of the femoral neck.

Smooth as silk.

You won't have to worry about a broken hip any more, little lady.

He stopped for a moment, wondering how he knew it was the leg of a woman. He shrugged his shoulders and resumed cutting away extraneous fat and muscle chunks until there was only bone.

Now he had the part he wanted.

He went to a large cabinet, opened the drawer, and looked at the stored bone parts he'd been drying. There were several pieces that were almost ready for coring out the marrow before he could create a bone-handled knife that he would sell on the internet.

Of course, he never claimed it was human bone.

Why would he tell anyone that?

His foster father had taught him how to work with animal bones. But one day Todd suggested they try human bone.

That's where Eddy first came in. He would gather thigh bones or sometimes arm bones and they would cut them into pieces.

Since Russell had to cut off the head of the hip this time, it meant he would have to stuff it into a grocery bag, along with the rest of the tissue he'd removed, and drop everything into a plastic garden waste bag.

Later on when the streets were deserted, he would carry it to a Dumpster down the block and get rid of it.

Bone Dust

He smiled when he looked at the length of the bone he'd just retrieved. He would cut it in half, then shape each segment before drying. Each individually fashioned for style.

Chapter 9

Gina buzzed Jenni into the building and ran down the stairs to help her carry some groceries and a couple of small suitcases. They met about halfway up.

"Is that all you have?" Gina took the food and nodded towards the two carryons.

"I don't plan on staying but a few days. Actually, I almost called to cancel even though I know for sure he's definitely following me now. I saw him in the lot at the dry cleaners ... and he knows I saw him."

"That's terrible, Jenni."

They walked into the apartment, dropped off the groceries in the kitchen. Gina led the way to the bedroom where Jenni would be staying. "This is it, in all of its glory."

"What a lovely large room." Jenni set her bags down and stepped over to the curtained window. There was a line of magnolia trees planted along the street and a couple stood tall outside the apartment complex. "It's like being in a garden, with the tree's leafy spread right outside the window."

"Leave that unpacking for later. Let's have a Coke," Gina said.

"How about some tea instead," Jenni said.

"Good idea."

* * *

They sat at the kitchen table, Jenni with her cup of green tea, Gina with a Diet Coke.

"Listen, Jenni, maybe it's time you went to the cops. I have a friend in the police department who might be able to offer some help. The last thing you need is to be the focus of some weirdo like Russell."

"I feel kind of silly. I never actually caught him until today. Most of the time I kind of sensed his presence." Jenny took a sip of her tea. "Stupid, huh? Who senses someone tailing them?"

Gina laughed. "I don't think it's stupid at all. You'll never know the kind of hot water I've been in because of a gut feeling. Did he follow you here?"

"That's the weird part. After I saw him, he followed me for a short while and then disappeared."

"That only tells us he knows where you live and doesn't have to stay on your tail."

Gina's phone rang. As she went to answer it, Jenni said, "Jeez, a Neanderthal who still has a land line."

Gina was laughing as she lifted the phone to her ear.

"Someone is happy."

"Oh, hi, Brad."

Jenni whistled. Gina turned to her and frowned.

"So what have you decided about Saturday?"

Gina hated the pounding of her heart. "How about a tentative yes?"

"It's a step in the right direction. I'll talk to you tomorrow. And remember, I know how to fatten up an Italian girl."

Before she could respond, he was gone.

Almost immediately the cell phone in her purse blared Gershwin's *Rhapsody in Blue*.

Gina said to Jenni, "I guess you and I are never going to talk."

"Hi, doll."

Gina's legs gave way when she heard Harry's voice. She sat down hard onto a kitchen chair.

"Hi, Harry." There were several beats of silence before she said, "How are you?"

Jenny stood, waggled her fingers at Gina, and went off to her room.

Thinking about you," Harry said. "Wondering about you. Wanting you."

It had taken time, but Gina had finally sorted things out. Harry had not only left, but told her he was signing on for an additional stretch. At that moment, she'd accepted that the two of them were never going to make it. It had almost stopped hurting ... until now.

"Why did you sign up for more time in Tucson?"

"You know why," he said softly.

"Is it because I wouldn't marry you or that you ... needed to stay away from me?" Gina could hear the catch in her voice and her chest was so tight she could barely breathe.

"I'm pretty confused right now, Gina. That's why I planned on staying."

"Well, my head is a mess, too." Her throat kept closing. She could barely swallow. "Maybe it's time to be grateful for the four years we had together and let it go." Tears were running down her cheeks and she swiped at her nose. "Time to let us go ... move on."

"Are you sure that's what you want, Gina?"

"What *I* want?" Gina's voice was rising. "I never wanted you to leave. You slapped me in the face with your ultimatums. Marry me, or else."

"I just want us to be together ... maybe it's better if we skip that whole marriage thing for now."

"Oh, I'm not going through that whole useless scenario again: I'm crazy because Dominick is out to get me ... and that he would kill you too." Gina was shouting. "I'm just not going to go through any of that again. Do you hear me?"

"Yeah, I think I finally do."

Then Harry was gone. Really gone.

Chapter 10

Harry liked Tucson General, liked to spend his dinner break chatting with staff members from the various departments. But he was lost in his own thoughts, couldn't even begin to think of food or light conversation right now.

He pocketed his cell phone and walked in a daze into the cafeteria.

Gina was finished with him.

Finished.

He sat down across the table from Abby, who usually matched his dinner hour so they could spend some time together shooting the breeze. Not tonight. Casual conversation wasn't going to do it. He looked at her and he didn't have to say anything. She already knew.

Been crying my heart out to her, ignoring the more-than-friends body language, all because of Gina. Shit!

"I can tell from your face you called your fiancée."

"Yeah." He couldn't think of anything else to say. Then it spilled out before he could stop himself. "It's over."

"Oh, I'm sorry, Harry. I know how much she means to you." Abby reached across the table and covered his hand with hers.

"I really thought she'd come around when I left, but her brother Vinnie warned me ... said when Gina was finished, she was finished." He looked around the room to slow himself down. "Vinnie also warned me that I didn't fully understand Gina's fear of her ex, said I'd have to know the man personally to understand."

"From what you've told me, it sounds like you understood the creep all too well." Abby took a bite of her enchilada; red sauce dripped onto her plate.

"I just wanted her to get on with her life, not be held hostage by a bad past relationship." He couldn't sit still anymore. "Hey, Abby, I think I'll head on back to the unit."

She looked surprised.

"I know it's weird, but I've got to get my head into something else. I'm sorry. Maybe I'll see you later."

* * *

Dominick was back in the El Peso after work. Manny the bartender looked him square in the eye. "No more of your shit, Machado."

"Hey, sorry. Yesterday was a rough day."

"Yeah, man, I hear you. But we don't manhandle women in this establishment. Got it?"

"Yeah, *comprendo*." He edged onto a bar stool. "How about a draft, señor. And hit me with a shot of tequila, too." He took several crumpled bills from his shirt pocket and spread them out on the counter.

Manny waited a beat before he drew up the brew and placed it in front of Dominick. Then he poured the tequila and snatched up some of the money.

Dominick downed the shot in one gulp and drank half of the beer. He saw the woman he'd been with the night before sitting at the other end of the bar. "Hey, baby, how about I buy you a hit?"

"I had enough of your 'hits' last night. Get lost, loser!"

Dominick smacked his lips at her, then made suggestive sucking sounds. She turned away.

Just another Gina.

"Manny, how about another?" He was feeling the booze tonight, more than usual, which was good because he'd already decided he was going to get blotto.

The bartender hesitated before filling his beer mug and reaching for the bottle of Cuevo. He filled the shot glass to the top. He set some lime and salt in front of Dominick, who pushed them away. "Come on, man, you know I don't like fruit with my booze." He raised the shot glass to the woman. "Here's to ya."

She continued to ignore him.

I don't give a rat's fuck about you, whore.

"Hey man, if you're driving, maybe you'd better shut it down and head on out," the bartender said.

"Nah," Dominick said. "Hit me one more time and then I'll call it a night."

Manny set up the drinks and took the last bill from the counter.

Dominick downed the shot, gulped the brew, and stood up next to his stool.

"*Hasta la vista, putas.*"

He headed for the door.

* * *

Dominick climbed into the '95 shabby pickup truck he'd bought from a down-and-out Mexican. It ran fairly decent for an old bitch. He patted the dashboard.

You look like hell—fenders beat up and all, but I'm not going to the Ritz or any place special ... and your price was right.

His head was spinning from all the drinks he'd practically inhaled. He sat still and let everything settle down. But damn, he was starting to feel good.

Really good!

He tried to latch the seatbelt, but couldn't get his hands to work the two ends. He shrugged and headed for the highway yelling, "Whoopee, motherfucker!"

The highway was practically deserted. He accelerated until the speedo read 50, which seemed to be where the engine was most comfortable, the one loose fender stopped rattling, and the rest of the truck's body stopped giving off weird noises.

At least it's a Chevy, not some dumb Feeeaat like Nursie Gina drives.

He was belting out a stupid country-western song that he didn't even know all the words to, when he closed his eyes for half a second. With a sudden *whump* he was thrown into the steering wheel.

"Oh, my God!" He screamed in pain as his ribs cracked and his chest was crushed. Wild bursts of red, orange, and flashing lights blinded him. There was a blast of sirens with a buzz of voices echoing. Excruciating pain pushed him into nothingness.

His mouth barely moved; he heard a choked voice mumble, "Where am I ... who ... what ... don't ... hurt .... pain ... stop ... stop!"

* * *

Dominick's eyes were slits, almost swollen shut; when he tried to move, a scream curled in his throat. Someone was tearing his neck from his head while his chest was clamped in a vice.

He knew he was in a hospital—that putrid smell was all around him. His eyes hurt as he tried to distinguish someone across the room in another bed.

He guessed he probably had the same tubes and wires, sending out signals to make wiggly graph lines on two or three monitors attached to him—like in the movies when some poor *shlub* was checking out.

No. Not that bad. Not that bad.

Man, it feels like a six-hundred-pound Sumo wrestler is sitting on me.

Son-of-a-bitch!

He couldn't see where the nurses were and his pain was getting worse.

"Hey," he called out. "How 'bout some juice for this pain?"

Some guy moved toward him with a syringe in his hand. "Hi, Mr. Machado. I'm going to give you some medication through your IV line. It'll take away that pain you're starting to feel again."

"Where am I?"

"You got rear-ended. You were in a pretty bad accident. You've been lucky. My name is Harry Lucke, and I'm your nurse. I'll be taking care of you." With that the guy pushed the needle into the IV line.

Dominick's head started to spin again, but the pain was already much better. "Harry Lucky?"

"Why does that name sound so familiar ... familiar ... familiar...?

He was barely able to get the words out. "My neck ... hurts."

The nurse's voice was so far away and as he spoke, it faded even farther away.

"Your neck took a real beating in the accident, Mr. Machado. Hard to believe, but nothing was badly damaged."

What happened? Did he tell me?

The voice was floating in and out, in and out. "Wuz ... your name ... again."

"Don't worry about it now, Mr. Machado. Get some rest."

Dominick barely heard him. He was falling, falling, falling. Down, down, down.

Chapter 11

The full moon was shining brightly on Gina's bed. Well, really her and Harry's bed. The light was eerie, mystically beautiful. It made her feel less lonely.

Harry. What will I do without you?

He'd seen her through so many crises. And her brother Vinnie loved him. And if Harry hadn't bonded with her brother, Vinnie might not be alive.

Harry was the one who got Vinnie into a special program a friend ran for vets with PTSD. Vinnie had been in it for a full year now and the word suicide hadn't been mentioned in a long, long time. Living with her friend Helen had also given Vinnie a real sense of security. He was even back to razzing Gina, giving her a bad time like he did when they were kids.

She reached out for the pillow next to her, Harry's pillow. She slid it to her and hugged it to her chest. Then she wrapped her legs around it and started crying.

* * *

Russell had been working on two sections of bone for three hours. His shoulders were killing him and his scalp was so tight it felt like flaming fingers snaking through his hair.

He had to stop.

Pulling the cord from his iPod, he put down his favorite carving knife and stood up. When he yanked out the ear buds, it killed the heavy metal with its booming heartbeat. The silence left him uneasy.

The half-full tequila bottle reminded him of his mother, made him angry. It had been untouched when he started.

Downed too much of that shit carving away and listening to the music.

He stood on wobbly legs and looked at the two chunks of bone. He brushed the loose flakes off the work space and grabbed onto the table to keep from falling.

Bette Golden Lamb & J. J. Lamb

As the dizziness eased, he noticed he'd disturbed the piles of dust bunnies on the floor under his work area. A squadron of them, covered in bone dust, now marched around the room.

He tried to remember the last time he'd cleaned, or done anything to spruce up his pad. No way. Impossible. It wasn't a great place, just a studio apartment, but it was his. He'd clean it when he damn well pleased. As long as he could pay the inflated rent, no one was going to take it away from him ... dirty or not.

A flash of anger spiked.

If Eddy had cut the hip like he was supposed to, I wouldn't be near as done in. The idiot was right there, right in the mortuary, handling all those stiffs, and he was too chicken to do what he was paid to do. High school buddy, my ass. Just some jerk afraid the boss will catch him. Wuss.

He reached for his cell phone and punched in Eddy's number. It rang four times before there was an answer.

"Hey, Russell. Somethin' wrong?"

"You ever do that again and it's *your* leg that's gonna get cut up, ya hear me?"

"Hey, man, cool it. No need to get so stirred up. Wasn't much left to do."

"Don't let it happen again ... or you'll be sorry."

With that he threw the cell across the room onto the sofa; it bounced and teetered at the edge of a cushion.

A faint breeze tickled Russell's neck. He did a 360, taking in all the shadowed corners in the room. He grabbed one of the knifes from his kit, the one he'd sharpened to an almost needle-like point, and walked on tiptoe to the double-sized closet. He shoved the door to one side.

Leading with the pointed weapon, he popped his head inside, pushing all the clothes aside until he was satisfied there was no one there. Then he stepped into the bathroom and shook the shower curtain, looked in the bathtub, eyed the small window to make sure it was latched.

Bone Dust

Even though he'd checked both hiding places, plus under his bed after he came home from work, he knew the Presence was here and could breeze in through a crack at any time.

Just a crack.

It was always tracking him. He felt its vibrations as it flew through the air and sliced through his brain. That's what it always did.

Sometimes he thought he'd cornered the Presence, but like the air, it slid through his fingers and was gone.

The Presence had first come to him in a dream. That was the day his mom died.

In his dream he'd covered her mouth with a pillow when she was out cold drunk. That's all he'd done ... at first.

Then he'd smashed his hand down between her breasts, expecting her to fight back. She didn't move ... didn't try to catch a breath.

He hadn't wanted to do it ... the Presence made him do it.

The Presence also told him she was already dead before he used the pillow ... and maybe she was. Maybe she wasn't. The memory of the dream always confused him

When he woke up his mother was gone and the police were at the door.

"Run over," they said. "Too much booze in her."

Abandoned me. All because she was a damn drunk.

* * *

Russell hadn't liked being a foster kid, but his foster dad, Todd Grotten, taught him how to use tools, taught him how important they were, how independent you could be with them, and how possessing that kind of knowledge could make you very powerful. Yeah, you could use a Swiss army knife, but tools were what made the difference between just plain old whittling and shaping art.

Sometimes Todd's stepdaughter, Ellen, would try to butt in and copy what they were doing. Todd would send her packing. Ellen was only a year older than Russell but she could shoot the

61

eye out of a squirrel with a bow and arrow from thirty paces away. She had no use for Todd, or Russell.

Dad Todd, as he liked to be called, was a real hunter. He'd also used a bow and arrow and could bring down anything that moved in the woods. The two them used every part of the deer, as well as the bones. Nothing went to waste—Russell learned to carve perfect bone handles for throwing knives, pocket knives, straight razors, and almost anything sharp.

Todd tried to be fair minded with Russell. When he arrived after his mother died, he refused to go to school and Todd worked with him, helped bring his schoolwork up to par, encouraged him to get his diploma.

Yeah, Todd turned out to be a pretty good dad except when he got into alcohol. For such a mild-mannered person, he became a mean, hard-cursing drunk. He beat Russell's foster mom and raped his stepdaughter.

One night, instead of shooting the eye out of a rabbit, Ellen put a clean shot through Todd Grotten's throat .

Of course, it wasn't really clean ... the arrow made it damn messy.

Chapter 12

Jenni and Gina rode to work in the Fiat. Gina could see that her new roommate was a lot more cheerful than she'd been in a long time.

They walked down the hall to the station, both laughing about Gina's car and the antics of the temperamental Italian lady.

"Hey, you're actually going to be on time today ... again." Jenni elbowed Gina. "And your car ran like a dream."

"Hah, hah," Gina said as they reached the nursing station.

The night shift team leader, Angie, widened her eyes in mock surprise. "Gina, again? Two days on time? And here I thought I'd forgotten what you looked like at report."

"All right, all right," Jenni said. "Leave the Mazzio alone."

After the 11-to-7 staff left the unit, Gina and Jenni were going through treatment plans when Russell set his tray, filled with the lab tubes and other phlebotomy equipment, on the countertop.

"Good morning, ladies."

Jenni kept her eyes fixed on the computer, but she squeezed Gina's hand.

Before Gina could stop herself, she blurted, "Why were you following Jenni? She's staying with me, so there'll be two of us watching out for you now, you creep."

His eyes became slits. "I don't know what you're talking about."

"Just answer the question." Gina's eye did its twitch thing.

"I'm here to do a job, just like you. None of it requires that I talk to you about anything that doesn't have to do with the patients."

With that he turned and headed down the hall to draw blood.

* * *

Goddam! Why is that cow butting in? Jenni must have told her about the grocery store incident.

He stopped outside a patient's room, his chest tight; he could hear air whistling through his teeth. He clutched the tray handle tighter.

Of course she did. Well, so what if I was following Jenni. BFD. They have nothing on me ... and it's going to stay that way.

But he couldn't help being angry, and couldn't get himself to calm down. Gina had no right to talk to him that way. Her with that stupid New York accent. He was so upset his hands were shaking. He couldn't draw anybody's blood like that.

Look like a damn meth-head.

He pulled out his patient slips with the names and various orders. He scanned the list trying to make up his mind who to go to first

He found a name, and from her lab tests he not only remembered her, he knew she was pretty damn sick. He took several long, deep breaths, found the right room, and walked in.

The woman was alone and the room was very quiet. He walked around the bed and saw a urine bag attached to the post. The output was scant and it was very dark. The patient most likely was having some kind of kidney problems. The piggyback of meds hooked into her IV was only half empty.

He had some time.

He looked at the order slip and whispered her name, "Ms. Baker? I'm Russell from the lab and I'm here to take some blood." He couldn't stop his hands from shaking, and he was still angry. His heart was pounding hard and fast.

She grunted, "Uh-huh," and started to moan.

He swayed in place, thinking.

Too soon. Should wait.

His mind jumped from Gina to Jenni and back again.

He felt something ruffle the hair on his neck and his mind became crystal clear. He took a 60cc syringe from deep inside the tray and wrapped a tourniquet around the woman's arm.

Bone Dust

Gina didn't like the look in the lab tech's eyes. There was something off about the man, and it was more than just anger.

"You know, Jenni, at first I thought you were being oversensitive about Russell, but now I think you were right about him. He seems more than a little weird."

Jennie said, "You don't know the half of it."

Gina looked closely at Jenni. The nurse was still hiding something. Gina picked up her pen from the counter, tucked it into her scrubs. "I'm just going to check things out."

She walked down the hall, smiled at the nurse techs returning to the station to enter vitals in the computers.

As she moved, she looked into each room, trying to find Russell. Now, she had a really bad feeling about him, just as Jenni did.

She almost passed up Ami Baker's room because it was so dark, but she saw the flash of a white jacket as she passed by. She turned and went back.

Was she imagining it? No, it wasn't her imagination. The phlebotomist was startled when Gina stepped in. He had a 60cc syringe filled with the patient's blood.

"What are you doing?"

"What are *you* doing?" he said. "Are you checking up on me?"

"That's the second time today you haven't answered a question I've asked," she said, noticing Ms. Baker was starting to fully wake up.

"Look, I didn't want to wake her, so I drew her blood all at once to inject into the tubes."

"That's not how you usually take blood," Gina said, watching him squirt blood into the half-dozen tubes lying on the patient tray stand.

"I know," he said with a smile. "But it seemed like the best way to do it today." He took off the tourniquet and folded it neatly and put it back in his tray. "She has difficult veins to find. The syringe was the easiest way."

Gina stood there and watched as he applied labels to each tube and placed a Band-Aid on the patient's arm.

Something was wrong ... for sure.

* * *

Gina tapped her fingers on the desk in the nurses' station waiting for the lab manager to pick up.

"This is Rod."

"Hi, this is Gina in Internal Medicine and I have a technical question I want to run by you."

Jenni walked into the station at that moment and gave her a probing stare. Gina shrugged and Jenni went into the medication room.

"Yeah, sure. What is it?"

"Do phlebotomists usually collect blood with 60cc syringes?"

"Sometimes. Veins can be hard to snag. It's individual." The manager paused. "What's up?"

Gina was holding the receiver so tightly her hands were sweaty and slippery. "Oh, probably nothing. I'm not used to seeing blood drawn that way."

"Who are you talking about?"

Gina hesitated, then blurted, "Russell Thorpe."

There was only a beat missing before the manager said, "I know, that guy's really strange. He takes getting used to ... and I'm not there yet. But he knows his stuff. You know the needle-in-a-haystack bit?"

"What?"

"Well, he can find a vein in there, too, if there is one." The manager thought that was pretty funny.

Gina was not laughing.

Chapter 13

Dominick was in a long, dark tunnel ... something, someone chasing him. No! He was chasing someone, something. Running, running so hard he could barely breathe.

Up ahead, a slim line of piercing light drew him in. The closer he got, the wider the stretch of blinding light. He opened his eyes, snapped them shut.

"Turn it off," he shouted and tried to turn away.

"Mr. Machado! You're in the hospital. If you don't lie quietly, you're going to hurt yourself."

Dominick's head throbbed, pounded. He drifted in and out of consciousness, but with each awakening things become a bit clearer.

Left El Peso loaded. Must have done something stupid while driving. How long have I been here?

Doctor talking to me ... something about my neck. Don't know about that, but my chest sure as shit feels all weird.

He tried to move, but felt glued to the bed. He rolled his eyes around and saw the edges of some kind of neck brace that had him trapped.

He snaked a hand up, moved it across his shoulders, touched the brace, and then felt thick bands of tape wrapped around his upper body. Every time he took a breath there was piercing pain, but he knew that without the tape he wouldn't be able to breathe at all; his ribs had been cracked before, more than once.

What did he say? That doctor? What was it he said? I was lucky ... lucky ... his name's Lucky. Harry Lucky. Not a doctor, a damn male nurse.

Heard that voice before. Where?

His mind jumped back to Frisco ... hiding ... watching Gina's ancient Fiat ... seeing her get into it ... some dude bending over, kissing her.

67

He remembered following her to her apartment, looking at the names on the lobby mailboxes. The anger came back with the visualization of the two names opposite on the bell-push button: Gina Mazzio & Harry Lucke.

He forced his eyes open, tried to ignore the harshness of the lights. Finally, the piercing eased and his eyes adjusted; he could focus on the name tag hanging from a cord looped around the nurse's neck.

Harry Lucke, RN was standing next to the bed, looking down at him.

Yeah, that's the guy that was living with Gina.
Right here, served up on a silver platter.

Chapter 14

Brad Rizzo sat at the telephone doing a should I, or shouldn't I while thinking about calling Gina Mazzio.

He knew he was in deep trouble the first time he even considered asking her out. He'd made it a point to avoid dating women from Ridgewood, knew it could turn into a real nightmare. Or at the very least problematic.

Way too much potential for messy and embarrassing situations at work.

His attitude had a firm foundation, started when he got into a tangled relationship with one of the pediatricians a few years back. It not only ended badly, it left him feeling gun-shy about any romantic involvement. He didn't blame her for leaving; one of them had to go. They'd both become nothing but raging egos that fought without an ounce of give or take.

When she'd left Ridgewood and headed for a Southern California hospital, he'd closed the door on the memories, left all his regrets behind, and dove into his work. Of course, there'd been a very brief fling with a nurse who was now camping out with Gina—Jenni Webb. But that hadn't gone anywhere.

Now, watching Gina Mazzio had become a habit. He'd eyed her in the cafeteria; he was drawn to her, couldn't help himself. Not beautiful in the classical sense, but striking, with her dark hair and dark eyes. More than that, she seemed so animated, so alive. When he heard rumors that Harry was out of the picture, he jumped in.

That alone surprised him.

He listened to the phone ring several times and just before it would probably go to message mode, Gina picked up.

"So how was your day?" Brad said, caught off guard.

"Hi, Brad. Jenni and I were fixing dinner."

"Well, before you get too entrenched, how about we go out for some deli? An ex-New Yorker like you should love that stuff."

He held his breath before she answered.

"Well, it's been a long time since I had some really *good* deli."

"Are you kidding me?" He knew he had her interested. "You haven't been to Schlomo's? Well, let's fix that right now. It's even there in your part of town."

* * *

When the bell rang, Gina turned to Jenni. "You sure you're okay with being alone?"

"I'm fine. Go have some fun." Jenni pointed a finger at her. "But stay out of trouble, Ms. Mazzio. You haven't been a single woman for a long time."

"Between you, my brother, and Helen, I'm suddenly being treated like a teenager."

She waved goodbye and hurried down the steps to open the front door to the apartment complex. Brad was all smiles, dressed in jeans, sports shirt, and bulky, rust-colored wool sweater.

"Hi, Brad. You *would* pick the one thing I can't turn down."

"You know, I knew I'd reel you in by dangling a little chopped liver as bait."

The MGA was double-parked in front. She dropped into the seat and started laughing.

"What may I ask is so funny?" he said.

"I still can't wrap my mind around your driving such a small car."

"My small mind finds it a fine companion."

It took them several circuits around three or four adjacent blocks in the Sunset before Brad could find a parking place. Finally, they snagged a spot about four blocks away.

Bone Dust

At the restaurant, the aromas knocked her over from the moment they walked in the door.

A surly hulk of a man in white coat and pants greeted them from behind the counter, if you could call it a greeting.

"You gonna eat somethin' here, or just stand around blockin' my door so payin' customers can't get in?"

Brad bent over and whispered in her ear. "That's Schlomo. Don't take it personally ... he's that way with everybody."

"Hey, I was raised with that kind of guy," she said, laughing. "But I've never been able to figure out why they're so gruff all the time."

Gina felt like a little kid back in the Bronx, looking through the glass front of a cooler filled with every kind of deli imaginable.

Not only that, there were trays piled high with half-sour pickles, the kind you can only find in a Jewish deli—the *right* kind.

"When I was a kid," she said, "I would run into a deli, buy a pickle, and walk down the street chomping on it."

"Yeah, I saw kids like that in New York; they're still doing it."

It took Schlomo several minutes to take their orders. Gina went for a chopped chicken liver sandwich on corn rye, with a large side of potato salad and three large sour pickles"

"Three?" Brad said.

"And I may have more, so be prepared."

Brad ordered pastrami on Russian rye with a side of kishka, better known as stuffed derma.

They could see their sandwiches being made—perhaps constructed was a better word—behind the counter. Schlomo created sandwiches that were so stuffed with food they looked more like mountains by the time he was finished. And all without once breaking into a smile, or changing expression.

"Chicken liver! Pastrami!" Schlomo yelled at them when he was finished.

"I'll take a bottle of Dr. Brown's cream soda, if you have it, please," Gina said.

"Same for me," Brad said. He picked up the plates with their huge sandwiches and carried them to a table in the back, but he had to return for the cream sodas and a large pile of napkins. Gina carried the plate of kishka.

"Wow!" Gina said. "Stuffed derma. That's an acquired taste, and I know you're not a transplanted New Yorker."

"I caught a residency at Mount Sinai Hospital." He filled his fork with derma and offered her a bite, took one himself, and gave her an OMG kind of eye-roll. "In four years I managed to get gobs of deli and Italian food. I liked to go to Central Park and pig out—no joke intended. Best people-watching spot in town."

"That *is* pretty close to Mount Sinai."

"What have you got against marriage, Gina?"

"Whoa!" she almost choked taking in a huge chunk of pickle. "That's a loaded question ... and from out of nowhere. Are you trying to ruin a fun evening, Doctor?"

"Hey, doctors and nurses ask all kinds of personal questions. And they flow from our mouths faster than a flash flood." He took a large bite of his sandwich, chewed on it slowly, and swallowed. "You don't have to answer. You know that."

"That's all I've been thinking about recently because marriage seems to be the focus of Harry's entire existence."

"You've been with him for a long time. It's not an unnatural thought if you love someone." He looked deeply into her eyes. "What's the truth, Gina?"

Gina finished her sandwich, dabbed at her mouth. "The truth?" She started picking at one of the stray napkins, not really knowing how to answer him. Finally, she just blurted it out. "The truth is, I probably can't have children and I think that not having them would be a real disappointment for Harry."

Brad reached across the table, took her hand. "Are you sure that's Harry's take?"

"I know him ... it would eat at him." Gina sat back in her chair. The rickety wood squeaked every time she moved.

"Why don't you tell him?"

"I have, but like most people, he hears only what he wants to hear. He thinks modern medicine can do anything. I don't have the same opinion."

"You don't?"

"Why are we talking about this, Brad?"

He took the last bite of his sandwich. Gina could see he was a very intense, measured man, the kind who probably never jumped into anything without thinking about every aspect, every possibility—really not unlike a lot of internal medicine docs she'd known throughout her career.

"I want to see more of you, Gina." He squeezed her hand. "You know?"

She looked into his intense green eyes and his smiling face, and for the first time in a long stretch of time Gina felt lighthearted.

Bette Golden Lamb & J. J. Lamb

Russell slammed the door behind him, stomped into his apartment and flung his backpack across the room. It hit the sofa and bounced onto the floor.

"That bitch! That fucking bitch!"

He looked around and realized he'd been screaming the words. He'd also begun to talk to himself out loud at work, sometimes in the bathroom.

What's with you, idiot? You're going to get caught if your mouth keeps flapping. Keep it shut, for crissake. If you don't get smart, you're going to get nailed like you almost did this morning when that nurse walked in on you.

That damn nurse, Gina Mazzio, had been jumping around in his head all day. He knew she didn't believe him this morning. She'd seen right through him with that large, blood-filled syringe in his hand.

Man, two minutes earlier and she would have nailed me red-handed emptying drained blood into the toilet. Damn good thing I had those tubes ready. She must have been the one who called Rod ... the bitch. Forced me to sit through another of his stupid lectures.

"Don't rile the nurses."

"Not smart to get on the bad side of the nurses."

Fuck the nurses! What does Rod know, all comfortable in his little spot in the world? He may be the manager, but he sucks.

"Thinks he can get away with telling *me* how to draw blood ... got another thing coming."

He dug his nails into his arm. "Stop it! Stop talking out loud!"

Russell paced around the room, heart thrumming. Nothing changed that feeling of raw malice he kept gagging on, nothing got rid of the pain in his chest. He tore off his shirt; two of the buttons popped off and flew out of sight.

"Stop it! Stop it!"

A current of cold air circled around him.

But nothing stopped ... stopped his head from exploding, stopped his stomach from turning into a flaming furnace.

He ran into the bathroom, dropped to his knees, and vomited his fast food dinner into the toilet. The retching continued until all that was left were painful dry heaves.

On watery legs, he went to the sink, rinsed his mouth, and looked up into the mirror at his eyes. There was no trace of his violent anger. It had drained from him, flushed away with his dinner.

Russell took off the rest of his clothes, piled them on the toilet lid, and stepped into the shower. He surrendered to the water's hot, stinging fingers. He rotated in place, allowing the moist heat to find and slide across every part of his body.

He pictured the smart-ass nurse's mouth while he soaped and rinsed every inch of his body, hands moving across his chest, down his sides, along his thighs, around his ass, back and forth on his cock. He visualized her spread out nude before him, her legs wide open, his cock entering her as smooth as silk. He rode up and down, up and down ... slowly at first, then faster, then faster and harder until he could hear her screams.

Water off, he stepped out of the shower to dry himself. The steam-fogged mirror held a smudged view of his dark, searching eyes

"No!"

He saw a dim image of his mother; she was holding a bottle of cheap gin.

I can't help it, Russie. Don't look at me that way. I love you. I love you.

"Sure, Mom. You love me. Sure."

* * *

Two short lengths of bone lay side by side on Russell's work table. He picked up a sheet of sandpaper and tried to smooth the end of one bone.

Bone Dust

It hadn't dried out thoroughly and was way too porous for his use, not the young bone he always demanded of Eddie. It was never going to make a strong knife handle. It would never be right.

"Screwed me over."

He punched Eddie's number into his cell phone.

"Yeah?"

"You owe me two hundred dollars worth of bone."

"Don't owe you nothin'. You got the bone."

"This is some old geezer's lifeless bone."

"So what's the fucking big deal? And stop calling me all day here or we're finished."

"Get me another bone."

"Sure thing, Russell ... but it's still gonna cost you another two bills. Take it, or leave it."

"Just do it!"

Chapter 16

Dominick was awakened by the clatter of ICU equipment and the beeping of instruments, but especially the sharp aroma of alcohol that made his nostrils sting.

More than anything, it was that voice.

He kept his eyes closed, but his focus was on Harry Lucke, his ex-wife's boyfriend.

Dominick had secretly watched the dude in action—taking care of patients, talking to other nurses. Sure as shit, he was one of those good guys Gina always used to talk about.

Yeah, like those medical people were some kind of heroes. What a bunch of crap. Hell, I listened to her run through all that hype when it was just them doing their job.

Nobody had ever called Dominick a hero.

Oh, that's right, he was *going* to be a hero, a Yankee. Didn't make it, though, because his bitchy wife ruined it for him.

So what if I drank a little, gambled a little? What's that got to do with anything? I could still work the ball. Isn't that what counts? It was her nagging that distracted me. That's what did me in.

Hell, maybe I can't get to Gina right now, but taking care of Harry Lucke will be a close second.

Harry was talking to another nurse. They were both standing by his bed. Dominick played possum and listened:

"I hear he plowed into a car and then got rear-ended," Harry said. "And no seat belt. Man's lucky to be alive."

"No, you're Lucke. He just lucked out."

"Aren't you a cute little thing?" Harry's voice was sharp. "Let's just get on with the change of shift report."

"All right, already. Lighten up, dude."

"Sorry, end of shift exhaustion," Harry said. "Anyway, the only reason he's still in ICU is there's no bed for him in Internal Medicine. He probably could use another day for meds and observation, but I wouldn't be surprised if they discharged him right from ICU tomorrow.

"Got it."

"Vitals are stable, have been most of today," Harry said. "That collar is more for comfort. Scans were basically negative, although I'll bet his neck took a helluva beating. Cracked four ribs ... miracle they didn't splinter and puncture his lungs."

"I see he's bound up."

"Got to keep him breathing, especially since he's on heavy-duty pain medication. I've never broken any ribs myself, but I know from patients that taking a deep breath hurts like hell."

"Yeah, again, I got it."

"Then I'm out of here," Harry said. "Hope things stay quiet for you."

They may stay quiet for her, loser, but things are gonna heat up for you when I get out of here.

* * *

It was the end of shift and Abby Singer was sitting on the hospital stoop waiting for Harry. She usually got out before he did. Orthopedics was a little more predictable than ICU.

In the few weeks she'd known Harry, it hurt to even be apart from him. She'd fallen for him.

Hard.

She knew he saw her only as a friend, and why on earth would she even consider having a serious relationship with someone on the rebound?

For some reason, she'd shoved all logic aside and continued not only to spend all her free time with him, but to allow herself to hope things would change between them.

Besides, he was fun, and adventurous, and when she first started hanging out with him, she didn't mind being an impartial listener to his feelings about ex-girlfriend Gina. He seemed to be what she called a deep guy, but solid and real. Abby didn't have a chance to meet too many men like that.

She hadn't been thinking about a long-term relationship of any kind. But here she was, falling in love with Harry Lucke.

That Gina has got to have a loose screw in her head. The man is crazy about her and she won't seal the deal. Some people don't know a good thing even when it's standing right in front of them.

Harry walked out of the hospital front entrance, saw her, waved, and gave her that wonderful smile of his. "Hey, how was *your* day?"

"Pretty routine. A couple of hip fractures, a fractured arm. The rest were post-op hip replacements." Abby shrugged. "It never ends."

"Ready for a ride in the Porsche?"

Abby hesitated. She really wanted to talk to him about the two of them.

Was their relationship going anywhere? Could she continue to be only a friend? At least get it all out in the open. It was time. Maybe past time.

"I'm still hungry," she said. "I ate dinner hours ago. How about we grab a taco and a beer at Picos. Is that all right with you?" She crossed her fingers behind her back as they headed for the Porsche.

* * *

Picos was a small Mexican restaurant a couple of blocks from the hospital. It was rare to find any place to eat at this hour, but they were open and served food until 2:00 a.m. Of course it was the bar that brought in the money, but they managed to get enough midnight snackers to make wee hours food service worthwhile.

Harry led Abby to a corner booth that two people were just leaving. They stood and waited while a waiter rushed in to clean off the dirty dishes, wipe down the table, and reset the silverware.

"*Buenos noches, mis amigos.*" The man handed them menus and hurried off.

"I've never seen it this busy at this hour," Harry said as they slipped into the booth.

He could tell Abby had something on her mind and he sensed what it was. What he didn't know was how he was going to handle it.

They each ordered a draft beer and supersize chicken tacos. The waiter had no sooner left than Abby said, "I need to talk to you, Harry."

"Sure."

The change of her expression from carefree to sad-eyed and questioning made Harry shift in his seat with worry. Before she could say anything more, the tacos and two Dos Equis arrived. Harry could tell she was as happy as he was for the momentary distraction.

Harry loaded his food with Tabasco while Abby used the green sauce that came in a little bowl.

"Man, this is really great," Harry said, biting off a large chunk and dribbling sauce onto the plate. "Nothing neat about eating a taco." He laughed.

Abby downed all of her food with a sense of urgency, as though she hadn't eaten in days. Finishing her last bite, she splattered salsa on her green scrub top and tried to wipe it away with a napkin.

"You must be kidding if you think attacking that juicy stuff is going to do anything but spread it around." Harry was laughing so hard he had to put down his half-finished taco before he spilled it everywhere.

Abby looked up at him, but she wasn't smiling. She pushed her plate aside, wiped her mouth, and without a word left the booth and ran out the door.

Harry was stunned. He quickly pulled some bills from his wallet, threw them on the table, and took off.

He could see her in the distance, running so hard she was already half a block away.

He fired up the Porsche and drove after her. When they were side by side, he called out, "Abby! Come on! Get in the car, please."

She stopped, and he reached across to open the passenger door. She just stood there, not moving.

Her shoulders lifted, she sighed, stepped up to the car, dropped down into the leather bucket seat. Seatbelt fastened, she turned to face him, eyes desperate. Tears were rolling down her cheeks.

Harry reached over and folded her into his arms.

Bette Golden Lamb & J. J. Lamb

Lena Dobbs had been feeling ill for the past two days, but swallowing aspirin helped shove the muscle aches and fatigue aside. She refused to let it hang foremost on her mind. She was used to pushing herself to the limit, no matter what or how she felt. A little bit of a temperature and a cough wasn't going to kill her, especially when she had finals staring her in the face. She knew the flu was running rampant, but she could not, would not accept that she was really sick.

She checked her iPhone to see if there were any new messages, but there it sat, the same one from her boyfriend, Benjamin—the one that she'd been ignoring all morning. She finally gave in and hit the speaker button.

"Hi, babe ... I'm sorry about last night ... I really missed you ... but it hurt when you didn't come to my gig."

There was a long pause.

"I know you've got finals ... I just thought ... anyway, let's talk later. You know I love you, baby."

Lena wasn't prone to headaches but after listening to Benjamin, her head started to pound and her eyelids grew heavy. She went into her parents' bathroom and grabbed two more aspirins from their medicine cabinet.

She was shocked when she looked into the cabinet mirror and saw dark circles under both eyes—the contrast to her golden brown skin was not what she had expected to see.

Mom and Dad assured her that she wasn't adopted—both of them dark-skinned African Americans—but Lena was about one hundred shades lighter. Family joke: Way back some slave trader inserted himself into the family tree. Lena never thought it was funny.

She ran a comb through her tight curls and spread foundation makeup around her eyes, trying to lighten the dark circles. She walked down the hall to her room to gather her books.

Benjamin kept popping back into her head.

At twenty-five, she thought her life was full of wonderful choices. Unlike Benjamin and many of her friends, who didn't have a clue about what they wanted to do after college, she'd always known exactly where she was going.

Her parents were both tax lawyers and in practice together, and loved living in San Francisco.

At first, Lena thought she would follow in their footsteps, not because they pushed her in that direction, but because she found the practice of law fascinating. If they'd tried to influence her in any way at all, it was to become a doctor and help people in a different way. That's what her parents were like.

But the more she studied, the more she realized that criminal defense was where she belonged. The idea that she could be responsible for saving innocent people from being executed or going to prison, made her feel inspired. If she could keep anyone from suffering any kind of injustice, *that* was what she wanted to do.

Benjamin.

He wanted to be a music teacher, but wasn't ready to tie himself down. Most of their fights were about his not jumping into his future, laying low and partying wasn't going to make anything happen.

Lena walked to her desk, sat, and started fingering through her notes on Criminal Justice Reform and Individual Representation. The words kept blurring and her headache stabbed at her; it was getting worse.

Maybe I ought to get some orange juice. A little vitamin C might help.

When she stood, the room tilted, then started spinning. Lena grabbed onto the desk to steady herself. After a moment, everything returned to normal.

Bone Dust

Shoot, I have two exams today ... have to get myself together.

She took her time, walked from her bedroom into the kitchen, navigating by holding onto furniture and the walls. She reached into the refrigerator and opened a large jug of juice.

The last thing she remembered was watching in amazement as it slid through her fingers, splashing all over the floor.

* * *

Lena heard the shifting of machinery all around her. She was so tired. She didn't want to see anything, she just wanted to rest, but there was such a racket, her eyes snapped open.

She was in a semi-chamber, stretched out on a table.

"Where am I?" she screamed. "Help!"

She couldn't move her head. Something was holding it down.

She screamed again. "Let me out of here!"

A disembodied voice spoke softly: "It's all right, Lena. You're fine. We're just taking a scan of your head. You have to lie very still; you'll be out very soon. I promise."

She stopped struggling.

"What happened?"

"You fainted and struck your head. The scan is just to make sure everything is all right. Your parents are in the waiting room and you'll be seeing them soon."

The voice faded and Lena closed her eyes.

* * *

Brad Rizzo pulled up a chair and sat down next to Gina in the nurses' station. Much to her disgust, she couldn't stop her face from burning.

Someday I'm going to stop morphing into a persimmon at the least little male-female interaction. But obviously not this morning.

"One of my patients, Lena Dobbs, is going to be admitted very soon."

"What's the problem?"

87

"Her parents found her passed out. Seems she fell in their kitchen and gave her cranium a royal whop."

Brad edged in a little closer. "She's fortunate they decided to come home for lunch for a change. Otherwise, she might have been there all day on the kitchen floor in huge puddle of orange juice. P. S. she also could have died. "

"Poor gal. It must have been scary for her."

"EMTs admitted her through the ER. The doc worked her up and had her head scanned."

Gina felt his knee casually brush against hers.

"She's had a concussion, but there's more to it," he said.

"There's more than a conk on the head?"

It was a poor time to joke, but Brad was making Gina nervous sitting so close to her, even though it was simply a normal medical conversation about a patient, nothing out of the ordinary.

"Lena has the flu, she's a rundown mess, and has a go-go-go personality."

"Quite a combination."

"Yeah, and like every Type A you've ever known, she's ready to burn the world down if she has to crawl to do it. We had to practically pin her down after she woke up. It's hard. She's a law student about to graduate, and has finals today and tomorrow. Or should I say, *had* finals. Which she's definitely going to miss."

"That's pretty rough," Gina said. "Will they let her make them up?"

"I'm betting they will. Her parents are both lawyers. I think they'll make sure she gets what she needs."

Brad gave her one of his dimpled smiles. Gina's heart started racing.

God, I hate this. He must have pheromones polluting the air.

"I've been taking care of Lena since she was fifteen. She's a very special person."

"How is she taking all of this?"

"Not well. But she's been walking around with a temp of one hundred and one ... finally got her to admit to severe chest pain and a gunky, productive cough. I'm sure a culture will reveal strep colonies, or other organisms that think they've found a home."

"X-ray?"

"Yup. Pneumonia for sure, and a pretty bad case of it ... we'll be drowning her in IV antibiotics." Brad chuckled. "That, after her giving me the third degree about why antibiotics were overused ... wanted to know if she couldn't just play it cool."

"I like her already."

"Normally, I'd release her after a night of observation and antibiotics. But I know if we release her she won't stay down. Bed rest is not in her vocabulary. One part of her brain says this is really serious. Another part says, I can get through anything."

He typed in the rest of his medical orders. "That's youth for you."

"I'm not sure I recall," Gina said.

He stood. "I had such a good time with you last night. I can't remember ever enjoying deli so much."

Gina looked up at him. "I guess we don't need to go out Saturday now."

"You're an imp, Ms. Mazzio. Do you know that?" He took her hand and pulled her up into his arms, kissed her right then and there in the nurses' station.

"Brad!"

"There's your answer." And then he walked away.

Chapter 18

Gina walked into the private room, stepped back as the ER techs transferred Brad's restless patient from a gurney onto her bed.

That is one sick twenty-five-year-old.

Although Lena Dobbs was a beautiful young woman, her face was drawn, her skin dull and slack.

Her face held a range of naked emotions—worry, anger, fear—and total exhaustion. To top it off, every movement caused a deep cough to rack her whole upper body.

Yes, she was very sick.

Gina was glad the patient was already hooked up to an IV because she didn't need one more moment of unnecessary pain.

As if anybody does.

When she stepped up to the side of the bed, Lena's expression shouted: *What now?*

"Hi, I'm Gina, one of the nurses who'll be taking care of you." She placed a hand on the young woman's shoulder—that was enough to make her burst into tears.

Gina grabbed several tissues from the bedside table and gently placed them in her hand.

"I can't be here," Lena said between sobs. She yanked the oxygen cannulas from her nose and blew into the tissues. "I have a final today. I can't not show up."

"You look pretty washed out," Gina said softly. "Too sick to do anything but rest and I think you know that, Lena."

"One of my friends had a concussion ... they didn't keep her in the hospital." Lena looked at Gina with a child's questioning face, but her eyes were very grown-up and piercing. "I'll bet my parents put Dr. Rizzo up to this."

"They want you to get well. You're very sick with a rotten upper respiratory infection. It's going to need some heavy-duty medication. "

Lena tried to say something, but her cough interrupted.

"They should be charged with false imprisonment." She burst out into laughter that ended with another roll of coughs. "Okay," she said when she could talk again. "*That,* I've got to admit, was pretty stupid."

"Yeah," Gina said. "In the hospital, you're allowed to be stupid."

"Probably the last time I'll get a pass for anything."

"I'm going to hook up some antibiotics and I'll bring you something for that rotten cough."

"That would be great. It's getting worse and worse."

Gina gently placed the oxygen cannulas back into her nostrils. "Also, your doctor ordered some respiratory therapy for you, so a therapist will probably be in here pretty soon."

"What will that do for me?"

"Probably loosen up that cough and let you get rid of the gunk that keeps you hacking. It should make your breathing a lot easier."

Gina poured water from a plastic pitcher into a tall plastic cup and planted a straw in it. "I'll be back in a few minutes. Why don't you drink some water or, if you want, I can get you some juice."

"I think I'll pass on the juice. That's what got me here in the first place."

* * *

In the station, Gina used the computer to open the doctor's orders. She wanted to double check Brad Rizzo's treatment for Lena Dobbs.

Satisfied with what she read, she moved into the med room. Jenni walked in as she was gathering a piggy-back med to hook up to Lena's IV, plus the rest of the ordered medications, most of which were for her cough.

"I saw you talking to Dr. Good Looking."

"Cut it out, Jenni. We're just friends. We were conferring about his patient, who was just admitted to the unit."

"Yeah, I saw. Another damn flu case."

"She's pretty sick, but she's young; this bug seems to be killing mostly older people," Gina said. "Still, she has the ugliest cough you've ever heard. She must have a ton of goop in her lungs."

"Did she have a flu shot?"

"I checked that out in her history and saw she had been vaccinated. Why?"

Jenni tugged at a loose strand of hair. "I'm really paranoid these days ... and who would know that better than you? But I swear the CDC is messing in some way with the flu vaccines."

Gina laughed. "It would be an effective way to cut down the population."

"I don't really know what they're doing, and it's probably better I don't know, or I'd be on someone's hit list." Jenni rolled her eyes. "Oh, wait. I'm on Russell's hit list ... you suppose he works for the CDC?"

"Jenni, you're beginning to sound as nutty as me," Gina said. "Harry says that's what I do to people."

"What, make them crazy?"

"You got it."

As Gina walked down the hall, she thought about Harry. It was now six weeks since he left for the wilds of Tucson. Normally, he would be returning from his assignment about now. But he'd said he was signing on for another hitch at the same facility. That is, unless she asked him to come back. They both knew what that meant.

After being together for four years, Gina knew what Harry was thinking—it was now or never. She could either back away and move on, or marry him and ruin his life.

It was time.

Time to stop thinking about Harry. Time to stop working and reworking all the useless scenarios that ended up with her being without Harry.

Gina felt like she was choking. Would she ever be rid of that ache in her heart when she thought of him?

She waited a moment to pull herself together before walking into room 114. When she moved through the doorway, Russell was standing by Lena Dobbs' bed.

Chapter 19

Aaron Dobbs had been feeling run down for the past twenty four hours. But he kept it to himself. He hadn't wanted to worry his wife when she was already on overdrive about their daughter, Lena.

When Brad Rizzo suggested hospitalizing Lena, Barbara and Aaron Dobbs were right on board. Anyone who knew their daughter was aware of her driving ambition, knew she would keep going until she dropped—which is exactly what she'd done.

After Lena's admission to Ridgewood, they drove back to their office. Aaron's eyes were so heavy he had almost fallen asleep at the wheel and he was grateful when they arrived in one piece.

"Hey, Barb, I'm going to go lie down in the back room for a while."

"Sure." She squeezed his arm. "Are you all right?"

"Fine, fine. It's this whole thing with Lena, you know. I'm worried, same as you."

He could see she was unconvinced, but he took her in his arms. "Maybe when you get caught up, you could join me back there for a quickie."

"Oh, go on, Aaron. Someone has to be responsible in this practice."

He was smiling when he walked down the hall past their two compact offices, each decorated to reflect the personality of the Dobbs who used it.

Barbara's had an overstuffed leather chair for clients, a solid oak desk, and three walls of bookshelves with essays and philosophical discourses about the law.

Aaron was the modernist, with a glass-and-chrome desk, Eames chairs, and a wall of books similar to his wife's collection.

In the back storage room—never used for storage of any kind—Aaron took off his shoes and pants and crawled into the double bed, the sole piece of furniture in their flake-out room.

The place felt cold—he shivered a couple of times, then wrapped himself in a blanket.

His chest was tight and he was having some trouble breathing. But he closed his eyes and let his mind drift. Right before he fell asleep, his thoughts drifted back to his daughter. He wondered if he might have picked up her bug.

* * *

"Are you all right, Aaron?"

He heard the voice from far away. It was like he was in a deep hole, so deep he couldn't see out.

He tried to ignore the babble of words and go back to sleep, but the voice kept nagging, over and over and over.

Then once more, louder, "Aaron!"

He turned, saw it was Barbara tugging at his sleeve.

"I went to the hospital to see Lena," she said. "You were so out of it, I left you alone."

"You should have woke me up." His voice sounded thick, even to him.

"I tried, but you wouldn't budge."

"How's our baby girl?" He tried to sit up but he couldn't manage it.

"She seems better now that they've gotten the antibiotics into her system. But she's still very ill."

"Poor thing."

"At least they're satisfied the concussion did no real damage; they've started to give her medication to make her more comfortable." She ran a hand across his forehead and leaned over to kiss him.

"Is she still angry with us?"

"You could say that. But the good news is, I've spoken to the dean ad have arranged for her to take her finals after she's well."

Bone Dust

Aaron laughed. "I guess it pays to be contributing alumni."

"You can bet your booty on that. But it's also her class work and test scores. She's a great and gifted student."

Aaron inched to the edge of the bed and forced himself to sit up, but as soon as he did, he started coughing. He was hurting.

He balled a fist and held it to his chest. "Barbara, I don't think I can stand." A frisson shook him; he grabbed the blanket and clutched it to him.

"Aaron, are you having trouble breathing?" She pulled the covers up and around his shoulders. "What's going on with your chest? Are you in pain?"

"No, love, I'm just tired." His voice sounded thick and mushy. He tried to speak again but the words were even more garbled.

"Let me help you lie down. I'm calling 9-1-1."

Don't! Don't! Don't! It's only Lena's bug.

He couldn't speak and he didn't resist when she forced him to take two aspirins before she gently pushed him back down again.

* * *

Brad Rizzo was standing over him when Aaron opened his eyes. The doctor turned from him to check the EKG strips.

"Am I going to live?"

"For now. No one gets out alive, you know that."

"You would remind me, wouldn't you?"

"Well, at least you can speak again. Barbara said you were having chest pain and couldn't articulate."

"Just tired. This thing with Lena has been really stressful." His words ended in a roll of coughs.

"I hear what you're saying, but let's talk about *you.*" Brad held up the EKG strip. "You're not having a heart attack. That's the good news, and by the way, you can give Barbara an extra kiss. Pretty smart of her to give you the aspirin and get you here so quickly."

"She's the really smart one. Without her, there'd be no Dobbs law practice."

"Yeah, I'll fly with that."

Aaron eyed Brad. "I hear a 'but' waiting in the wings."

"I just want to get a scan to make sure we're not missing some kind of vascular event in that hard head of yours."

"Hey, doc, I just want to go home."

"And I want you to. But we'll get the scan, keep you overnight so you can stay in bed and rest."

"Okay, I'll admit I'm beat. We've been putting in long hours at the office ... but I can go home to rest."

"Like your daughter, you'd never get any rest at home, and also like your daughter, I think you're very run down. Your chest sounds congested and I'll bet my last buck, that you're coming down with what Lena has."

"I knew it! And it's damn unfair."

"Whoever said life was fair? Lawyers usually know that better than most people."

Chapter 20

Stop whispering in my ear! Hear me? Stop it!

Russell bolted to a sitting position on his lumpy sofa bed. All night the steel rods and straps had cut into his back— stabbing knives searching for vulnerable soft spots.

His gaze poked into the corners of the room. Then his attention settled on the slit of an opening in the bathroom door.

He brought his knees to his chest, thrust his arms around his shins, and hugged himself. Squeezed tighter and tighter.

"Nonononono!"

Help me! Someone help me! I'm afraid. The bathroom door! Why is it open? I never forget to close it. Never! It's in there ... in there!

He forced himself to carefully shove the blanket aside, slip out of bed, and tiptoe to the bathroom. He stood there shaking. Pee ran down his leg.

Breathing hard, he flung the door open.

The blackness stared back at him.

"You're in there! I know you're there. You're in there!"

In the darkest of the dark ... in the darkest of the dark of night ... that's where The Presence hides. That's what his foster dad said, and Russell believed him.

The Presence used to whisper to Todd. Now it wanted to whisper to Russell.

He snapped on the light, saw nothing. A gust brushed his neck.

It whispered as it passed, "Doitdoitdoitdoit!"

Russell balled his fists, pounded at his head until he was dizzy.

"Go away! I don't want to do it! Leave me alone!"

Silence, then another gust—softer this time.

"Go away! Go!"

Chapter 21

Dominick's bottle of Vicodin was emptying far too fast. He'd been overdosing with the prescribed pills because the pain wouldn't ease up, let alone go away.

It was bad, so intense in his neck that he had to constantly wear the collar brace the hospital had given him. It was either that or hold his head up with both hands. And his ribs? Even with them bound, it was tough to breathe deeply without the pain medication.

Damn doctor said it would be at least six weeks before my neck was healed.

Five more weeks of pain? He'd never been too good at handling pain.

Well, he sure as hell wasn't going back to work for awhile. Just thinking about picking up a shovel or an axe made things worse. Good thing he'd been stashing the dough from his craps winnings for the past year. It had been one long, lucky streak since he left Frisco.

Just starting to get it together.

Had his phony ID; people thought he was a Mex, and he was getting ready to go back to Frisco. Now this new shit comes down on him.

Yeah, well, it's been worth it to find Gina's man. That son-of-a-bitch is gonna take the heat for her. And I'll be damned if he's gonna get away from me.

Dominick carefully undid the support collar and massaged his neck for a few minutes, tried to relax the muscles.

Fortunately, he'd managed to sweet-talk José, one of the gardening crew, into picking him up from the hospital and bringing him back to his room. He didn't have much in common with those Mexicans, and they weren't too keen on him, either.

Had to slip the asshole a twenty. Thank you very much, hombre.

Dominick rubbed his hands together, feeling a little better. The Vicodin was doing its thing, giving him a buzz.

I found the dude. Found that Harry Lucke. Now I'll track the sucker down, see where he hangs out, then nail him.

Poor little Gina. That bitch can't seem to hang onto any man.

His mind started drifting, jumping from one thing to another.

Gonna have to get me some wheels ... my truck looks like a kinky accordion about to stand up and run.

That was pretty funny. He laughed hard. That brought him up short. He pressed the flat of his hands against his ribs.

Gotta take it easy ... winner or no winner, gotta let up on the drinking and gambling. If I don't cut the spendin' and save more dough, I'll go bust in no time.

Not much fun hanging out in this two-bit room.

Shit! Gonna find me a woman and buy me some company.

* * *

Harry knew he and Abby had reached dangerous crossroads in their relationship. Neither wanted to talk about what had happened at the Mexican restaurant. He'd read the signals she'd been putting out, knew what was up. He simply wasn't able, or didn't want to hook into it.

He thought about how he'd chased her down in the Porsche after she ran out of the restaurant, how he'd gathered her in his arms, felt her body tremble as he tried to calm her sobs.

He'd become a lifeline as she buried her head in his chest, hands touching all of him, nothing held back.

He understood that horrible feeling of desperation, that feeling of wanting someone so badly you could barely breathe.

She'd held onto him with grasping arms, hands that clutched at him while he tried to comfort her. And he wanted to feel the way she did, to love her, need her. He wanted to want her.

But he didn't want her.

Bone Dust

Nothing could erase what he felt for Gina. And that truth, whether he verbalized it or carried it silently within his soul, would never go away. It would eventually drive Abby—or any woman—away from him.

He knew Abby wouldn't want it that way.

* * *

Dearest Gina,

Please, don't turn away from me.

I know this whole marriage thing has always been a wedge between us, has always put you off. But I don't understand why. You've tried to explain, said many things that really shouldn't matter if we love each other. If you can't have children, that's not an issue for me. It's not a reason to keep us apart.

If Dominick is out there looking for you, that's all the more reason to be together. I know we've had our differences during the four years we've been a couple, but it's never been about loving you. I'll always love you.

Please! Let me see you. We can work this out.

Yours,

Harry

Harry punched *Send* and the email was gone, travelling through the ether, on its way to San Francisco. For better or worse.

Bette Golden Lamb & J. J. Lamb

Chapter 22

Gina knew she looked wasted. Her eyes were red-rimmed, her skin splotchy and dull, and no matter what she tried, whether rinsing her eyes with cold water or camouflaging all the imperfections with makeup, she still looked like she'd been crying all night.

She didn't want to think about Harry, but couldn't get him out of her mind.

"What's going on, Gina? You look like you haven't slept a wink for days," Jenni said on the drive to work.

"I didn't get much sleep. Harry sent me an email last night."

Waiting at a red light, Gina turned to look at Jenni. "He won't leave me alone ... let it go. He wants us back together again."

When the light turned green, she moved ahead, had to work hard to keep her focus on her driving—her agitation made her restless, she had difficulty trying to sit still.

Jenni touched her arm. "Does he even have a chance?"

"No! It's over! For God's sake. He has to let it go so we can get on with our lives. This back-and-forth communication by emails and telephone is not helping. If anything, it's making it worse."

"The guy loves you and you've been a twosome forever. What do you expect?"

"I expect him to move on ... do whatever he needs to do ... leave me alone."

Gina snagged a parking space very close to the hospital. She checked her watch. "Let's grab some coffee in the cafeteria. We're early for a change. Way early."

* * *

105

With cups in hand, Gina and Jenni found a vacant table near the window. Before Gina could take a sip, she spotted Vinnie and Helen wending their way to them.

"You've been avoiding me," Vinnie said, glaring at Gina.

"Vin, that's not a good way to start a conversation with your sister," Helen said as they pulled up a couple of seats they'd snatched from another table. "Here I am, being Mommy Helen with the two of you. Can't you treat each other with a little civility?"

A scolding from Helen was usually good for a laugh, but today Gina wasn't smiling. She ignored Helen and said, "Have you two met Jenni?"

"I've seen her around, mostly right here," Helen said with a big smile. Vinnie nodded and reached out for a handshake.

"Jenni's staying with me for a while."

"Oh?" Vinnie said. There were unspoken questions in his eyes.

"Someone's been stalking me," Jenni said. "So Gina's taking me under her wing for the time being."

"It's kind of nice having company, and also not having to drive to and from work alone," Gina said. "Better yet, she's a good roommate."

"And Harry?" Vinnie asked, coffee cup halfway between the table and his mouth.

"Harry and I aren't a couple anymore, Vinnie. You're going to have to accept that."

Helen placed a hand on Vinnie's arm and squeezed.

"You know I love the guy," Vinnie said.

"I understand," Gina said.

"No one has ever been there for me the way Harry has. It's not only that he jumped in and helped me with the PTSD, he took a genuine interest in everything that's been going on in my life."

Gina said nothing.

Bone Dust

Vinnie couldn't stop. "He's been there for me day and night ever since I left the military. No matter how you look at it, he's a damn good person."

He shifted in his seat, took another hurried sip of coffee. "You probably don't have a clue as to how many middle-of-the-nighters he's spent talking me down from bad places."

"I do know," Gina said. "I'm sure that will never change no matter what goes on between Harry and me."

"Maybe it's better if I went on up," Jenni said, half rising.

"No, forget it. You've already heard a lot of this. No reason for you to leave."

Jenni dropped back down into her seat, but it was obvious she'd rather have left.

Gina reached for Vinnie's hand. "Please try to understand, I'll always love Harry, but I can't marry him. And that's that!"

All conversation shut down and they sat there quietly drinking their coffees.

Jenni broke the silence. "So how are your units? Are you guys overrun with secondary infections from the flu the way we are?"

"That's the truth," Helen said. "I've never seen Internal Medicine this crowded. I swear, if this keeps up we're going to be stacking patients on top of one another.

"The latest word," Gina said, "is that this is the worst flu outbreak San Francisco has had in years. I've never seen so many people with pneumonia. Most of the older patients are not doing well."

"Problem is," Vinnie said, "most older people don't come in until they're already half dead from dehydration and raging pneumonia. They can't breathe on their own, so they're already beyond the early treatment stage."

"I hear the ER is drowning, not only after hours, but throughout the whole day, even when the doctors are in their offices," Jenni said.

Bette Golden Lamb & J. J. Lamb

"I know," Helen agreed. "When they can't squeeze anyone else into their office schedules, patients automatically head for the ER. It's getting impossible to handle the crowds."

While Jenni and Helen talked, Gina studied Vinnie. She could tell he wasn't letting the Harry thing go; it would take him a long time to get over her breakup. He also looked like he might be coming down with something. His eyes were glassy and he kept trying to suppress an insistent cough.

Helen, the peacemaker, hit the table with the heel of her hand, gave everyone a big, toothy smile, and said, "Enough of this depressing talk. Why don't you two roomies come over for dinner tonight? We'll have hamburgers, big, fat juicy hamburgers with all the fixings and a mountain of fries on the side."

Jenni and Gina glanced at each, and then gave Helen enthusiastic nods.

"Sounds great," Gina said. "What time and what can we bring?"

"Make it around six. And bring along a bunch of those deli pickles, the half sours you and Vinnie scarf up like they were peanuts."

Chapter 23

Gina and Jenni came in after doing some light grocery shopping and rushed to put everything away so they wouldn't be late for dinner with Vinnie and Helen. Before they could change out of their work clothes the phone rang.

"Please get that, Jen. If it's Harry, I'm not here."

Jenni gave Gina a look that told her what she thought of being put in the middle of her and Harry's mess, but she answered anyway.

"Oh, hi, Helen. We're just getting ready to pop over to your place."

Jenni's smile morphed into a frown. "Oh, sorry." She held the receiver out to Gina.

"What's up, Helen?" Gina said.

"Your brother's just plain out of it. He actually turned sour on our way home from work, but insisted all he needed was a nap."

"And?"

"And, it didn't work. I'd say he's got what everyone else has been coming down with."

"Maybe if you—"

"Bite your tongue, nurse. I don't need you to lecture me on how to take care of the man ... and no, you don't need to come over, thank you very much. Stay away and stay well."

"I wasn't about to do that," Gina said, knowing full well that's what she was about to do. "He's in your good hands. Just give him a big hug and tell him I love him."

"Will do. Promise."

When she hung up, Gina said to Jenni, "Weird. Vinnie's the one who never got sick when we were kids. It was always me who came down with any and every bug. Well, we'll just make our own hamburgers."

Before she could put down the phone, it rang again.

109

"Man, I wish people would leave us alone right now." Gina checked the window on the receiver, sighed, and said, "Hey, you're getting to be a habit, Dr. Rizzo."

"A good one, I hope."

"That's still up in the air," Gina said in a quiet voice.

"If you haven't already eaten, come on over and we'll have dinner at my place. Give us a chance to have a long talk."

"Sounds nice, but I promised to eat in with Jenni tonight— big fat homemade hamburgers." She looked up and saw Jenni waving her hands and shaking her head.

Gina mouthed *what?*

"Go ... go!" Jenni said softly.

"Well?" Brad said.

"Somehow I think you know that you're further complicating my already screwed-up life?"

"Maybe, but you can't hide from me, forever."

* * *

"Good evening, Ms. Mazzio," the doorman said as he pushed open one of the tall, double glass doors to the condominium's main entrance.

"I'm here to—"

"Dr. Rizzo is expecting you."

He held the door open until she stepped into the foyer, then moved past her to show her to the elevator. He used a key to unlock one of the buttons; the elevator door slid open, and he directed her inside.

Gina started to ask which floor, then saw there were only two choices: *Up* and *Down.*

"Thank you," she said after pushing the *Up* button.

"I'll call Dr. Rizzo and let him know you're on your way."

It was a smooth, fast ride, with no indication of how many floors she'd traveled when the elevator slowed and stopped. The door slid silently to one side and there was Brad, smiling and waiting for her.

Bone Dust

The elegance of the condo, at least from what she could see at first glance, made her self-conscious for the first time in many years. She felt underdressed with her sweater and jeans, even though Brad was dressed pretty much the same way.

"Hey, glad you decided to come." He reached out and took her hand, led her to a plush, white sofa.

She stared out of a huge panoramic window where a spread of the San Francisco cityscape was alive with sparkling lights.

Brad sat down in a chair on the other side of a glistening, free-form glass coffee table.

"This is truly awesome," she said, pointing to the window. "I didn't realize you're one of those rich doctors, what with the old MGA and all. I mean, I didn't know internal medicine paid so well at Ridgewood."

"It doesn't. Believe me." He swept a hand through the air from one side of the room to the other. "This was once my parents' pad. If it wasn't already mortgage-free, I really couldn't afford it."

"What happened?"

His face paled. It was long moment before he answered. "My parents died last year in an automobile accident. Some drunk rear-ended them ... slammed their car head-on into a tree ... a rather large tree."

"Oh, Brad, I'm sorry. Just like me to put my foot into my mouth. It's a Bronx thing, I guess."

"There's no way you could have known."

"Was your father a doctor also?"

"No, not even close. Dad was heavy into real estate, and, as you can see, he did all right."

"I'll say." Gina felt awkward and sorry she'd ever agreed to come over. She'd only said yes to get away from the phone, to avoid any chance that Harry might call. Now she was having second thoughts.

"I hope you're still in the mood for burgers. I already had all the makings for turkeyburgers and a Caesar salad, if that'll do it for you."

For the first time since walking into the building she relaxed. "That's pretty funny, you know."

"Funny? Burgers aren't funny, they're an essential food group ... top of the pyramid."

"No, no. As I told you, I'd already signed up for that meal when you called. Turkeyburgers must have been my destiny. Jenni and I were supposed to have them with my brother and his girlfriend at their place, but he came down with the flu and we had to call it off."

"How about a glass of wine? I have red or white."

"What a classy invitation?"

"You want class, we could hop over to my uncle's restaurant," Brad said, his soft green eyes making fun of her. He set the two wine glasses down.

"I'd love a glass of red."

Brad brought their drinks, set them on the table, and eased back into his chair. "Vinnie Mazzio is your brother, right?"

"Yeah, that's the schlub."

"He has real talent when it comes to taking care of patients ... kind of runs in the family, it seems." He raised his wine glass to her. "So, Vinnie's sick with the flu?"

"Yeah. That's what his girlfriend Helen said."

"This whole flu situation is getting harder and harder to deal with. We can't handle too much more. We're running out of beds, and the ER is being overrun with sick people who can't get in to be seen by their own doctors."

He took a sip of his wine. "And today there was another announcement from the CDC saying the vaccine is a poor fit for this flu outbreak. Like we couldn't figure that out for ourselves."

"I heard about that."

They gravitated to the kitchen. Brad went to the refrigerator and pulled out a plate with two burger patties, plus a bowl of Caesar salad ingredients. He popped the burgers into the broiler, then whipped up the Caesar salad dressing.

"You just happened to have all this ready and waiting when you called me?" Gina said.

A shrug and a smile were his noncommittal answer.

After the turkeyburgers were flipped, Brad toasted a couple of ciabatta buns, prepared the plates of salad, complete with garlic croutons and anchovies.

When the turkeyburgers were ready, he put a thick slab of cheddar cheese and thick slice of onion on each one. He arranged everything on the counter, which was already set with silverware. The final touch was organic ketchup and Dijon mustard.

Gina took a seat on one of the tall counter stools, looked at everything, and said, "This is fantastic, but it does raise a lot of questions."

"We can discuss your questions now, or eat before the burgers get cold and the salad gets warm."

Gina's response was to take a huge bite out of her turkeyburger. It took several moments before she could speak. She wiped ketchup and mustard from the corners of her mouth tried the salad, and took a second bite of the burger.

"This is delicious."

"Thank you."

"So, tell me," Gina said, "are the flu shots useless?"

"For the most part. Also, the really sick ones have avoided medical care until it's too late for anti-viral drugs to do anything of much value."

Brad paused to take a forkful of salad.

"When they come down with secondary infections, like this virulent pneumonia we're seeing, then they rush to the hospital. By the time they get to us, they're so sick they need to be treated on the spot—oral meds take too long to kick in."

"This is definitely the worst outbreak I've seen," she said.

Gina was starting to feel a satisfying glow, and not only from the meal. Just relaxing, hanging out without any pressure of any kind was what she'd needed.

They finished the meal and sat quietly at the counter, listening to music and sipping from snifters of Spanish brandy.

Brad was the first to break the silence. "So, no marriage for you and Harry?"

"Nope, no marriage."

Brad stretched and twisted on the high stool. "Let's go into the living room where the chairs are more comfortable."

He stood, took her hand, and led her back to a sofa that faced the window and the panoramic view beyond. The lights around San Francisco Bay twinkled and sparkled, creating a fantasyland. It was pretty spectacular.

Gina hadn't noticed that Brad had brought the brandy and their snifters into the living room until he bent over and poured more of the dark amber liquor for them. He sat down on the sofa next to her.

She knew she should be nervous or at least think about what was going to happen in the next five minutes. But she was totally surprised when he took her glass and stood it next to his on the coffee table.

"Gina, I really want to kiss you. I've been thinking about it day and night ... until it's all that I can think of."

"Brad ... I—"

"I've really enjoyed our time together ... especially this evening." He took her hand in his. "I don't want to do anything to make you uncomfortable."

She looked into his green eyes, they were soft, kind, and it was such a relief to be with someone who wasn't constantly pressuring her to do something she knew could be the worst possible thing.

"We can end the evening now," he said smiling. "I've had a wonderful time, and hope you have, too." He squeezed her hand, brought it to his lips, and lightly kissed the backs of her fingers. "Or, we can just see how the rest of the evening turns out."

His lips on her hand were soft and warm and sent shivers through every part of her. She let herself fall back into the sofa.

I'm not ready to leave."

* * *

Sunlight fell on Gina's face; its warmth awakened her.

It's late!

In a panic, she half sat up. A bedside clock showed it was a couple of minutes past eight. She also saw she was lying next to Brad in a king-size bed.

Work!

The panic started to do a number on her stomach until she remembered they both had the day off.

Brad's arm stretched out across her pillow. She watched him sleep, studied his relaxed face. A dark, day-old beard delineated his jaw, chin, and upper lip; twin smudges of long, curved lashes softened the fine lines around his eyes, and a curl of dark hair was looped on his forehead.

She wanted to feel guilty about last night, but instead, she remembered how they had listened to music and kissed until she was breathless.

At some point, he had picked all five-feet-ten of her and carried her into the bedroom. She'd wanted to protest, but when he set her down on the edge of the bed, she was as eager as he was. They tore each other's clothes off and fell onto the bed.

Gina remembered his hands moving softly all over her body, followed by his lips. Everywhere he touched her, thrilling stabs of pleasure cut through her. She couldn't stop from drawing him inside.

The memory made her breathe more heavily.

"Hey," Brad said, looking into her eyes.

"Hey, yourself."

"What are you thinking?"

"Last night."

He smiled and pulled her down until she was lost in his arms.

Chapter 24

Helen picked up the phone, ready to tear into whatever telemarketer was calling at this hour of morning.

"Hi, it's Jenni. Sorry to bother you so early, but I'm really worried. Gina didn't come home last night. I don't know what to think."

"Last night? Did she say where she was going?"

"To Brad Rizzo's for dinner."

Helen hurried out of the bedroom, not wanting to disturb Vinnie. He was finally asleep after a restless night of tossing and turning. She hadn't slept much herself worrying about him. "Did you try to call her?"

"Soon as I saw she hadn't come home. Her cell goes straight to message mode."

"Look, Jenni, Gina has the day off and she might have stayed over with Brad. I wouldn't worry about it if I were you."

"Yeah, Brad has the day off, too, so I guess what you're saying makes sense. I tried his answering service, but they told me he would be unreachable today." After a long beat, Jenni said, "You really think she might have spent the night with him?"

"Gina's a big girl. If that's what she chose to do, it's all right with me."

Jenni was silent.

"I don't spend time judging my friends," Helen said. She was feeling pretty damn prickly about Jenni's attitude. "She was having a rough time with Harry, and now they've broken up. As long as she's safe with Brad and not out there being hurt or murdered, that's all I care about."

"Well, I—"

"Do we understand each other, Jenni?"

"I just thought—"

"Forget what you've been thinking. Just leave all of this to me. I'll find a way to make sure she's all right."

"Okay, but please call me the moment you find out anything."

"I'll let you know," Helen said, running a comb through her hair. "I promise. Right now I've got to get ready to go to work." She quickly hung up the phone.

"What's happened to my sister?"

Helen spun around. Vinnie was standing in the bedroom doorway in pajamas, wiggling his bare toes. She rushed to him, took his arm, and led him back to bed.

"What on earth is the matter with you?" Helen helped him crawl under the sheets and blankets, placed a hand on his forehead, and stared into his droopy eyes.

"Tell me about Gina," he mumbled.

"She's off today and she hasn't come home from a date."

"A date?" he said, his voice thick and raspy. "Harry's not back. He would have called me first thing."

"Listen to me, dear boy, just get it through your head once and for all, Gina and Harry are kaput. Sad as that may be, that's the way it is. So, if your big sister wants to go out with another man, she has that right."

"I get it! Gina's a grown woman, and I ought to just butt out of her affairs."

"Now, you *are* getting it." Helen tucked the covers around him. "If you want to have any kind of relationship with her, you have to respect her decisions."

"I know ... if I didn't feel so lousy, I'd probably be up and out looking for her."

"And that's something her little brother is going to have to stop doing. You can't run her life just because *you* think she should spend it with Harry." She smiled at him. *"Capish?"* She laughed. "See, you've even got me talking Italian."

Vinnie gave her a weak smile; his eyelids blinked a couple of times, then stayed closed.

Helen went into the living room and gathered up her purse, reached for the phone, and called Gina's number.

Bone Dust

"Little phone freak that you are, I know you'll be checking in for your messages," she said when she heard Gina's recorded message. "Well, dear girl, here's one for you. Call me right now. And I mean now!"

* * *

Jenni put her phone back into her purse after talking to Helen.

She didn't seem all that worried, and she and Gina are best friends.

Jenni stared into space, tried to remain calm and centered. Mostly, her thoughts were on the kind of life she'd led before Gina started working in her unit. She'd made bad decision after bad decision. She was worried Gina might do the same thing now that Harry was out of her life.

When Jenni first came to San Francisco she was angry at everything—her ex-boyfriend, who'd dumped her for her best friend; her parents, who blamed her for the breakup.

She'd wanted to get lost in a new life. She moved to San Francisco from Reno and took a job at Ridgewood. As soon as she settled into her new digs, she started dating. But she didn't just date, she slept around—a lot.

Most of the men were nice enough and she was excited to be in a magical city like San Francisco. Everyone seemed so buoyant. But she'd had a couple of close dating calls, almost been raped.

One of those men was Russell Thorpe.

* * *

Second thoughts had plagued Jenni about going on a second date with Russell. They'd gone to a movie on the first date and there wasn't a lot of interaction and she'd been a little uneasy with him. When he'd asked her out again, she'd said yes, on a whim.

He really hadn't done anything *bad!* Besides, he'd said he was going to teach her how to use a bow and arrow. Sounded like fun, even a little romantic. Like Robin Hood and Maid Marian.

"Hey, Russell, where're we going?" she said when he came by to pick her up.

"Something real special, Jenni," he said. "Not a city date. You'll see."

He took the coast road and drove north—drove and drove and drove.

"You promised me something different, but all we've been doing is riding around in your truck for an hour. Kind of boring, you know?"

"We're almost there. You're going to love this place, Jenni." He pulled off the highway onto an auxiliary road, and after a while they turned onto a dirt road that wound itself deep into the woods.

"It's beautiful here." she said. She clutched her sweater tighter around her, protecting herself from the cooler air under the shadow of the redwoods.

"And this is it!" He sounded very proud when he slowed down and then stopped in a small clearing about one hundred feet in front of a rundown log cabin.

A pile of wood was stacked haphazardly in front of the structure and litter was scattered all around the grounds surrounding the parking area—rusted out cars, broken farm implements, concrete blocks, a jumbled pile of bricks, tumbled trees, and broken limbs poked up out of tall weeds.

Jenni was disappointed, wished they would just turn around and leave. But Russell was out of the car, motioning for her to follow him towards the cabin.

She'd accepted that he was a little strange, but she'd never felt intimidated by him ... until now.

Russell waded through the weeds and went inside. Jenni sat in the truck, trying to make up her mind whether to follow him, or just sit and wait until he came out, then tell him she wanted to go home. The keys were in the ignition and she was tempted to start the truck to hurry him along.

Bone Dust

But when Russell came out carrying a bow and quiver of arrows, she got interested again and climbed out of the truck.

She walked on the uneven ground, kicking aside the weeds. As she got closer to the pile of wood, she not only saw shards of bone tossed everywhere, but on one side of the cabin there was a stack of bones waist high.

"What's that about?" She pointed to the bones.

"Deer bones." He gave her a measured stare.

Why is he looking at me that way?

He raised the bow and arrow over his head and headed for the woods. "Come on, I'll show you how to shoot."

Jenni's heart started to race and her breath was coming fast and hard. All the blanched deer bones were creeping her out. Before she followed him, she picked up a fist-size jagged rock and stuffed it into her sweater pocket.

They had been walking for a while when they came to another small clearing. A tree trunk had a white bull's eye painted unevenly on the bark. Russell took a shooting stance and fired an arrow.

Bull's eye.

"Come on," he yelled. "Give it a try."

"I don't think so."

"Aw, come on, Jenni. You can do it."

She walked up to him and he handed her the bow and a steel-tipped arrow. He moved behind and pressed against her.

Ugh! Smells like greasy fried food.

Russell wrapped his arms around her, positioned her hands on the bow and bowstring, and showed her how to set the arrow.

Jenni pulled back on the bowstring, and was ready to release the arrow when his hand shot down between her legs. The arrow fell to the ground.

She dropped the bow and tried to get away, but Russell grabbed her with both hands and threw her to the ground. He fell on top of her, held her down with one fist and ripped open her jeans.

"Stop it! Get off of me!"

"Word gets around, you bitch. You put out for all those other guys ... now it's my turn."

He unzipped his pants, pulled out his cock, and tried to wedge himself between her legs. She grabbed the rock from her sweater pocket and bashed the pointed end against his head.

She struck him again and again until he went limp.

Jenni pushed and shoved to get out from under him. Once up, she ran back to the truck, pulled her purse from under the seat, found her cell, and punched in 9-1-1.

No signal.

Russell was crashing through the woods. He would be on her in no time.

She jumped into the driver's seat, turned the key, and started the truck.

He came out of the woods yelling, "I was only kidding with you. Come on, Jenni."

"If you ever come near me again, I'll kill you! You hear me, Russ?"

"My name's not Russ, you bitch." He raised the bow and aimed an arrow at her. "Get out of my truck. Now!"

The arrow whizzed past her nose and out the passenger window. She stomped the accelerator and took off.

Before she could report Russell to the police, they were waiting for her at her apartment. Russell had out-maneuvered her, reported that she'd stolen his truck.

It was a real mess.

Jenni got a good lawyer and managed to avoid getting into deep trouble; it cost her a bundle. Criminal records didn't sit well with the Board of Registered Nursing.

No one believed that he'd tried to rape her. Not even her lawyer.

* * *

After morning report on the unit, the first thing Jenni did was go through the database for Dr. Brad Rizzo's home telephone number. She jotted it down and took her cell into the workroom where no one else was around. After three rings he picked up.

"This is Dr. Rizzo."

"Hi, this is Jenni Webb; I work with Gina."

"Oh, hi, Jenni. Hey, I'm off today, so if there's something you need, Dr. Grayson is on call."

"No, no, that's not it. I've been rooming with Gina and I'm a little worried. She didn't come home last night and I know she was having dinner with you. So—"

"Hold on a sec."

Oh, boy, if Gina's there, I'm going to catch hell.

"Jenni?" Gina said. "Is there problem?"

Oh, that voice.

"I was worried about you when you were gone all night."

There was a heavy pause. "Well, now you know I'm fine. I appreciate your keeping track of me. I'll talk to you later."

One day I'll learn to keep my nose out of other people's business.

* * *

Jenni picked up the nurses' station telephone. It had been ringing for a long time, but with everyone running back and forth trying to keep up with the increased patient load, answering the telephone had dropped far down on the priorities list.

"This is Jenni Webb."

"And this is Helen Trent."

"Oh, Helen. I meant to call you, but I've been too busy with patients. This flu epidemic is driving us crazy. Anyway, Gina's okay."

"I know that already," Helen said coldly, "especially since she called me, fuming about your calling Brad Rizzo at home."

"I'm sorry, Helen. I was worried."

"Both of us appreciate your concern, but the next time I tell you that I'm taking care of something, I'd expect you to have the decency to listen to me." Helen hung up.

Oh, shit!

Chapter 25

"You have a fabulous view from almost every room," Gina said, placing their bacon-and-cheese omelets on the dining room table. Brad followed with English muffins, orange juice, and their coffee.

She smiled her thanks as he pulled out her chair, a curved piece of clear acrylic. She sat on the cushion of purple, blue, and abstract swirls.

"This is really cool, dinner in the kitchen and now breakfast in the dining room."

Before Gina could take her first bite, Brad asked, "Why did you give Jenni such a bad time on the phone? She's a nice gal, and a great nurse."

"I know I came on pretty strong, but everyone is freaking out over my breakup with Harry."

"Can't really blame them," Brad said, reaching for his orange juice. "You two were an item for a long time."

"Don't tell me you're trying to make me feel guilty like everyone else."

"Of course not." He reached under the table and gently squeezed her thigh. "But it's hard for people to move on, even if you have."

"Have I?" She finished the last of her omelet.

"After last night and this morning ... it feels like you have. Am I wrong?"

"I think it's going to be a while before I have an answer to that." She put her fork down and leaned back in her chair.

"Not too long, I hope."

"Right now it's almost a fulltime job dealing with Vinnie, Helen, and Jenni. And they're merciless."

"As am I," said Brad, smiling. "But for different reasons." His cell phone rang, he picked up, looked at the window, and threw his napkin down in the table. "This is supposed to be my day off," he growled. He tapped the button to answer the call. "This is Brad Rizzo." He nodded. "Yes ... okay."

Gina could see he was listening carefully; the lines in his face deepened.

"Who told you she was here? ... yes, I'll ask her."

He hung up the phone and started clearing away the dishes. "I have to go back to the hospital."

"What's happening?"

"The ER is swamped with influenza patients ... the staff can't keep up with the crush. They're diverting, but so is every other hospital. They want you back, also."

"How did they know I was here? It's supposed to be my day off, too."

"Jenni told them," Brad said with a smile. "They tried your phone, but you had it turned off."

"Oh, well. I guess the whole world knows now that I spent the night with you."

Brad bent over and kissed her. "There are no secrets at Ridgewood."

* * *

Russell was packed in the elevator with the extra staff who had been called back in to work. There were rumors the hospital had to pay top dollar to the temp agencies to bring personnel from other states to help cover the increased patient load.

He hated being trapped in this confined place where he was so physically close to everyone.

They were all bumping against each other, and him. They gave off disgusting aromas of annoyance and agitation. It reminded him of the dead animals he and his foster dad had cut up at the cabin; they also had reeked of fear. He could smell some of that stink here, too.

After he stepped out of the elevator, he could breathe again. He spotted Jenni talking on the phone in the nurses' station but he kept on walking down the corridor before she could focus her attention on him.

Bone Dust

With the hospital's overloaded census, he had to cover larger numbers of patients, plus more than the usual number of tests being performed on each individual.

His tray was very heavy. He could have taken one of the carts, like most of the other lab personnel, but they didn't have anything to hide, and the tray made him more mobile.

People might start asking questions.

No, they would definitely ask questions.

Usually, his day started early when the staff was involved in taking report from the night shift in the nurses' stations—normally there weren't too many people out on the floors working with the patients. Today, at every patient room, staff members floated in and out.

It was too busy for him to drain anyone. But nothing could stop him from observing each and every individual, in each and every bed, looking for his next victim.

The first name listed on his assignment page: *Room 214. Lena Dobbs, Blood cultures.*

The room's blinds were closed and a reading light was positioned so it shone on the wall behind the patient. She was sitting up and coughing, her face contorted by a worried expression.

She gazed over at him, played with the tubes in her nostrils that provided oxygen. He could see she was scared and physically exhausted. Her arms dropped away from her face and lay limp by her sides.

"Lena, I'm here to take blood for some lab tests."

"They took blood from me when I was admitted." She began to cough again. "I don't want to be stuck again."

"Sorry." He lifted her wrist and verified her name, went to the sink and washed his hands. "They have to do repeat blood cultures. I won't be able to talk much with a mask on so why don't you just let me do what I have to do."

Why do these patients always give me these strange looks when all I'm doing is telling them the truth?

Now he was annoyed with her. He turned away and slapped on his mask.

I'm the one in charge here, little girl, and don't you forget it.

Snapping on his gloves, he removed the cap from the culture solution bottle and replaced it with an alcohol pad.

"How long is this going to take?" Lena asked, tears running down her cheeks. "I'm cold."

He said nothing.

Jenni walked into the room and glared at him when she saw the patient crying.

"Hey, Lena," Jenni said softly. She took an extra blanket from the bedside chair and covered the patient's shoulders. "This will be over soon."

Goddam bitch! She would have to show up.

Jenni took Lena's hand and glared at Russell. "Don't worry; I'll stay right here with you."

I'll bet you will.

He quickly wrapped the tourniquet around her arm and found a good vein right away.

He circled and scrubbed the site with alcohol, let it dry, than opened an ampoule of 1% tincture of iodine and scrubbed again.

Waiting for that to dry, he replaced his gloves with a fresh sterile pair.

The patient started to cough just as Russell was about to puncture her vein. "You'll have to hold still or I can't do this."

Lena started to sob and then she was coughing at the same time. He could see Jenni was furious and Russell's head started spinning.

A blast of hatred and memory was building. Every time he saw Jenni, he remembered her stealing his car, the long walk from his cabin, the reporting her to the police. She'd gotten away with it when she should have been locked up for bashing him on the head. She should have had to pay.

Bone Dust

He looked at Jenni and the sobbing patient. If he didn't get out of the room soon, he would start screaming at both of them.

"It's all right," Jenni said. "Let's just get through the next few minutes and it'll all be over."

Russell took the 10cc syringe and had to keep himself from stabbing the needle into her arm instead of calmly finding the vein and getting what he needed.

He struggled with his anger as he gently pulled the blood into the syringe, and then discharged it into the culture solution before removing the tourniquet.

"It's all done." He placed a cotton ball on the puncture site. "You should hold this on the spot for awhile."

He was still angry as he looked down at Lena.

I'll be back for you.

Chapter 26

"That wasn't terribly good, was it?" Harry said, pushing away a half-eaten taco.

"You'd think the people who run the cafeteria would consult with some of the Latinos who work here and learn how to make good Mexican food," Abby said. She'd eaten only half of her taco also.

"I suppose it's better than going hungry," he said and glanced at his watch. "We still have a little time left. What say we get out of here and take a walk. I'm feeling kind of sluggish after that so-called meal."

"Sounds good to me."

They walked out the back door and started down a trail that took them to the edge of the open desert.

"Abby, I'm sorry to be such a disappointment to you."

"It's my fault," Abby said. "I knew you'd just ended a long-term relationship and that I would have to be patient if we were ever going to get together."

"What I hoped for," Harry said, "was friendship. I'm just not ready to really give up on Gina ... no matter what she says or does."

"Has she answered your email?"

"No. She made it pretty plain on the telephone that we were finished." He took in a deep breath. "But I can't seem to let her go."

Abby squeezed his arm. "I'm willing to wait."

"Right now, Abby, I need a friend, not a lover. If we can just spend some time together, have that kind of relationship, it would be nice. I mean, I really like and admire you." Harry squeezed her hand. "But I don't think that's what you're looking for. Right now, I can't offer you anything more than that."

"I won't lie, Harry. I'm disappointed we haven't become more than just friends, but I don't want to be here alone. I've been a travel nurse for many years, the way you have. I've worked all over the country and I've met some really great guys. In fact, I was engaged for a while."

"I didn't know that."

"He was a nurse, like you."

"What happened?"

Abby looked away.

"You don't have to talk about it if you don't want to."

"We waited too long," Abby said. "In many ways, like you and Gina. We kept putting off a wedding date. It was always going to be after the next assignment, or there was a special bonus sign-up and we thought having some extra money would be great."

"Only in my case," Harry said, "Gina had a bad marriage and she couldn't surrender to the idea of another marriage. Trust has been a big issue with her."

Abby picked up a rock and threw it at a spreading Saguaro cactus "In my situation, we sort of lost our long-term commitment to each other and went our separate ways."

"I swear," Harry said, "I'll never understand people."

"Me neither."

* * *

Dominick was high. Way out in space, floating. Vicodin had taken the edge off the pain and the pot was making him feel light as a feather.

His thoughts jumped around. He was missing his family back in the Bronx again.

No one here knew who he truly was. To them, he was just some dude named Dommi Machado, with absolutely no roots in Arizona.

If any of these people ever suspected he was an ex-con or had broken parole in New York, they would turn him in for the price of a beer.

He missed New York with all the fast talk, the intense people, and his drinking buddies.

He'd never ever been on his own except when he was in prison. There was always his mother and father, his sister, and the guys he hung out with.

There was nothing here.

On an impulse, he pulled out his cell, punched in the numbers.

"Hello."

"Hi, Mamma. It's me."

The silence between them was almost unbearable.

"Why you call me now, Dommi?"

"It's been a year, Mamma. I miss you and Papa."

"Oh, Dommi. Why you have to run away?"

"I couldn't go back to jail. I just couldn't."

"No!" his mother said. "You went to California because you couldn't leave Gina alone."

"She has to pay, Mamma. She sent me away to jail. She's the one who did it." He wiped away a tear. "Don't you think she has to pay? It was her fault."

"No, Dommi. You beat your wife. She almost die." He could hear his mother crying. "It was your fault. *You* the one who has to pay."

Dominick cut the connection. The high was gone; all he felt was sadness. Gina had destroyed his life, taken his family away, turned them against him.

Standing at the window, he looked at the blue sky and the desert landscape. He inhaled and held the smoke, then again, and again. In a little while, not only his neck and ribs felt better, he felt better.

He would take away what Gina loved, too.

Bette Golden Lamb & J. J. Lamb

Chapter 27

Gina went through the double sliding doors into the ER waiting room. The place was packed with people of all ages, of every shape and size. It was standing room only.

For just a beat she felt euphoric.

This was what she signed on for when she became a nurse. She wanted to help sick people, be there for them.

But the sounds of choking coughs and screaming babies, along with the sight of exhausted, fearful faces, blurred some of those simple ideals.

As she stepped into the middle of the crowd, she was surrounded by very, very, sick people.

One person was being eased into a wheelchair while she kept her place in line. Others were shifting back and forth from leg to leg; many just stood and stared into space, their faces drained of color.

When the door opened to the treatment area, all eyes focused on the person calling the names of those who were going to be taken inside to be examined. Everyone hoped it was his or her turn.

Sounds of disappointment rippled throughout the room when they realized they weren't going to be called this time.

Gina felt the first twinge of panic. Did she really want to expose herself to this snake pit of humanity?

For one fleeting second she thought about running back to her car. She'd had that feeling a few times in her career, but she'd never given in to it; the urge was gone by the time she walked into the treatment area of the ER.

She spotted Brad and caught his eye; he gave her a brief smile and was gone in an instant into a curtained space where a baby was screaming.

Gina stopped a passing nurse. "Hey, sorry to bother you. I was called in to help. Who's giving directions in this madhouse?"

The nurse pointed to a woman at the medicine cabinet. "Donna's the one you want to see. She'll put you into the right slot. Sorry, I've got to run."

Gina walked up to Donna and tapped her on the shoulder.

"Yes?" she said irritably and turned. She looked at Gina, then at her ID. "Oh, Mazzio! Boy, am I glad to see you."

"It's a mob scene out there," Gina said.

"You noticed? I mean, it's been pretty wild around here." Donna locked the narcotics box and slipped the keys into her pocket. "I looked up your personnel file and man, was I was happy to see that you've done triage before."

"True."

Donna placed a hand on Gina's shoulder. "That's exactly where we need you right now. Actually, we could use two or three of you. Are you up for it?"

"Sure. Wherever."

They hurried out the door, walked through the reception area to a triage room. "Gina, I want you to meet Pamela Cavanna. She's been holding down the fort in this loony bin."

The triage nurse barely smiled at Gina. She looked really stressed. Her stethoscope was like a skinny blue snake curling around her neck. Gina smiled at a man sitting in a chair next to Pamela's desk having his vitals taken. He kept rubbing his throat; it was obvious he was having trouble swallowing.

"She'll be glad you're holding down the other spot." Donna pointed to another desk set-up. Next to it was a portable piece of equipment to assess B/P, pulse, temperature, oxygen intake, and the usual computer equipment, same as Pamela's.

"Welcome," the triage nurse finally said. "I'm really so glad you're here. I was about to go under. Donna, would you please take Mr. Pronzini to the treatment area? He's going to need immediate attention."

"See you later," Donna said, taking the arm of the man, leading him out the door.

Gina stuffed her purse in the desk drawer and hung up her coat. She snatched the next-in-line patient information sheet from the crammed-full intake rack. She stood at the doorway. If it was possible, there were now more people than when she arrived. "Ms. Podolsky," she called out.

A woman stood on shaking legs and moved toward Gina, who took her arm to guide her into the triage room.

* * *

Jenni called out to one of the nurse techs, "Help me move this man, please?" She was swamped and frustrated with the crowding ... everywhere.

"Where're you gonna put him?" the tech asked. "There's no more room."

"He's going into Lena Dobbs' room," Jenni said, walking down the corridor. "He's her father ... that will open a bed for us."

The tech looked agitated. In fact, every one of the nurses and nurse techs had been moving nonstop. They were having to squeeze in too many patients into too little space and it was taking a lot of creative rearranging.

Father and daughter will just have to tough it.

When they wheeled Aaron Dobbs into his daughter's room, Lena's eyes widened.

"Dad, I didn't know you were so sick. Mom didn't tell me."

"Just like my dorm days at Cornell, only my roommates were not my daughter." He smiled at her. "And this definitely is not going to be fun."

Jenni didn't like the way Aaron looked. His black skin had a gray tinge and his eyes were drooping like most of the others on the unit with high temperatures.

"How are the aches and pains since we dosed you with anti-inflammatories?"

Aaron looked at Jenni and began to cough. "Don't you worry about me ... just take care of my little girl."

The nursing tech left after the bed was positioned to form an isosceles triangle. Not the usual conformation, but the only way to leave some room for patient care.

"Don't you worry, Mr. Dobbs, we intend to take good care of both of you." Jenni fussed with his pillow. "In a few minutes we're taking you down for an x-ray."

Jenni was about to leave when Russell walked into the room with his lab tray. He set it on the Dobbs' shared bedside table. She looked at him and felt her arms explode with goose bumps.

"I don't recall any additional lab work ordered for Mr. Dobbs," she said gruffly.

He pulled out his order sheet and held it up so she could see it.

She slipped into the space on the other side of the bed, determined to stay until he was finished.

"Did you want something?" Russell asked her.

"I'm just going to wait and see if you need any help," Jenni said, ready to pounce on the creep.

"I'm fine."

She gave him a big smile. "You've never been fine." Her cell vibrated in her pocket.

"I hear you have a bed available," Brad Rizzo said. "If so, I've got an elderly woman the police brought in. No ID and she's burning up with fever. Not only that, I'd bet my last buck that she has pneumonia. They're taking her to x-ray first, but then I need a place to put her."

"Send her here; we can handle her." She took a deep breath and said, "Gina there?"

"Yeah, she's doing triage."

"Brad, I—"

"Stop worrying, Jenni. I forgive you, and I'm sure Gina will too."

Bone Dust

Jenni was flabbergasted, couldn't speak.

Brad laughed.

"What's so funny?" Jenni said.

"Let it go, Jenni. We're up to our eyeballs with people going down with the flu. Every one of us is too busy for that kind of stuff."

* * *

The old woman clutched Brad's arm. "Where am I?"

Brad looked at the veined hand and sparse gray hair. The x-rays had confirmed his diagnosis: Pneumonia.

What troubled him more than anything else was that she seemed malnourished and there were fresh bruises on her arms.

"We brought you into the hospital because you're very sick and we need to treat you."

"Yes, I'm really not feeling well ... can't catch my breath."

Brad looked into faded blue eyes that were flitting from one spot to another, never quite settling on any one thing. How many times had he seen patients with breathing problems look exactly the same way—like panicked animals about to take off and run?

"Can you tell me your name?" He tried to smooth her smattering of hair and reassure her, but he knew this kind of confusion was most likely part of a dementia syndrome. He hoped for her sake it was only her high temperature.

"I don't know." She placed a shaking hand on her bruised arm and rubbed. "I just want to go home."

"Where do you live?"

She pointed to the corner of the room. Over there, in my purse ... the address is there."

"There was no purse with you."

The woman began to moan and her cheeks were awash with tears.

Brad tried to remain objective about her situation, but the Bay Area hospitals were full and all the ERs were sending patients away, just passing them back and forth.

Bette Golden Lamb & J. J. Lamb

He felt a sudden flash of fear grip him.
How the hell are we going to take care of all of them?

Chapter 28

The score was tied, bottom of the ninth. Fans at Yankee Stadium were wild with excitement. They were screaming his name: Dominick! Dominick! Dominick!

Gina was in the front row behind the dugout, shaking her fist, yelling louder than anyone else.

But she was distracting him. Every time he'd look up at a fly ball, he'd hear her shriek his name—it tore at his head. But he knew the ball would drop solidly into the pocket of his glove. If he could just keep it together.

This one was high, highest of the afternoon. When it reached its peak, it paused for an instant, then started back down. Dominick stationed himself under the falling ball, moved a little to his left, then a little back. Soon it would be safe in the pocket of his glove. The ball was gently floating down towards him, but then it changed. Like a falling missile it started coming down really fast, and getting faster. He was ready, he was there. His glove was positioned perfectly.

"Get it, Dominick! Do it, do it!" Gina's screams were tearing at his brain, a banging, a pounding in his head.

He watched the ball barely miss his glove, fall to the ground, and roll away.

His eyes snapped open.

His heart was thumping against his chest; he sat up, looked around in confusion. Someone was pounding on the door to his room.

When he opened the door, there stood José, the only friend he'd made since coming to Tucson.

"*Hola, Machado. ¿Que pasa?*" José said. "Am I gonna have to stand here all day, or are you gonna ask me in?"

An illegal immigrant, José had helped him get a fake green card so he could fend off any cops or immigration agents who might stop and question him. The main thing was to keep from being identified as Dominick Colletti and sent back to New York.

It had cost him a bundle for the ID, almost every penny he had, and he'd gone around scared to death until he earned the money to pay for a new social security number and driver's license. Now, he sort of fit in and was relatively anonymous.

"Did you come to gloat?" he asked. He stepped away from the entrance so José could come inside.

"Nah. I'm here 'cause I miss your ugly face." He sat down on Dominick's bed, since there were no chairs. "You look drugged up."

"Yeah, well I feel like shit even with the stuff they gave me for pain."

"Listen, you keep taking that shit and you'll never get better."

"What are you talking about, dude?" Dominick sat down next to him. "How am I gonna sleep or move around if I'm in so much pain? Man, I'll never get over this."

"Bullshit, Machado! That stuff makes you need it. I'll bet you're not even getting a high on it anymore."

"Well, that's for damn sure. In the beginning it was good for a buzz, but I'm used to the shit now."

"Damn right you are."

Well, what the hell am I gonna do? I need to get my ass back to the job. I'm running the fuck out of bread."

"I got something for you in a couple of days, man. Think you can keep it together until then?"

"I don't know, man. My neck is okay. But my ribs. It's hard to breathe, dude."

"Look, just stop taking the dope and I'll tape you up real good so you'll be able to at least dig a hole in the ground."

Dominick didn't like the thought of either. "Are you sure?"

"I'll pick you up, but so help me, man, if you're stoned ... that's it."

"Okay, man."

"Machado, you need to grow a pair if you're ever gonna get on your feet again."

"I said, okay. Enough already."

* * *

Talking to Gina had done nothing but bring Harry down. Really down. He should have left her alone, not pressed so hard about getting married—it was a blind spot for both of them and it had caused brief separations before. This time, it might be forever.

Idiot! Had to get my own way. Couldn't keep my big mouth shut.

When he'd called the apartment again, Jenni answered. She reluctantly told him Gina was dating again. It left him feeling icy cold and desperate.

Have to talk to her face to face before it's too late.

He arranged to have three days off, threw some clothes in a suitcase, and was out the door.

In the Porsche, he checked his watch. The plane for SF left in a couple of hours. He had just enough time to make the Tucson airport, buy a ticket, and check in.

Abby reached through the car window and placed a hand on his shoulder. "I hear you're going to San Francisco. Is that true?"

"Yeah. I'm sorry. Can't talk about it now. Got to get moving or I'll miss my flight."

"Are you going to see Gina?"

"Yes." He put a hand on hers. "I need to try to put everything back together again."

"We've been good together, Harry." Abby looked into his eyes; there was just a hint of a smile.

"You've been a great friend. If things had been different ... if they were ..." He shrugged.

"Yeah, if only you weren't still in love with Gina."

"Something like that." He started the car. "Listen, I really need to get out of here. We'll talk again when I get back."

"Sure," she said, stepping back.

"See you later."

As he pulled away, he heard her shout, "Come back, Harry! Please come back!"

Chapter 29

Russell hurried through Ridgewood. The corridors were crawling with medical personnel—and there were rumors that more beds would have to be set up in the hallways. The whole city's medical system was drowning in sick people.

He'd heard there were no hospital beds available anywhere in Ridgewood, perhaps even in all of San Francisco.

He wanted to run but his legs wouldn't move fast enough to escape the horrible blast of sound that followed him everywhere.

It was the roar of an angry carnivore, running loose and chasing him from room to room, from floor to floor. He was surrounded by urgent voices of doom, surrounded by fear, surrounded by panic. His chest was caving under the crush of people.

Stop! You're killing me!

The overhead speakers blasted constant requests for Code Blue teams and "Dr. Gray," the emissary of death.

Moaning, coughing, gasping resounded everywhere, like the sounds of the dying animals his foster dad insisted he help butcher.

Listen to them. Listen! Listen! They're dying. Say it! They're dying!

Todd would repeat it over and over until Russell's ears heard nothing but the grunts, the cries, the last breaths of the hunted, doomed creatures in the woods. Todd made Russell kill, kill all the wounded creatures that quieted only when their blood drained away.

Everyone suffers until their blood drains away.

Russell hurried into the nearest restroom, locked himself in a stall, and covered his ears with shaking hands.

Get away from me, Todd. I don't want to do it anymore!

145

A voice cut through the noise in his head. "Are you all right in there? Do you need some help?"

Russell rubbed hard at his ears, forced his eyes open. "Yeah, I'm good ... stomach problems."

"Well ... long as you're okay."

He heard the outside door to the restroom squeak shut. A sudden whoosh of air slid past his neck and down his shirt. It left behind an icy chill that crawled down his spine.

The Presence was with him. Here, in the stall.

He shook his head and the roar quieted. The Presence quieted the noise.

Why don't you show yourself? I need to see you, know that you're real.

He picked up his work tray, surprised because he couldn't remember setting it down on the floor. He left the stall, went to the sink, and splashed cold water on his face again and again. He pulled several paper towels to dab his face dry.

He was in control again. He took a deep breath and slipped back out into the hallway traffic.

* * *

The laboratory was a madhouse. So many people were waiting to have their blood drawn; the line snaked down the corridor, spilled over into the x-ray area.

Rod looked at him, but instead of being angry, as Russell assumed he would be, his manager appeared relieved to see him. Russell set his tray on the counter and waited for whatever was going to happen next.

"Man, am I glad you're back," Rod said. "We have three or four patients that I swear don't have any veins. I have them waiting for your magic touch."

"I'll be there in a moment," Russell said.

"Three of the staff are out sick, can you believe that? The patient load has become impossible to handle. How is it out on the floors?"

"Pretty bad. People are everywhere you look." Russell chuckled softly.

They all need to have their blood drained.

Rod gave him a strange look and said, "Well, maybe you'd better get to it, Russell. We need to get these people out of here to make room for more."

Russell took a couple of deep breaths and carefully restocked his tray in case he was called out to the floors again. He walked over to the drawing area, where all six chairs were filled with patients waiting to give their blood for a variety of tests.

He smiled at the first person in line.

Bette Golden Lamb & J. J. Lamb

148

The ER was like a battlefield—bodies everywhere. Gina thought if she saw one more person with pneumonia, she would scream.

Many of those who came through triage probably should have been hospitalized. Most of the younger ones were given IV antibiotics for their secondary infections and send home with prescriptions.

She'd been working twelve hours straight and was out the door before they could try to talk her into staying another hour, or more. It was a good thing she hadn't come in Brad's car or she would need to take a bus home. She didn't think she could handle that.

When she slid into the Fiat, she rested her head on the steering wheel for a moment. Now that she'd slowed down, she realized she wasn't feeling so great herself.

Get on with it, Mazzio. Go home, have some hot soup, take a hot shower, and crawl into bed. You'll be fine. After a good night's sleep, you'll be ready for tomorrow.

She drove in a daze; the only thing that kept her awake was a pounding headache that was impossible to ignore. She parked her car and walked the short distance to the apartment complex.

Brad was standing beside the entrance, waiting for her. He held out a hand.

"Hey, how are you doing?"

"Not too good, really. I hope I'm not coming down with this horrible bug."

"Come on. I'll walk you upstairs." He took hold of her arm and they went through the entrance door. She leaned heavily on him as she forced herself up the flight of stairs.

"Brad, I'd ask you in but I'm really too done in. Tomorrow, okay?"

She'd barely got the key in the apartment door when it opened suddenly; she almost fell into her apartment.

Harry!

"What ..." Gina backed up a step, glared at him. "You have one hell of a nerve showing up here like this."

"You're Harry Lucke, right?" Brad said. "I've met you before." He held out a hand to shake.

"And your name?" Harry's voice was crisp, icy; he ignored the hand being offered to him.

Gina patted Brad's shoulder. "Thanks for seeing me upstairs. I'll see you tomorrow, Brad." She kissed him on the cheek, stepped into the apartment, and closed the door behind her.

"What in hell are you doing here, Harry?"

He pulled her into his arms and squeezed her to him. "Baby, I missed you so much. I had to see you."

"Where's Jenni?"

"She went to bed."

Gina stepped around Harry, her heart pounding wildly. She set her huge purse on the sofa, ignored him, and walked into the kitchen. She poured a can of minestrone soup into a sauce pan and put it on the stove to heat.

Harry followed her to the kitchen and leaned against the door frame.

Gina turned and gave him her full attention. "Was I not clear about our situation when I spoke to you on the phone?" A chill raced down her spine, leaving her tense and angry.

"Gina, we've been together for more than four years. Did you think I'd let you go without a fight?"

"Did Jenni put you up to this?"

"I did talk to Jenni ... so what?" He sat down at the kitchen table and looked up at her.

"So, it's none of her damn business."

Jenni walked into the room, towing her suitcase.

"Gina, I know I've interfered. Maybe that's unforgivable in your eyes, but you don't realize how fortunate you are to have someone like Harry. I was only trying to help."

Gina wanted to reach out and slap her in the face, tell her she never wanted to see her again.

Why does everyone think they know what I need more than I do?

"Well, you need to wise up, Jenni. Really, get it straight once and for all. All you did was make things worse."

"I was only trying to help."

"Did Helen or Vinnie have a part in this?" Gina asked.

Jenni's face was scrubbed clean of makeup, her dark eyes were large and fearful. "I spoke to them. They told me to leave things alone, that you would make your own decisions. But—"

"But you couldn't keep your two cents worth out of how you think I should live my life."

Jenni said nothing. Her silence was like a heavy blanket smothering the air in the room.

"I think packing your stuff was an excellent idea." Gina picked up a spoon and stirred her soup before her gaze cut back to Jenni again. "Just go!"

"Gina, maybe you ought to reconsider," Harry said. "It's not her fault. I'm the one who asked about you. Asked all the questions."

"She didn't have to answer or interfere in my life. And maybe it's time you left, too, Harry."

Gina stared at him, then at Jenni. Tears streamed down Jenni's cheeks. Harry looked like he was in shock. Gina knew she would regret it, regret what she was doing. But right now, she didn't care.

Harry stared back at her. Jenni quietly pulled her suitcase out of the kitchen.

"Both of you ... go!"

* * *

Jenni felt like an idiot as she walked with Harry down the steps. It had been really stupid to interfere in Gina's life. She shouldn't have said a word to Harry about Gina's dating.

Dumb, dumb, dumb. That's what happens when you don't have a life of your own.

"I'm sorry, Jenni," Harry said. "It's my fault you had to leave."

"No, Gina was right. She told me to butt out. I refused to listen, stuck my nose in where it didn't belong."

They walked together to Jenni's car.

Harry's face was drawn and unhappy. "So, Brad is the one she dated? I met him once before, and as much as I hate to say it, he seems like a nice guy."

"He is nice."

"And good looking, too, dammit."

They reached her car. Harry threw her suitcase into the trunk and stepped back up onto the sidewalk.

"Can I give you a lift someplace, Harry?"

"That would be great." He threw his shoulder bag into the trunk next to her things.

"Where are you headed?" she asked.

"I'll probably stay with Helen and Vinnie," he said. "They're not too far from here." He gave her directions and they took off. "Why were you staying with Gina?"

"Some creep from work has been stalking me; she offered to let me stay with her for a while."

"Hell, Jenni. I wouldn't mess with that. Go to the police and get some help."

"If it keeps up, I will."

"There it is!" He pointed. "That's Helen and Vinnie's complex. You can double park while I get my things."

She pulled the latch to open the trunk; he got out and grabbed his bag.

"I really hope things work out, Harry," she said.

He gave her a quick hug. "I do, too. Thanks for the ride."

* * *

Helen served Vinnie a bowl of hot chicken noodle soup, then sat down at the kitchen table next to Harry.

152

Bone Dust

She watched Vinnie spoon-toy with the noodles, picking them up and letting them slide back into the bowl without ever taking a bite. It was irritating her, but she bit her lip to keep from saying anything.

"Sorry you're sick," Harry said. "Damn, you look terrible. I guess you've got what's hitting everyone else so hard."

"Hey, man, don't worry about me. I'm getting better. Really."

Helen let out a long sigh. "If you don't start eating that soup, Vinnie Mazzio, I'm going to dump it on your head." She picked up the chicken sandwich she'd fixed for herself, took a big mouthful, and glared at Vinnie. "Eat the soup!" she said with a full mouth.

"She's beautiful when she gets her Irish up, isn't she?" Vinnie gave her a brilliant, toothy smile.

Harry was sipping on a glass of chardonnay and, like Vinnie, was barely eating.

"This is great of you guys to put up with me. I don't know what I'm going to do now. My whole life has been wrapped around Gina. She's all I really care about."

He looked away, but Helen saw his eyelids were rimmed with tears.

"I love my work, but Gina ... I need her ... need her so I can breathe."

"Focus on the now, Harry," Vinnie said. "That's one of the major things I've been getting out of therapy. As long as I remember to do that, it helps quiet the noises in my head."

"So things are going well with your sessions?"

"I'm not as angry, or as scared, but it's all still with me. I can't stop thinking about those guys in my crew that I left behind. I can't stop feeling that I deserted them ... they're there, I'm not. I can't let go of that."

"At least the nightmares have gotten less and less," Helen said, reaching across the table to take his hand.

"I have to thank you again for that, Harry. And you, too, baby," he said to Helen. He smiled at her, picked up his spoon and slurped up a spoonful of soup. "But I'll never figure out why a bunch of miserable, traumatized men and women spilling their guts makes all of us feel better."

"No one can *get it* like they do," Harry said. "Sharing traumatic experiences is healing. And there's always someone who's had it worse than you."

Vinnie took another shot at the chicken soup. "What are you going to do about Gina?"

"I don't know where to begin ... how to make her listen." Harry lifted his wine glass and took a large gulp. "I mean, she's already dating Brad Rizzo. Jeez! What if he hurts her?"

"He's a nice guy," Helen said. "I know that's not what you want to hear, but she's been so down; he's been good for her. "Have *you* considered dating again?"

"Honestly, I have thought about it. I work with a great gal and when I needed a friend to talk to, she was there. We spent a lot of time together. But she wants a lot more than I can give ... to her, or anyone else, except Gina."

"Gina loves you, Harry," Vinnie said. "I don't doubt that for a second. But I'm her brother; I saw it all ... saw how Dominick treated her. He destroyed a part of her, changed her in so many ways. It's not only soldiers who suffer from PTSD."

"Yeah, I know," Harry said. "She still has those horrible nightmares. Gina's a pretty tough person and can handle most things, but those dreams really beat her down."

"They're quite a pair of siblings," Helen said. "One goes off to Afghanistan, one stays in the Bronx, and they both end up a mess."

"Listen to me, Harry," Vinnie said, "If you want to win her back, you have to be willing to take her the way she is."

"Don't I do that?" Harry ran a hand across his eyes. "I'm in love with her. I'm always there for her."

"Not if you keep hounding her about getting married," Helen said. "Why can't you just be with her ... be her lover ... be her friend?"

Harry bowed his head. "I'll do anything." He looked up at the both of them. "Do you hear me? *Anything.* But how can I make her stop thinking about Dominick, stop her from thinking he's going to come kill her ... kill me?"

"If I knew, if I could think of a way, I'd tell you, man," Vinnie said.

Chapter 31

Jenni walked into her apartment. Everything seemed to be all right. She felt really dumb about overreacting. Russell was probably following her just to frighten her.

Must be something wrong with me to torment a rapist.

She set her suitcase down on the end of the bed and unpacked. She carried her things to the dresser and when she opened the drawers, everything was a mess.

She stared at it for a moment, shrugged, blamed it on having packed in such a hurry.

After she put everything away, she still felt something was off. She couldn't pinpoint what it was.

Standing silently in her bedroom, she listened, turning her head from side to side.

Nothing.

Maybe she was simply nervous about being alone again. She'd never thought of her place as empty or minded living alone ... until now.

It was nice staying with Gina, having a friend to talk to at the end of the day.

Guess it's back to the television for company.

She wandered into the kitchen and started searching for something to eat.

Screw it! I'll order out. Pizza.

She pulled out a delivery menu from a local pizza parlor. As she scanned through the menu food items, she absently opened the fridge.

Inside, a dead rabbit stared back at her, eyes bugging out, its pelt covered in blood.

* * *

What's Harry doing here in San Francisco? Why can't he leave me alone?

Gina was numb standing in the shower, relentless hot water pounding every part of her as she turned and turned. The steamy heat loosened her muscles and the tight, twisting knot in her stomach began to ease.

Thoughts, good and bad, swirled through her head, spinning like flashing lights on a runaway merry-go-round.

Confused, so confused.

Tonight, when Harry held her in his arms, it ... it ... was like coming home again. Just his touch made her feel safe and warm. He was her Harry.

Harry!

Was now the time to admit that ending their relationship had messed up her life even more, sending her off into nowhere land?

All I wanted was to protect him from Dominick. Protect him from the sadness of not having children. Protect him from ... me.

Long, slow moments passed as she soaped herself, let the water flow over every part of her as it washed away the foaming suds.

Am I that controlling? Do I think I can plan his life for him, decide what will give him peace of mind? Damn! Only idiots think like that ... idiots like me. Fix other people's lives? I can't even fix my own.

She needed to let go, accept that Harry could make his own decisions about what he wanted to do with his life.

Isn't that what Vinnie has been trying to tell me?

It may have been stupid to marry Dominick, but maybe it's even more stupid to not marry Harry.

And dating Brad?

All I've done is muddy the situation by bringing him into this whole mess.

Yes, he was attractive, intelligent, and understanding, enough so that she should have been able to forget her problems and immerse herself in sex. It hadn't worked.

Bone Dust

Gina stepped out of shower, dried herself, and hoped that her flu-ish feeling would disappear. She was better, but still not her usual self. Her muscles were achy and she felt like she was coming down with *something.*

She wrapped herself in a terrycloth robe, slipped her feet into a pair of fuzzy slippers, and shuffled into the kitchen to put on water for a cup of chamomile tea. Maybe it would help her sleep.

Tuva curled around her ankles and meowed, letting her know her cat food bowl was empty. She also needed to give the poor thing some fresh water.

When the tea kettle gave its little chirp, she poured the boiling water over a tea bag and let it steep for a moment. She took the cup, sat down on the sofa, and picked up her cell phone. She allowed the phone to drop into her lap without making a call.

The apartment was silent. Too silent.

Nothing's going to change unless I do something about it. Moping around isn't going to do a damn thing for me.

She sipped the soothing tea, ran her fingers through her damp curls, and picked up the phone again. Before she could dial, Tuva jumped up into her lap. Once the cat was settled, she called Vinnie. He picked up on the first ring.

"Hi, Vinnie."

"Hi, Sis. How you doing?"

"Not so great." Hearing her brother's voice brought tears to her eyes. "You know, Vin, I'm really an idiot."

"Yeah? I've known that for a long time ... but I love you anyway."

"I've sent Harry away and I don't know how to get him back again ... or even if I should try."

"What's going on in that spaghetti-for-brains head of yours? I'm supposed to be the fucked-up one. Harry's nuts about you and you know it. Why do you keep pushing him away? And, what's up with Dr. Brad?"

"It was a mistake ... that's all it was." Gina kept dabbing at the tears that wouldn't stop. "I just didn't want to ruin Harry's life."

"Well, you're doing a helluva job of that anyway. You couldn't make it much worse."

"You don't get it ... Harry doesn't get it. No one seems to understand that Dominick is going to kill me if it's the last thing he does because he thinks I messed up his life. And you know as well as I do that one way or another, that's what he'll do. What eats me alive is that Harry will be a target, too, if we're together."

"Yeah, so what?" Vinnie was laughing so loud Gina had to hold the receiver away from her ear. "You listen to me, big sister ... fuck Dominick! Harry's not a wimp; he knows how to take care of himself. Face it: The one you're worried about is you."

"I didn't know you had such a great opinion of me." Gina wanted to fling the phone across the room, never talk to her brother again.

"Just trying to shake you up." Vinnie waited a tick. "What's the real reason, Gina?"

She felt like someone had crushed her chest. The words were jammed inside. "You know I can't have children."

"You're not back on that again, are you?"

"Harry loves kids and it would be a miracle if I could ... could have a baby."

"Always trying to take control. Jeez, Gina, I bet you think the world would stop turning without you. Get a grip, will you?"

"I'm only trying to do what's best for Harry."

"Bullshit! Again, you're only trying to do what's best for Gina."

"Damn it, Vinnie, I am *not* that self-centered."

"Maybe not, but in some ways you're a typical nurse—think that if you do everything just right, you can save someone. You can't out-think destiny."

"What the hell does that mean?" Gina said.

"It means stop over-thinking every decision you make, every step you take. That's why you trip and fall flat on your face."

Gina started sobbing, she couldn't stop.

"Come on, Sis. You know sometimes I have to conk you on the head to get you to understand what's real."

"I don't know, Vin. All I know is I feel so lost ... lost without him."

"Well, if you really want to find him again, he's right here with us."

Chapter 32

Gina couldn't stop moving. She paced and paced around her living room, agitated and restless. She stopped, stared at the purple couch she and Harry bought at a garage sale. She remembered how much fun they'd had finding it, and then getting it home.

A replica of Rodin's *The Kiss* sat on the coffee table. It began to haunt her.

She and Harry would sit in the same position as the sculpture, wisecracking, pretending to be the couple Rodin had used as models. It usually ended up with them in the sack, doing a lot more than kissing.

The phone interrupted her reverie.

"Damn it," she muttered. It was Jenni. She let it ring a few more times, not sure if she wanted to talk to her. But in the end she picked up just before it went to message mode.

"Listen, Jenni—"

"In my fridge!" Jenni shouted. "What should I do ... a bloody dead rabbit ... he came into my apartment—"

"Calm down, Jenni." Gina plopped down into the sofa. "Tell me what happened."

"I came home...and..."

Gina could hear her taking long, slow breaths, trying to calm herself.

"I knew something was off ... but I was tired, upset ... didn't really pick up on it."

There was a long pause.

"Go on, Jenni."

Jenni sobbed into the phone, trying to get the words out. "I ... I opened the fridge and there it was—a dead ... a dead rabbit. It was smeared in blood. The whole inside of the fridge is covered with blood."

"Okay, okay. Sit down and wait for me. I'll get dressed and be right there. No more than twenty minutes."

"Hurry!"

"Have you called the police?" Gina said.

"I ... I—"

"Never mind. I'll take care of it." She spoke calmly and softly to Jenni, like talking to an injured child. Gina wasn't sure she was getting through. "Did you hear me, Jenni?"

"Yes, I'll just wait for you to come over here."

* * *

A familiar gruff voice answered Gina's phone call. She knew she'd just awakened him.

"Hi, Mulzini?"

There was a long pause before the SFPD Inspector answered. "Gina ... Gina Mazzio? Is that you?"

"None other."

"Must be near a year since I last heard from you," he said. "And, of course, you must be in some kind of mess again, because that's the only time I hear from you."

"Thanks for the vote of confidence."

"Don't tell me you've lost your sense of humor. Besides, how did you get my home number? That sergeant is in for a pop on the chin—"

"Before you go all crazy on me, he didn't give me your home number. You did ... a long time ago ... and you told me to call you anytime."

"Me and my big mouth."

"One of the nurses I work with was staying with me because someone had been stalking her."

"Isn't that nice. Now he has two women to stalk," Mulzini said in a sour voice.

"Anyway, she went back to her apartment tonight, opened her refrigerator, and found a dead rabbit inside, covered with blood."

"Heck, she should have gutted and stuffed the damn thing. She could have had it for dinner."

"She's not going to appreciate your gallows humor, Mulzini. She'll definitely freak out if you say something like that to her."

"You forget, Gina, I'm a sensitive guy. Would I say something like that to someone I don't know?" He laughed into the phone. "Well, maybe *something* like that."

"Would it be too much to ask you to meet me at her apartment? She needs to feel someone in authority is on her side."

"Don't we all?"

* * *

Gina, Mulzini, and Jenni stared at the gruesome rabbit inside the refrigerator.

"I've got to get out of here," Jenni said, her face white on white.

"Why don't we all go back in the living room," Gina said. "I'll put on water for some tea." The refrigerator scene had left her stomach feeling unsettled.

In the living room, Gina and Mulzini sat on a sofa across from Jenni.

"So this Russell guy, what makes you think he did this?" Mulzini said. "And even if he did, maybe it was just some kind of prank. Did he have a key? I mean, there' no evidence of a break-in. "

"Absolutely not," Jenni said.

"And a dead animal for a prank?" Gina said. "That's sick." The tea kettle began to whistle. She got up, went into the kitchen, and fixed three cups of mint tea.

"Russell hates me," Jenni blurted. Her hand was shaking so much she almost spilled her tea as she lifted the mug to her lips.

"Come on, Jenni, do you really think he'd do something like this?" Gina said.

"Yes!" Jenni's face turned a bright red. "That man tried to rape me a couple of years ago."

"What?" Gina stared at Jenni, her mouth hanging open. "You never said a word."

"Did you report it?" the Inspector asked.

"I did. But we were out in the woods and I had to take his car to get away. He reported the car stolen and the police acted as if that was more important than the attempted rape."

Mulzini kept nodding, but said nothing.

"So it was something more than your calling him Russ instead of Russell." Gina's voice was harsh. "I always thought that sounded lame."

"I wanted to forget about it, be done with it."

Gina took a sip of her tea. She could tell Mulzini was just being polite when he reached for a sip. When the tea hit his lips, that was the end of that. He set the cup on his coaster. It was plain he wasn't returning for more.

"So, Gina, have you picked up any vibes from this lab guy?" he said.

"Before this, I only thought there was something weird about the way he acted around patients. He may be very good at his job, but he's obviously a creep.

"Are you staying here tonight, Jenni?" Mulzini asked.

Jenni looked at Gina with pleading eyes."Heck, no," Gina said. "she's coming back home with me."

"Good," he said. "I'll get our CSI people in to see if they can pick up any evidence that he was in your apartment. And if you want, I can arrange for one of the clean-up crews to come in. It'll cost you, though."

"I don't care," Jenni said. "I can't go in the kitchen again ... not with all that blood."

"Isn't that what nurses do?" Mulzini said with a wry smile. "Don't you clean up messes like that all the time?"

Gina leveled her worst glare at him. "You really are a caveman, Mulzini."

Bone Dust

"Yeah, but right now I'm the only caveman you've got."

* * *

Russell had just finished sanding down two bone segments. He didn't like the way they came out.

The bone was porous and chalky. He swore he'd never use Eddy again as a source. But it was not going to be a snap to find someone else who worked in a funeral home, someone he could trust. Maybe he'd have to go back to using deer bones.

The door buzzer rang.

Who the hell's that?

He never had visitors other than when he had an appointment to sell his custom-made bone handles.

He started for the front door, stopped, then turned around and scooped the bones into the table drawer. He bent over, blew the fine bone dust off of the table.

The buzzer sounded again. This time, whoever was out there, kept a finger down until Russell could no longer stand the sound.

"Awright, awright, awright! I'm on my way, damn it!"

He flung the door open. A man stood there holding a wallet with a SFPD shield showing. The hair around Russell's neck stood up and with it came a chilling breeze across the back of his head.

They stood there staring at each other. Finally, the man said, "Are you Russell Thorpe?"

"Yeah, that's me."

"My name is Mulzini. SFPD."

"Mulzini?"

"Yeah, that's all I'm ever called. I know it's late, but do you mind if I step in for a moment?"

Shit, this has got to be about the rabbit.

Russell hesitated.

"Hey, I'll be in and out in no time," Mulzini said, edging through the doorway.

Russell stepped back out of his way.

167

"I've always liked these studio apartments," Mulzini said. He moved to the sofa. "Bet you pay a pretty penny to live in this neighborhood."

"Pretty penny?" Russell mumbled.

Mulzini sat down. "Oh, you know, one of those expressions that went out in the nineteen hundreds ... in other words, you pay a lot of rent, right?"

"Rent control. It's not too bad," Russell said.

"Uh, huh. Why don't you sit down. It's murdering my neck to keep looking up at you."

Russell sat down at the other end of the sofa.

"You know a nurse named Jenni Webb?"

"Yeah. She's one of the nurses at Ridgewood Hospital where I work."

Mulzini stretched his legs out in front of him. "Yeah, you know her all right. She the one you tried to rape?"

"That's her story," Russell snapped. "She could never prove it."

"Yeah, yeah. So tell me, you don't like her, do you?"

"Not one of my favorites."

"Why is that, Russ?"

"It's Russell, *not* Russ."

"Yeah, that's what Jenni says. Claims you've been following her around lately, just because she calls you Russ." Mulzini snickered. "Sounds pretty stupid to me. Probably hate her because you couldn't get into her panties. Now *that* I can believe."

"Seems to me it's only polite to call people by the name they want to be called. Is that too much to ask?"

"Seems that it is." Mulzini was checking out the apartment. His eyes were everywhere, finally resting on the floor around the kitchen table. "I kind of like the name Russ."

"Well, I don't."

"Does it make you mad enough to stash a dead rabbit in Jenni's fridge?"

Russell laughed. "Why would I do that when I could easily dress it and eat it myself?"

"Now you see, Russell. That was exactly my thought. Why waste it on trying to scare someone."

"So did it scare her?" The words just slipped out; he couldn't help himself.

"Uh, huh." Mulzini rubbed his face with the palms of his hands. "So, you've been stalking Jenni Webb?"

"No! We've ended up in the same place at the same time. But I wasn't stalking her."

"How'd you get into her apartment, pick her lock?"

Russell stood."I didn't do anything. Now get out of here and leave me alone."

Mulzini stood also. "Okay, man. I'll leave you alone."

They both walked to the door. Russell opened it quickly.

"Just remember, I've got my eye on you," Mulzini said as he stepped through the doorway.

Chapter 33

Gina couldn't believe that this was the same Ridgewood Hospital. It was the same building, but it didn't look anything like the place where she'd worked for several years.

There were people lined up everywhere trying to get into the facility for medical help.

Right now, there was a huge line outside the ER and it snaked around a tent that had been set up for triage. Several police cars were at the curb and officers were wandering among the crowd.

It looked more like a Civil War battlefield, with *everyone* needing immediate medical attention.

"Is this for real?" Jenni blurted.

"Hard to believe. I mean, we all knew there was the possibility of a massive outbreak. Especially if the CDC vaccine didn't match up with the current flu bug. Well, guess what? There was another report this morning that this latest vaccine is definitely not a match for the virus that's flooding the city."

"This is horrible," Jenni said.

"I'm glad I'm back on the unit today," Gina said. "Triage wasn't nearly this bad yesterday; at least we were in the building. Things have really escalated and I don't envy the nurses in that tent, having to sift though all these people, decide who gets immediate care."

The two of them crossed in front of the line, trying to get to the hospital entrance. Jenni took hold of Gina's arm and squeezed. "They all look really sick ... and scared."

Almost everyone was coughing or sneezing or both, some right into the faces of aides who were handing out masks.

When Gina and Jenni tried to slip in the entrance, no one would move out of their way until they held out their IDs.

"This is panic," Jenni said.

"Fear. It's always the greatest enemy."

Inside, a large crowd stood around the elevator, waiting. Most were wearing masks. Everyone was silent.

"Come on, Jenni. Let's hoof it up the steps or we'll never get to the station."

Up on the floor, the nurses from the night shift and the oncoming day replacements were huddled in the nurses' station.

Gina looked down the corridor and saw a rumor had turned into reality—there were beds outside the rooms and in the hallway. The sounds of moaning, crying, coughing, complaining patients became a surrealist nightmare.

"Welcome to Ridgewood's nightmare alley," the night shift team leader said. "This has been indescribable." She pulled out a room index of the patients on the unit. "I thought this would make it easier for all of the staff to identify everyone, both in the rooms and in the hallways. Computers alone won't cut it."

"I'd heard every hospital in the area is now trying to divert," Gina said, her headache getting worse. "No one is accepting patients."

"Hospitals and urgent care centers are sending medical teams out into the community," the head nurse said. "Wear your masks all the time, wash and sanitize your hands with every blink of the eye. If we get sick ... well, we have to at least try to take care of ourselves so we can take care of others."

"This has really spread quickly," Jenni said. Most of the gathered nurses nodded in agreement.

Another nurse popped in, "This is the second year in a row they've developed the wrong vaccine. What's the matter with those Big Pharma geniuses? They're supposed to know their stuff."

"Let's get on with it," said the outgoing team leader. "I need to get home and crawl into bed."

"Sounds like most of these patients have severe complications from the flu," Gina said. She could see the team leader had had it.

"That's pretty damn obvious, Mazzio."

172

Bone Dust

The team leader turned and spoke to the whole group: "As I said "I've indexed every person on the floor. Read through it. But I think, mostly you're looking at pneumonia, and all kinds of severe respiratory symptoms in-between." She paused, then added, "I said mostly because, as you already know, thrown into the mix is a continuing outbreak of some kind of intestinal bug."

Everyone moaned.

* * *

Russell couldn't stop thinking about that Inspector. When the cop had left his apartment, he'd spent an hour cleaning up all the bone dust on the floor and from his tools.

It's a good thing I got rid of that hacked-up femur right away.

Doing that had made him feel better ... at least for awhile. Then that Inspector showed up.

Fuckin' dumb to put that rabbit in Jenni's fridge. Couldn't help it. I wanted her to be scared. Guess it worked. She was scared enough to call the fuckin' police. Didn't think she'd do that after the way they treated her before. Worth it just to break into her apartment ... go through her things. I own her now.

Hope there's no way they can trace that rabbit back to the pet store where I bought it.

He ran a movie through his head of what had happened, watched while he gave the rabbit a shot of fentanyl, put the animal in a bag, and drove it to Jenni's place.

Man, did its eyes ever bug out when I set it on the cold bottom shelf of her fridge.

He'd positioned the rabbit just right so that when he sliced through its carotid, blood would spurt all over everything and the bunny would look like it was ready to jump out at her.

Thinking about it made him smile.

Russell looked out at the sea of bodies that were lined up outside the blood drawing area. He called the next patient to have her blood drawn.

Looks like there's a million of them out there needing to be drained.

The manager moved in and stood by Russell's blood-drawing-cubicle. "There's a whole bunch in Internal Meds that needs drawing. Why don't you get it? I'll do this."

* * *

The unit was crawling with patients. The minute Russell stepped out of the elevator, the sound of the sick and dying stunned him. The moans of pain, the choking coughs made him short of breath. These people were all dying.

Dying.

And so many. How could he stop it? How could he stop them? Stop their pain!

He looked for Gina or Jenni, but he didn't see either of them. Mostly he saw nursing techs flying from one end of the corridor to the other and it didn't look like nearly enough staff.

Maybe I can slip through the unit without either of them seeing me.

He took out his lab sheet with the names and the tests that were ordered. Lots of tests but only for four patients. One of them a Jane Doe.

He moved from room to room; no one seemed to notice or care who he was or what he was doing. With his lab coat and meds tray, he fit right in.

The first three patients looked feverish, but they were silent, eyes closed, and trying to sleep past their coughs.

For the last lab order, he entered a private, darkened room. The patient was sleeping.

At the foot of the bed, patient information read: *Jane Doe. Restraints required.*

She was restless and talking to herself between whimpers of pain and deep coughs that kept her spitting up mucus-like gunk all over herself.

Bone Dust

Russell wanted to turn around and run. Instead, he set his tray down on the patient stand. She raised her hand as far as her wrist bindings would allow.

"Please, please, please ... help me."

Thin white strands of hair were plastered to her skull and her eyes pleaded with him.

"Please, please make it go away."

He set up his equipment and took a pail from the cleaning closet, set it close to the bed. There was room underneath to hide the bucket if he had to.

The noise outside in the corridor, along with the old woman's loud moans, made him jumpy. He needed to do this. Do something to make it better for her.

He wrapped a tourniquet around her skinny arm, which was covered with dry, flaking skin.

He dampened her arm with alcohol, not to sterilize, but to make it easier for him to search for a vein. He kept moving farther up her arm, looking for a good spot.

It was hard to concentrate with all the soft, whimpering noises she was making. He could hear Todd in his head.

Get it done, you fool, get it done! You gonna let that animal suffer?

She's suffering. There was no doubt about that.

Then, like magic he felt a big rubbery vein.

Can't hide from me.

He carefully pushed the needle in and attached a clear catheter to the hub. The blood coursed into the bucket at his feet.

Even in the dim light the blood looked too red for a vein, and it was gushing out of her arm into the tube. He had tapped into an artery.

Now, her moans and whimpers took on a different tone. To Russell, it sounded like she was humming herself to sleep.

Soon even that sound was gone. Without even taking her pulse he knew she was dead. The blood had stopped running only because her heart had stopped pumping it.

He carefully removed the needle and placed a cotton ball over the puncture, sealing it with a tight elastic bandage.

It felt like he was awakening from a trance.

Forgot to fill the tubes for her lab work. Have to take some from another patient.

Russell moved very quickly now, grasped the bucket, went into the bathroom, and carefully spilled the blood into the toilet. It took two flushes before there was no trace.

Pleased, he rinsed the bucket and put it back in the closet. He looked again at Jane Doe.

Yes, she was sleeping peacefully now.

Chapter 34

José came over after work; Dominick was up and ready. Today he was going to buy a gun from a friend of a friend of José's. No registration, no papers, no nothing except good old American bucks changing hands for a pistol.

The two of them sat in José's truck in the Wal-Mart parking lot on the southwest end. It was pretty much deserted in that section.

"So do you know anything about guns?" José asked with that smart-ass grin of his.

"Nah, but he doesn't need to know that."

"I hope you know which end to use," José said, poking his shoulder.

"You'll be my target. I'll practice on you, asshole."

It wasn't long before a slick BMW came tooling into the area.

Man, that's a good lookin' car.

José nudged him. "That's the dude. Watch your mouth with him."

"Yeah, well at least the car looks good."

They opened their doors, stepped out, edged to the front of the truck, and just stood there waiting.

Pretty soon Señor BMW got his legs planted on the cement and turned to them.

He looked like any businessman, not some thug selling guns on the sly. He barely nodded, but José tapped Dominick's side, sending him into a time warp of pain.

They walked to the rear-end of the black car. The driver sort of ignored them, opened the trunk of the Bimmer, and indicated they take a look inside. He moved aside a pink towel to show them a lineup of weapons.

"That's really cute," Dominick said, pointing at the towel. "Nice touch, the pink."

"You want to flap your gums, or do you want a gun, huh?"

"I was only kidding."

"For you, Mr. Big Mouth, I have only one gun I'm willing to sell you: a 9mm Beretta. There, at the top. Take it or leave it."

"How much you asking?" José said.

"For your big mouth friend, nothing less than fifteen hundred. No dickering."

"Shit! That's high ticket," Dominick said. "I could buy it cheaper in a pawn shop."

The man looked at José and said, "If your loudmouth friend here had been able to go through all that legal purchase shit, you wouldn't have called me out here." The man flipped the pink towel over the weapons again. "Just turn your walkin' boots around and hike your asses back over to the ride you came in on."

"No, no, wait," Dominick said. "I'll buy it." He shifted from one foot to the other. "How many rounds."

"Ten in the clip, one in the chamber. And it's clean."

Dominick pulled the money roll from his pocket and counted out 15 Benjamins. "What about some bullets?"

"Well, I usually give a box with the purchase. But seeing how it's been goin', you get just the gun."

The man turned to José. "Don't bring his sorry ass to me again—ever. You got it?"

"Yes, Señor."

* * *

Dominick was damn irritable after the transaction. He felt like punching someone, putting his fist through the wall.

Goddam José! Why'd he have to pick that wiseass?

Dominick had dropped 1500 C-notes for the Beretta because he couldn't buy a pistol legally. Any records with a fingerprint would send him back to the slammer. And that BMW asshole had treated him like a loser. Him and his smart-ass car and expensive clothes.

Dominick walked around his small room with the worst fuckin' headache he'd ever had. Coming off of the Vicodin had been a lot tougher than he'd thought it would be.

Chrissake, it's not heroin. This should have been a walk in the park.

But going off the drugs seemed to make him real angry, even hotter than he usually was. And right now, instead of just his ribs hurting, every single part of him was on fire. He almost grabbed a couple of pills just to get comfortable in his own skin again.

But he needed to work, needed the money, so instead, he paced back and forth in front of his dresser where the bottle of pills stood taunting him.

After meeting with the gun dude, he wanted to swallow the whole damn bottle. But he held back.

He carefully rubbed at his ribs, where his skin was itching under the tape. He'd better get moving. José would pick him up soon—they were going out to hit the bars.

Probably will check to see if I'm still clean. I'll bet he didn't think I could do it.

But it didn't matter why José was coming. It was a good thing because Dominick was ready to put a fist through the wall.

He flashed on throwing a ball to first base. Man, that used to feel good. Everything would snap into place. If he tossed a ball now, they'd hear him screaming all the way back to the Bronx.

He chose a black tee shirt with a Yankee banner design splashed across the front of it and put himself into a new pair of jeans he'd been saving before all of this happened.

Standing in front of the mirror, he combed his hair flat and slick. He really did look like a Mex.

* * *

The bar was a little classier than El Peso. Actually, it was a lot classier. José waved to a couple of guys in the back. There were a few single women but most of the people were paired off. There was even a gay couple sitting in a booth holding hands.

"Now take a look at that," Dominick said. "I never could understand a guy getting it on with another guy. Seems to me their dicks would always get in the way."

"Listen, man, try to keep that mouth of yours shut," José whispered. "You don't want what these people will toss your way if you fuck up."

"They don't look so tough to me."

"Look at yourself and get real," José said. "You dropped a wad of cash today and you're still a mess." He laughed. "You might as well hang yourself as start a fight."

"Okay, you said your piece. I got it."

They slipped onto bar stools and ordered tap beers. The bartender looked them over real good before grabbing two glasses. José paid for the round. Dominick couldn't help it, he kept slipping a glance at the gay couple.

"You plan on picking up those two?" José said.

"What, are you kidding me?"

"Well, why don't you feast your eyes on those two chickies at the other end of the bar?" José turned away from Dominick, turned on the charm, smiled at the girls. "Now that's got real possibilities."

Dominick noticed that when he was on drugs, he didn't even think about pussy. But after a few days of being clean, things were working again. Not that he ever really worried. His buddy down there always knew when to stand at attention. Looking at the dark-haired girl at the end of the bar got him moving in the right direction.

* * *

Dominick couldn't remember the last time he'd been this drunk. What had started out with just beer had quickly turned into boilermakers the minute he and José started hitting on the girls.

Bone Dust

The four of them left the bar together and after the girls stop making fun of José's brother's beat-up car, they all jumped in and took off. They parked on the edge of the desert on the outskirts of Tucson and started groping each other.

He could hear José and his girl in the front seat. She was sucking him off, giggling while he was aye-yah-aying.

Dominick tried to get comfortable, but everywhere he turned, his ribs would send out daggers of pain, stopping him from moving too much. He turned on his back, unzipped his pants, and let it out for her.

"Come on, honey, take it in your mouth. Do it for me."

"Oh, Dommi, I don't do that."

"Why not, baby?"

"'Cause it tastes funny."

Dominick was loaded and loose, but his cock was hot, hard, and throbbing. He locked her head between his hands and started squeezing.

"Hey, Dommi. Stop that! You're hurting me." She began to squirm and try to get up.

"You get those lips where they belong or you're gonna hurt a lot more, and in places you never dreamed of." He squeezed harder and shook her head again, pulled her face down where it belonged.

Soon she was sucking away just like she was supposed to.

Chapter 35

Gina must have washed her hands a thousand times between patients, and used an extra puff of sanitizer each time for safety. All of those precautions probably weren't going to do her any good.

She was starting to have severe muscle aches and they were getting harder and harder to ignore. People were coughing all over her, and even with her mask on, she knew she would have to go into a decontamination booth, if one existed, to get rid of all the pathogens that were crawling on her skin.

Beyond that, she was really tired from running around the unit the whole shift. There never seemed to be a down time, but she did manage to squeeze in a short lunch break.

She ran to the cafeteria for a large bowl of thick bean soup. She piled a huge mound of crumbled crackers into the bowl and took quick sips of a giant cup of coffee, all while waiting in line to pay.

She spotted an empty table in a far corner of the room and managed to latch onto it before anyone else could get there.

Finally, off her feet, she breathed a sigh of relief.

She didn't want to talk to anyone, but she'd no sooner started eating then Brad pulled up a chair and sat down across from her. They stared at each other silently for a few moments.

"So how are you, Gina?"

"Not too good today."

"Look, I don't want to be a problem or cause you anymore complications." He reached out and took her hand. "But you know I care about you. I'd be lying if I said anything else. And I really want you in my life."

Words caught in her throat. It took her a while to speak.

"Brad, I've enjoyed being with you. It was such a relief to just go out and have fun without any strings attached. And you're a wonderful guy ... warm, intelligent ... sexy." The last word she said with a smile.

"I hear a *but* in there."

She nodded. "I have to straighten things out with Harry first, or at least come to some kind of understanding."

"Do you love him, Gina?"

She knew whatever she said would hurt him, but he had to know the truth. "I'll never stop loving Harry, no matter what happens, and that's whether he and I are together or not."

She took a long sip of her coffee, and then looked deeply into his eyes. "Everyone else is an also-ran ... and always will be. Everyone."

He bowed his head for a moment. "Thanks for leveling with me, Gina. And I do understand." He stood, bent over and kissed the top of her head. "If you ever change your mind, or need a shoulder to cry on ... you know my number."

He walked away.

* * *

After work, Jenni and Gina walked into the apartment. Gina collapsed on the sofa, put her feet up on the coffee table, and closed her eyes.

Jenni sat down next to her. "Are you all right?"

"Actually, I'm so beat I don't think I can even get up to take a shower and eat before I crawl into bed."

"Phooey! You've got to eat." Jenni was up and moving. "I'm going to take a shower and wash off all the hospital bugs and then make you dinner. I'm staying in your home, I've got to do something to earn my keep."

"Sounds like a plan. As for me, I'm going to sit here and veg out. Maybe just watch you work."

The doorbell rang.

"I didn't hear the downstairs buzzer, did you?" Gina said.

"It's me," Harry said on the other side of the door.

Jenni looked at Gina.

"Let him in, please, Jenni."

Bone Dust

Harry nodded at Jenni as she opened the door. He walked inside and sat down next to Gina, took her hand, and brought it to his lips. "Not feeling too well, babe?"

Gina's eyes filled with tears. She turned into his arms, put her head on his chest, and sobbed.

* * *

Jennie made a big bowl of minestrone soup when Gina refused to eat anything else. She looked so run down Harry suspected it wouldn't be long before she would be very sick.

She leaned on him as he undressed her and took her to the shower. He got completely soaked while he washed her hair, back, and all the rest of her.

Gina couldn't stop crying. All she would say over and over was "I'm sorry, Harry."

"Forget it, doll."

"Harry you'll end up sick, too. I can take care of myself."

"I don't think so." That's all he said, but he had to hold her up several times to keep her from collapsing.

Gina had really hurt him. He'd spent the last six weeks not only missing her, but almost paralyzed with loneliness. It was difficult to accept that she could be with another man so quickly, so easily.

Abby had been there for him, wanting to be with him, and he'd turned her away. Maybe it was time to accept that Gina not only wouldn't marry him, but that he'd become someone who was truly only a friend.

As he towel-dried her, she looked into his eyes. "I'm just so tired. I haven't been sleeping much without you, and the nightmares have gotten worse when I do sleep. "

He tucked her into bed, started to lie down next to her, but his shirt was soaking wet. As he removed it, he could see she was drifting off. "Some of your clothes are in the bottom drawer if you want to change," she mumbled.

"I'm going to go take a shower."

"Don't leave, Harry."

185

"I won't."

* * *

Harry lay in the dark trying to think about what his plan should be. He had to return to Arizona the next day. He'd signed up for an extended contract—a minimum of two, but possibly four, more weeks in Tucson. He wasn't sure about anything as he started to drift off into sleep.

"No!" Gina screamed at the top of her lungs. "Stay away from me, Dominick! Put that bat down!"

Harry reached out for her, pulled her into his arms, and held her tight while she shivered and sobbed.

There was a knock on the bedroom door. "Is everything all right?" Jenni called out, then started pounding.

"It's okay, Jenni. Gina's had a nightmare, but she's fine."

Gina looked at Harry and even in the dim streetlight he could see the fear in her eyes.

"It's Dominick. He's coming! Coming for me! Coming for you!"

Chapter 36

Gina forced herself out of bed the next morning to get ready to go to work. She felt somewhat better, even after a night of chills and burrowing into Harry's chest to try to warm herself.

She knew she was needed at Ridgewood—there were sicker people than her and the hospital was seriously short of staff. Seemed everyone was coming down with this bug.

She stood next to the bed, looking down at Harry. His dark curly hair was in a tangle, and he lay with his arms spread out, taking up a huge part of her side of the bed.

He was like a sleeping child, assuming that all was well, all was safe. Gina never felt that secure anymore. That sense of freedom had been missing from her life for a long time.

Evil was out there and she knew real safety was out of the question as long as it existed. One day her nightmares would turn into reality and Dominick would find her and kill her.

Harry opened his eyes. One moment he'd been sleeping like a child, now his eyes were fierce, intense.

"You're not going to work, are you?"

He reached for her hand.

"Harry, I have to leave."

"I'm going back to Tucson today."

"Go."

He looked at her with pleading eyes. "Gina—"

"Go back, Harry." She turned and ran from the bedroom, through the living room, and out the apartment door, with Jenni straining to keep up.

* * *

The hospital grounds were a swirl of movement. Patients were milling around, most of them looking deathly ill. Several open canopies, along with a large Red Cross cabin tent, had also been set up next to the hospital as triage units.

Doctors and nurses dashed in and out of the temporary facilities, trying to care for the huge number of sick people who kept crowding in like apparitions out of nowhere. With every blink of the eye, the numbers seemed to double.

Like yesterday, police cars were parked at various locations around the hospital. As they drove by to find a parking place, Gina and Jenni could see the officers moving through the crowd on foot. People were pushing and shoving to gain better positions in the long lines.

"Oh, my God! If this keeps up they're going to have to bring in The National Guard just to maintain order," Gina said. "These people are starting to hit each other just to get in."

"This is awful," Jenni said. "Some of them can barely stand."

"I'll bet the floors are like a madhouse." Gina bit her lip. "You can almost smell the desperation."

They drove around the side streets; all of the usual parking spaces were gone. They finally drove into the underground hospital employee parking garage. It, too, was almost full.

Gina hated driving into the bowels of the hospital and always parked on the street. It always made her think of Dante and the final circle of hell. She slipped the Fiat into an empty slot next to a wall. Not a favored spot, but at least one side of her car was protected.

They walked to the elevator and when the doors snapped open, there was only enough room for the two of them.

Someone in the back of the car said, "In or out!"

At the first stop, a few people got out and Russell stepped in with his tray.

She gave Jenni a reassuring smile, but she could feel her eye start to twitch.

Gina was squeezed smack up against Russell. As the doors closed, he whispered in her ear, "I'm coming to get Jenni, and then you're next."

Gina half-turned. "What did you say?" She could feel everyone's eyes boring into her.

Russell looked around as though he didn't know what she was talking about, or even if she was talking to him. She wanted to stomp down hard on his foot but was afraid he would react violently, harm someone on the crowded elevator.

When the door clunked open again, it was their floor; Jenni tugged at her arm. "Come on, Gina, let's go."

She was furious with Russell, wanted to strike out at him, but she let Jenni guide her to the nurses' station, which was surrounded by personnel waiting for report.

Russell, who had followed them out of the car, scurried past them and went on down the corridor.

"Did you hear what that lab rat said?" Gina said, nodding toward the departing Russell.

"No, but I could tell something was going on," Jenni said. "What did he say?"

"Some gobbledygook I couldn't understand." But she'd heard every word; she kept watching the lab tech until he entered a room at the far end of the corridor.

* * *

Russell's stomach was churning.

I hate those two nurses. Bitches!

Hate them.

Lately, finding a way to get rid of them was his first thought when he woke up, and the last thing on his mind before he fell asleep.

Their constant scowls of disapproval stirred up that familiar hot lava in his stomach—it bubbled up inside of him, threatened to expand and scald the rest of his insides.

At home, when the pressure became too much, he would grab one of his X-acto knives, find a virgin spot on his thigh, and slowly move the blade across the skin. As the pain and the beads of blood welled up through the slit skin, he surrendered to a wild orgasmic explosion; its powerful release always brought a sense of control.

Blood was powerful.

Blood was his savior.

Here, people in the corridor were pushing past him like he was unimportant, like he was nothing. The whole hospital was alive with movement, like an ant hill with hurrying drones.

Russell took a deep breath and looked at his lab sheet and the orders for blood samples.

He needed blood.

He needed blood *now*!

He checked his lab sheet against the last room number at the end of the corridor—patients Lena Dobbs and Aaron Dobbs.

Inside the room, he found them squeezed into a space that was barely adequate for a single patient.

He had no orders for Lena, who was sleeping quietly, but Aaron Dobbs had a string of ordered tests. The patient was coughing and moaning, suffering obvious severe pain. Russell moved to the side of the bed away from Lena, set his heavy tray down on the stand.

His mind raced ahead, projecting the outcome of what he had to do. He was intent, focused on how he could empty this man, empty himself.

He *needed* to empty himself.

A voice cut through his thoughts like a penetrating laser.

"What are you doing?"

It was Gina Mazzio.

"What do you think I'm doing? I'm drawing blood for lab work." He dragged the necessary tubes from his tray, put on the identifying stickers, and wrapped a tourniquet around the patient's arm. Puncturing the vein was easy and he was done in a few minutes.

RN Mazzio never left the doorway.

His insides were ready to explode.

Chapter 37

By the end of the shift, Gina was near exhaustion. She kicked herself for getting cornered into agreeing to stay two extra hours.

But she could tell that the evening shift supervisor was desperate for staff. That's what usually happened to Harry, and she would give him a bad time about it. Now here she was doing the same thing.

Harry, I've got to stop thinking about you.

She could barely plow her way through all the patients housed in the hallways; the madhouse of activity all around her was beating her down.

She was actually bruised from running into people, turning blind corners and smashing into them. The place was like a snake pit, with everyone on top of each other, slithering around, looking for a way out.

But there was none.

Every time she saw Russell on the unit, she made it her business to keep track of his movements. Her gut told her he was up to something ... something dangerous other than tormenting Jenni. But what?

After the change of shift report, Jenni, purse in hand, said, "I can't believe we made it through. Get your things and let's get out of here."

"Sorry, Jenni. Haven't had a free moment to tell you that I agreed to put in another two hours."

Jenni's face sagged. "Are you kidding me? How could you do that? You're totally beat." She leaned against the wall. "Well, I'm not doing it. I can barely lift my arms."

"It's okay." Gina pulled her car keys out of her pocket. "You'll be doing me a favor. I hate leaving the Fiat there ... something bad always happens to it in that damn garage. I'll grab a cab home."

"Really? That's the most temperamental car in the universe and you want *me* to drive it?"

"You can do it. I'll give you my emergency info if you need help."

"But, Gina, it's got a stick shift. I haven't driven one of those in years ... and I wasn't too good at it then."

"It's up to you. It's that, or you can grab a cab."

"Oh, I'll do it." Jenni took the keys from Gina, started to turn away, but instead took Gina's hand. "You know, Gina, I just wanted to say how much I appreciate you're being such a true friend to me." Tears welled up and spilled down her cheeks.

Gina hugged her. "Hey, glad I could be there for you."

Jenni smiled and walked away, then waved goodbye when she reached the elevator.

* * *

By the time Jennie made it into the underground parking garage, she was thinking the whole place was much too eerie ... and much too quiet.

It also seemed darker than she remembered as she walked down the aisles, moving toward the far section where Gina's car was parked.

Jenni finally realized some of the overhead lights had burned out, which added to the creepiness of the place.

The stupid hospital's probably trying to save money on their electric bill.

She laughed at her cynicism.

She began to enjoy the silence. The day had been filled with so much noise—patients in distress, one Code after another.

Thoughts of a hot shower popped into her head. That was the first thing she was going to do when she got to Gina's apartment. Then maybe she'd make a grand attempt at creating her Italian-style lasagna from scratch.

For an Italian like Gina, that should be good for a laugh or two.

Bone Dust

At least it will be something special ready to eat so she can just flake out when she comes home.

The more she thought about it and all the preparation it would take, she changed to spaghetti.

The underground garage echoed her laugh.

When did I get to be so lazy?

She thought about Gina. You couldn't say that about *her*. Jenni didn't know how her friend could have agreed to put in *any* overtime.

How does she keep going? She looks sick. I swear, nurses are the worst when it comes to taking care of themselves. We're all demented.

The car was just ahead. She slid her hand into her pants pocket and took out the keys.

Man, it seems like days ago instead of just this morning that we came to work.

She turned, looked back in the distance she'd covered, couldn't see any other departing employees lined up in their cars ready to leave the garage.

No one hangs around one minute longer than they have to. Don't blame them for wanting to get away from this snake pit as quickly as possible.

Her watch said it was a few ticks past 4:30. All the incoming shift workers were already parked and the place was peaceful. Maybe she would curl up in the car and take a nap. She studied the Fiat for a moment.

No one's curling up in that car. No way.

She quickly opened the driver's door, tossed her purse onto the passenger seat.

I hope I don't strip the gears driving this little baby.

With one leg in, she was distracted by a noise at the rear of the car. She turned her head and stared into the stone-cold eyes of Russell.

"What the hell, Russ?"

He grabbed her by the arm, yanked her out of the car, and wrapped both hands around her throat.

Jenni tried to turn away, could barely speak. "Let ... go of ... me ... you ... bastard!"

"What did you call me, bitch? It's Russell. My name's Russell."

"Leave me alone!"

Her leg was caught in the car; she couldn't pull it free.

She let herself fall to the pavement to get away from his strangling hands.

He wouldn't let go.

Russell squeezed her throat harder and harder. She couldn't breathe. Everything was fading.

She tried to jab the car key into his arm. He grunted a laugh, held her down with one knee, and pulled out his jackknife. He shoved it in front of her face and opened the largest blade.

"You little bitch."

He slashed across her throat; a spray of red flew around her head.

"That's ... my ... blood," Jenni sputtered as darkness closed in. "No!"

* * *

Russell ran to his car, drove out of Ridgewood's garage like the devil was chasing him. He screamed Jenni's name over and over, the sound bouncing off the insides of the small car. He could barely coordinate his movements to keep the Civic on the road.

Rapture curled into every fiber of his body.

He'd watched in fascination as her blood sprayed from her neck, pumped by each fading heartbeat. It was the most beautiful sight he'd ever seen.

He'd done it to animals when his foster dad was with him, made him do it. But this was different. Nothing compared to the vibrant spray of thick, heavy blood coming from a person's neck. Jenni had been a human fountain.

It hadn't lasted long enough.

Bone Dust

The front of him was covered with her blood. It was viscous and he couldn't stop smearing it all over his shirt and arms. Warm. Thick.

Draining patients didn't compare. This was what he really craved.

He was several blocks away from the hospital garage when the glow began to fade. Reality smacked hard.

They would be after him. That Inspector, the one who'd come to his apartment, would come looking for him.

The thought of getting caught made him frantic. He shucked his shirt and jacket, threw them on the passenger-side floor, reached for his lab coat from the back seat to hide his nakedness.

He drove, checking his speedometer and rearview mirror again and again, all the way to the back entrance of the mortuary where Eddy worked. The area was deserted except for the broken-down hearse that seemed to be stored there permanently.

He stopped a moment to think it all through. First, he thoroughly cleaned his jackknife, then stuffed his blood-splattered clothes under the garbage in the mortuary's disposal bin. He knew this was just regular trash. Eddy told him that human scraps were in special contamination units inside.

Still, he was certain that no one, homeless or otherwise, was going to go searching through a mortuary disposal bin looking for soft drink cans to recycle. People simply didn't want to have anything to do with a morgue. Most probably avoided this back entrance to the building all together.

He tried to slow down, to remember where he might have left any evidence connecting him to the crime.

He was nervous, his mind scattered, and he needed to get going. He didn't want anyone seeing him fooling around in the alley behind the mortuary.

What he needed to do right now was go home, clean himself from head to toe, and check through his car for anything of Jenni's.

He knew the police would eventually come to question him.

Chapter 38

Mulzini drove into the garage of Ridgewood Hospital. He'd never admit it to anyone, but nothing spooked him more than driving into an underground facility of *any* kind. It felt like he was being dropped into a mine.

I got to find another way to make a living. Only crazy people do this.

He'd gotten himself involved in this whole mess by taking someone else's on-call shift. He could still hear his wife Marcia when he told her where he was headed.

"That's what you get for being Mr. Nice Guy."

All he could think to say was, "I know. I know."

"Kisses, big guy. I'll see you when I see you."

He didn't tell her about Gina Mazzio's involvement. She would have only laughed harder.

Yeah, Mr. Nice Guy.

Up ahead, uniforms were setting up floodlights and stringing yellow tape to cordon off the crime scene.

Oh, yeah. Looks like Mazzio's little Fiat. Damn, blood smeared along the left side of the car.

CSI people were all over the place when he stepped out of his unmarked car and walked over to the murder scene.

He nodded to everyone and after looking at the woman, he thought she was probably the gal he'd interviewed about being stalked by that lab guy in Ridgewood.

He couldn't be positive because most of her face and body was doused in blood.

Mulzini stepped closer. "From what I can see it must have been a razor. Looks like a pretty thin cut," Mulzini said to the ME, whom he recognized.

"Don't jump the gun, Inspector. I see one finger mark on her throat, but the rest is coated in blood. Going to have to wash her down to get a better look. But you're probably right. Bet you a tenner that the perp tried to strangle her first and couldn't bring it off."

"Must be a Boy Scout," Mulzini said. "Always prepared ... to kill ... no matter what."

"Yeah, sure looks that way."

* * *

Mulzini took the elevator up to the top floor of Ridgewood Hospital. He knew the deal. If he was going to try to keep this quiet, at least for a short time, he'd have to go through the bigwigs. It wouldn't take long, though, before the whole hospital knew about the death.

He introduced himself to the administrator's assistant, who buzzed her boss and noted who wanted to see him.

Alan Vasquez met Mulzini at his office door, told his assistant to hold his calls, and followed Mulzini inside.

"We've met before, Inspector."

"I remember. It was about your niece. That was rough," Mulzini said as they shook hands.

Vasquez waved him to a chair and slid into another chair next to him. They both stared at the photograph of a young girl.

Mulzini knew it was the administrator's niece and he knew what had happened to her. It had been really ugly. He was thankful he'd not been directly involved in the case. He and Marcia were on vacation in Hawaii, but he met Vasquez when he returned home.

"I still miss her ... very much," Vasquez said. He turned his attention back to Mulzini, who nodded his understanding.

"Well, I'm sorry to say that right now we've got a messy situation in the garage of your hospital."

Vasquez glanced quickly again at his niece's picture, then turned back and said, "I know. I was told to stay out of it while the police did their job. Normally, news of something like this would spread like wildfire throughout the hospital."

"Yeah, I'll bet with this epidemic no one has time to breathe. The whole city is practically in lockdown."

"It's been pretty intense," Vasquez said.

"I'm gonna need to speak to Gina Mazzio. Probably a good idea if I took her home. She won't be able to use her car for a couple of days and she may or may not know what's happened to Jenni Webb, but either way it's gonna hit her hard."

"Let me get hold of the facility supervisor and check on her status."

Mulzini nodded.

Vasquez stood, reached down for his phone, and punched in some numbers. "Hi, Hillary. Listen, is Gina Mazzio still in the building? Oh, I thought she worked the day shift."

He looked at Mulzini and nodded.

"Okay ... I'm glad it was only a couple of hours overtime ... but she's going to have to leave." He gave Mulzini a shrug and looked up at the ceiling. "You can't have her for another two hours, Hillary, you're going to have to let her go now."

Mulzini could tell Vasquez was getting an earful of protest.

"Do the best you can." He hung up. "Poor, Gina. It's always one thing or another." His eyes were sad as he looked at Mulzini. "The fates need to give that woman a break."

* * *

Gina was rushing around the unit trying to finish handing out her meds. She'd just given the last injection when one of the nurses pulled her out of a room.

"There's someone here to see you. He's at the nurses' station."

"Who is it?"

"Don't know him, but administration sent him down."

What did I do now?

When she turned the corner and saw Mulzini, she broke out into a smile. "Inspector, what are you doing here? And from administration?"

Mulzini wasn't smiling. "Get your things. You're off duty."

"No, I've been asked to put in more time, sort of indefinite. I can't leave now."

"Yeah, you can. I've cleared it with the head honcho."

Gina was puzzled. She went to the Nurses' station, took the keys from her pocket, and unlocked the drawer where her purse was stashed.

A sudden chill jolted down her spine when she returned to the Inspector and studied his face.

He took her arm and led her to the elevator. "Jeez, is there anywhere we can talk. This place is too damn crowded."

"We can go to the cafeteria. It's probably the emptiest it's ever been. No one is getting any time off." Riding down the elevator, Gina tried to read Mulzini's eyes, but he kept turning away. She gave up as they reached the cafeteria and the doors popped open.

It was more crowded than Gina had expected, but most of the people were family and friends of patients. Everyone was glum; she'd never seen the place so quiet.

"You want something?" Mulzini said.

"What I really want is for you to tell me what this is all about."

They grabbed a corner table and when they were seated, Mulzini reached for her hand. "Jenni's dead."

It took a beat for it to register, and then her mind went blank.

"Did you hear what I said, Gina?"

All she could do was nod until his words registered. "You said Jenni is dead? The Jenni that's staying at my apartment?"

"Unfortunately, yes."

"Oh, my God. Was it my fault? Should never have given her the keys to the Fiat. She really didn't want to drive it. Oh, my God, what happened?"

"It wasn't your fault, Gina. She was murdered."

Gina took in a deep breath and for a moment thought she was going to vomit. She swallowed a couple of times and said, "Murdered? Who?"

"We don't know yet."

"How?"

"Maybe it's better if we skip that for now."

"No, tell me!"

"Someone slit her throat," Mulzini whispered.

Gina's head dropped onto her folded arms; she kept it there for a long moment, then looked up at Mulzini.

"Where did it happen?" She sat up straight.

"In the hospital garage as she was getting ready to drive your car home."

Gina stared at the Inspector.

"I was hoping you might have a clue as to who did it."

"Who? Who? I'll tell you who. It had to be Russell, the lab rat! He threatened both of us."

* * *

"You won't be able to use your car for the next few days," Mulzini said, walking Gina to his car. "I'll give you a ride home."

"Thanks."

"They'll be going through it with a fine tooth comb to see if the killer left any evidence."

"I'm telling you, it was Russell Thorpe. He killed her."

"How can you be so sure?"

"You know they had history—he tried to rape her once. And you also know about the stalking. Dammit! He hated her." Tears ran down Gina's cheeks.

"But why, exactly, did he hate her?" Mulzini thought Gina was more than emotionally distraught—she looked physically ill. He hoped she wasn't coming down with the miserable flu that was hitting everyone, including his own department. He was working double shifts like several others who were still standing.

"Isn't what I told you enough?"

"No. It's not hard evidence."

"Okay, well, she's been digging at him lately, pissing him off by calling him Russ instead of Russell."

"I know about that, too. Big deal. I mean, isn't that stuff kind of childish? Working up a real sense of killing hatred usually takes a lot more than that," Mulzini said. "Don't get me wrong. I'm not saying it's not possible. People can get crazy over the weirdest things."

"Exactly. He *is* weird ... something's just not right about that guy."

"And if anyone is going to pick up on it, it's certainly going to be you," Mulzini said with a smile. "Look, I'll be checking out this Russ-Russell guy again. He's the only suspect we have right now."

"I know you think I'm nuts, Inspector, and maybe I am. But I can't help thinking that if I hadn't agreed to work a couple of extra hours, Jenni would still be alive."

"Maybe. And maybe you'd both be dead." He squeezed her hand. "You've got to stop torturing yourself. It is what it is. If you keep going down that *what if* road, it's just going to make everything harder for you."

"I know that coward would never have tried to take us both on at once."

The Inspector bit his lip, then said, "Where's Harry? Is he off on an assignment? This would really be a good time for him to be here with you."

"Harry and I are not engaged anymore."

"What? Are you kidding me, Gina?"

"No."

"You mind telling me what happened?" Mulzini pulled up and double-parked in front of Gina's apartment complex.

She was sitting up straight, staring out the windshield. She looked like she could start crying again at any moment. He wasn't good with that, women crying.

"We have some basic differences about our relationship that just aren't working."

"Okay, that's the cleaned-up version. What really happened?"

Gina shifted in her seat. "Harry wants to get married, has wanted to for a long time." She sighed, blowing air out between her lips. "Thing is, I'm simply not ready to get married. That's it in a nutshell. I don't know how else to describe it."

He took her arm and held it tight. "I'm the last one in the world to give advice about love and marriage, but I've always thought you two were a great match."

"I'd better go in now," Gina said.

"Is there anyone who can stay with you?"

"I'm fine," she said. "I can always call my brother and his girlfriend. But thanks for asking ... and for giving me a ride home." She started to get out of the car, stopped, and looked back at him. "It means a lot to me that you took the time to find me and tell me about Jenni. Nothing's going to take away the pain, but ... but ... you know what I'm saying."

Mulzini could feel his face redden. "Well, you're not only one of my favorite people, but Marcia likes you, too, and she *never* likes any of the women I do." He started to get out of the car.

"You don't need to come in with me," she said.

"Yes, I most certainly do. You're not going in there until I check it out."

Chapter 39

Mulzini drove straight to Russell Thorpe's apartment after dropping off Gina and making a couple of phone calls.

"What's this all about?" Russell demanded when told he was being taken to the police station. "I haven't done anything."

"I need to ask you some questions," Mulzini said.

"Can't you do that here?"

"We're going down to the station."

When they got there, Mulzini planted Russell in a stuffy interrogation room and left him there alone in the cramped, intimidating hole.

The Inspector watched through the one-way mirror as the lab rat, as Gina Mazzio called him, glanced at the one-way mirror a couple of times, shook his head, and returned to staring at the blank wall opposite him. Unlike most people, guilty or innocent, he didn't become jumpy or impatient after several minutes went by.

Not this creep. He knows he's being observed ... and doesn't give a shit.

Russell spent most of the time tapping out some kind of rhythm on the table to music only he could hear. If he was in any way ruffled, he didn't show it.

Mulzini got tired of the game after almost 20 minutes and went back into the room. "Sorry to keep you waiting, Russ. Would you like something to drink—water, soda, coffee?"

There was only the slightest twitch of his upper lip that might or might not indicate a negative reaction to not using his full first name, as Gina had mentioned.

"No. I'm good. I'd just like to get out of here. I start work early tomorrow and the way things are going, I'll probably have to work overtime." He looked at his watch. "It's getting late, man."

"Yeah," Mulzini said. "It must be really hard on the hospital staff, what with this flu epidemic and everything. I've never seen Ridgewood that pushed before."

"Yeah. That's why I need to get a good night's sleep."

Mulzini smiled at Russell. "Well, I won't keep you here much longer."

The Inspector, sat down across from Russell, placed a file folder on the table, and opened it. "I assume you're aware that Nurse Jenni Webb was murdered in the garage at Ridgewood."

"Murdered? Jenni Webb?"

"Yes." He let that hang for a moment, then said, "What time did you leave work today?"

"Regular time," Russell said. "About four."

"Regular time? With all this flu going on?"

"That's what I said. You can check with the department."

"Already did that."

"Then why—"

"We both know you didn't particularly like Ms. Webb, is that correct?"

"She was all right."

Mulzini continued to stare at Russell, keeping his head level and lowering only his eyeballs ever so often to glance at the file's contents.

"So what's this all about?" Russell looked him square in the eye. "Why'd you bring me in?"

"I understand Jenni almost took out a restraining order on you. Were you stalking her? That's what she told some of the hospital staff?"

"I thought she was cute so I followed her one day."

"I think you're lying to me, Russ. We both know you've known Jenni for a long time." Not even a lip twitch this time. "We've already had a conversation about the attempted rape."

"Can I go now?"

Mulzini stood so quickly the chair he'd been sitting on flew back and hit the wall. "No, God dammit, you cannot go."

Russell's jaw dropped. "What do you mean I can't go?"

"You hated Jenni Webb." He took a deep breath. "I think you killed her."

"I didn't!"

"You stalked her, threatened her, and when she still didn't come around, that didn't stop you ... you killed her."

"Stop what?"

Things had been going the way Mulzini wanted until Russell asked that question.

This guy thinks he's slick.

Mulzini leaned over the table until their faces were up close and personal. "You didn't like the way she treated you. And as stupid as it sounds, the ignition point was that she called you Russ, instead of Russell. You couldn't stand that, even hated her for it, according to some sources."

"So?" Russell glared back at him. "She was one wacko chick, Inspector. Just because she fucked around with my name doesn't mean I killed her. That's plain nuts."

Maybe it was, but Mulzini was definitely getting the same bad vibes as Gina about this lab rat. But that was not the solid evidence he needed.

* * *

Russell felt damn good about himself when he left the station, got into his truck, and headed for home. He knew the Inspector didn't have anything on him, and neither did Gina. Otherwise, he'd be locked up.

He'd been heavy into Dad Todd's game with the Inspector.

His foster dad taught him well. Look people in the eye when you talk to them, especially when you're in the hot seat. They always think you'll give yourself away by doing or saying something stupid.

Well, not me, man.

Russell saw right through the Inspector. The man had him sit in that room to make him jittery. Well, it didn't happen. And he'd made a point of staring that cop right in the eye.

Standoff, man. Big fuckin' standoff.

* * *

At the hospital the next morning, Russell drove into the employee parking section of the garage and tried to go by where he'd finished off Jenni. He couldn't get near the spot, though, because it was still cordoned off by yellow police tape. He circled around and found a parking place on the other side of the garage.

When the elevator got to his floor, he saw right away that conditions in the lab were just as bad as they'd been the day before. People were crawling out of the woodwork, waiting to have their blood drawn.

Controlled chaos. Barely.

It was all good ... for him. Ridgewood lab was his safe zone. The only place in the world he could slip in and out of unnoticed. Here he could blend in, appear to be like any of the other staff. He was as invisible as the walls.

He took a fresh lab coat from the stash in the back room. He still had his old lab coat, the one with a few blood smears on the inside from when he covered his nakedness after killing Jenni.

He'd stowed it under the back seat of the truck until he had more time to get rid of it.

Thinking about the lab coat and Jenni put a damper on the elation he'd felt earlier with the Inspector. He was slipping back into the weak little Russell that he usually was.

Rod was waiting for him as he walked into the blood drawing section.

"Boy, am I glad to see you."

Russell nodded.

"Maybe you could help us out down here for a while and then pop upstairs to Internal Medicine. I have a whole block of lab tests ordered and you're the best blood man we have."

The manager was trying to butter him up for something. He knew Rod didn't even like him, and the feeling was mutual.

Bone Dust

"I may have to ask you to put in some overtime. I've never seen anything like this. We've been swamped the past twenty-four hours. It would really help us out."

"No problem, Rod."

* * *

By the time Russell got up to the Internal Medicine unit it was after 9:00.

The hospital was still mobbed and there was no sign it was going to let up. The unit was the focal point of the frenzy, with staff and patients filling the rooms and hallways.

He was getting tired by the time he walked in to take the final blood draws from Lena Dobbs and her father. He'd saved them for last.

The girl was sleeping peacefully. It looked like she was going to make it unless something unusual hit her and caused a relapse.

Aaron Dobbs, however, was on his back, moaning in his sleep. A light positioned against the back wall gave off a dim glow. Russell could see a sheen of sweat coating Dobbs' face.

Russell set his tray on the food stand and lifted a covering towel from atop all the vials, tubes, syringes, and other equipment he used in his rounds.

The noise from staff and patients moving up and down the corridor was muffled by the closed door.

He looked at the array of bags attached to Aaron Dobbs' IV. This man was sick, totally wasted. They were pumping him with everything they had in order to turn him around.

Well, I'll save them the trouble.

Looking at the man energized Russell. He would do something good ... release this man from his pain ... finish what he'd left undone yesterday.

Suffer no more, Mr. Dobbs.

Russell wrapped a tourniquet around Dobbs' arm, took an alcohol sponge and thoroughly wiped the arm.

First things first, no matter what.

After he set an 18-gauge needle in Dobbs' arm, he drew and filled the ordered blood samples into their specific tubes.

He placed the filled tubes into the tray, then selected a large syringe and attached it to the needle.

In a moment he would suck off more blood and collect it in an emesis basin. Just enough to further weaken Dobbs. In his condition, it wouldn't take long for him to die.

"What are you doing to my father?" Lena Dobbs demanded. Her voice cut through his focus. When he looked up, her piercing eyes were searching for an answer.

"I'm collecting blood for, uh, several tests the doctor ordered." He forced a smile.

As he spoke, he put the syringe back into his tray and set the emesis basin back on the stand. He pulled the needle from Dobbs' arm and shoved it into a small sharps container. He held up the tubes for her to see.

Lena appeared to relax somewhat even though there was still suspicion in her eyes.

"I hope I didn't disturb you."

"Where are the nurses?" she asked. "I haven't seen one for hours."

He picked up his equipment and started for the door. "I'll let them know you asked."

He felt her eyes on his back as he walked out.

Chapter 40

Dominick was digging in an old broad's desert garden. It was in one of those places where two people were living in a big expensive house with handicap walkways. Pretty much like every other one on the block.

The sun was already hot early in the morning and he was sweating his brains out. Every time he tried to push the shovel through the *caliche*, his damaged ribs would make him want to scream out. But that was the last thing he would do with his macho Mex friends working beside him.

Friends? Yeah, sure. The only *compadre* he had in this crew was José. Didn't even trust that *hombre*, but he seemed to want to help Dominick when the others in the crew didn't give a shit.

It pissed him off that after the accident, he'd had to live off of his stash of money, which was supposed to be for his trip back to San Francisco. Now that wasn't going to happen for a long time.

The upside? He had accidentally found Gina's boyfriend. It may not be first prize, but it was a close second.

He'd lie awake in bed at night and try to figure out his life. He got it, knew why he was always angry—losing out on getting into the Yankees was plenty of reason.

But it bothered him that he'd hurt that shill in Frisco. He still didn't know whether she was alive or dead; it felt wrong that he might have killed her. She hadn't deserved that. She was only trying to earn a buck, like everyone else.

Okay. So he had a bad temper; he knew that. But people couldn't seem to stop ticking him off, and he wasn't about to let himself be a patsy.

But was he really such a bad guy?

When he was high on Vicodin, he would admit to himself that he'd deserved to go to jail for hurting Gina.

Those nights left him feeling low. Confused.

A sharp pain pierced his chest as his shovel hit a rock.

Damn! He'd been clean for a few days but he was gonna have to take a Vicodin. The hell with José, who seemed to think Dominick couldn't work while taking drugs. He stopped and reached for his water jug.

With his back away from José, he slipped a pill from his pocket, slipped it into his mouth, and took a long slug of water. It wouldn't get rid of all the pain, but it would help.

"How's it going, man?" José said from behind him

The guy's like a shadow. He moves from one place to another like the wind.

"It's fuckin' tough, if you must know."

"It's your first day back, man," José said. "Did you think it was going to be a breeze?"

"I don't like hurting." He looked José square in the eye. "It makes me want to put my fist into someone's mouth."

"A fist is one thing. A gun is another," José said. "When are you gonna stop carrying that thing around with you?"

"When hell freezes over."

José gave him the finger but Dominick ignored him. "Look, we've only got another hour," he said. "What say we go get a beer together, *compadre*?"

"I think I'm ready now."

"Hey, don't think I didn't catch you flipping that pill down your throat. Remember, I said no drugs."

"Just aspirin, you dick. What's wrong with that?"

José gave him that smirky smile that was supposed to let Dominick know he wasn't putting anything over on him. The dork was right. He did feel a lot stronger without taking the drugs. Not so weak and confused. Maybe the dude knew what he was talking about.

"Finish up planting that cactus," José said. "And don't forget to get all the way through that layer of *caliche*."

* * *

212

Bone Dust

Dominick sat in the passenger seat of José's truck, outside El Peso, their usual bar. He didn't want to get out; he was feeling down. Way down.

Taking the drugs didn't make him high anymore. Just the opposite. They made him feel bad. Bad about lying to his mother, taking her money. Bad about running away when he could have stayed in New York, been with his family, and not have to lie his way through every day.

Gina used to tell him to think about things. Stop jumping into everything. He hated when she said that.

"Come on, man," José said. "Let's go in and get a drink."

"I'm not ready."

José got out of the truck, opened the passenger door, and yanked at Dominick's arm. "Now or never, *pendejo*."

Dominick slid out of the truck and the two of them walked into the bar.

"Well, look who's here. Dumb and dumber," the bartender called out.

"Shove it up your ass," José said, laughing.

Dominick was silent.

One of the barstool-sitters yelled, "Snake, and I do mean snake, got your tongue ... usually can't shut that one up."

"Leave him alone," José said. "First day back at work ... just wonked out." To the bartender he said, "Give us a couple of drafts."

As soon as the beer hit the counter, Dominick snapped it up and swallowed it down without stopping.

"Hey, man, slow down. We've got the whole evening ahead of us. Pace yourself." José slapped him on the back and then sipped at his beer.

A couple of Latina women sitting at the far end of the counter were staring at the two of them. In a few minutes they were up and moving in their direction.

"Tell them to get lost," Dominick said to José.

"What's wrong with you anyway? Since when haven't you been interested in pussy?"

"Just not with it tonight."

"Get my man here a shot of tequila," José said to the bartender. "And let's get a pitcher of beer to go with it." He punched Dominick's arm. "Get with it, man."

* * *

They'd been sitting and drinking for hours. It was plain as day that José was going home with one of the women.

Dominick took hold of José's arm. "How about I borrow your truck, man? I need some alone time." He pointed at the woman hanging on José's arm. "She can get you where you want to go."

José looked at him as though he was a bug that just landed from Mars, but he nodded and held out the keys.

"You better pick me up in the morning, *mi borracho amigo*. If I don't get to the job on time in the morning, you and I are *término. ¿Si?"*

"¡*Si*!¡ *Si*! I got it!" Dominick said, snatching the keys.

* * *

Dominick was loaded, really loaded. Every time he opened his eyes the whole world was spinning.

He kept dosing on and off as he sat at the curb in front of the hospital. The seat of Jose's pickup was hard as a rock and he was about as uncomfortable as anyone could get.

Shit! Don't these fuckin' wetbacks drive anything newer than a twenty-year-old heap?

He laughed to himself as he remembered José's reaction to a turndown to go to bed with a pickup at the bar.

Dominick couldn't get it into the Mex's thick skull that he was still in pain from his accident. Screwing didn't have the appeal that it usually did. His neck was still stiff and his ribs never seemed to stop hurting. Fucking a woman wasn't going to make things better. Probably worse.

Bone Dust

What a dumb ass sitting here waiting for Gina's man. He could have come and gone and I'd still be sitting here like a boob. Well, the hours are right and I haven't got anything else to do. What the hell?

He shifted in the seat and pulled another Vicodin from his pocket and tossed it down his throat.

Even without José here at his side to nag him, he'd become reluctant to take the stuff. He didn't like the way it was making him feel lately.

But what about the pain?

* * *

The ICU was hopping and when Harry offered to go back to work a day earlier than scheduled, they practically snapped him up before he could get the words out of his mouth.

He was waiting for Abby outside the hospital at the end of the shift. It had been a good move to go back to work. It helped take his mind off of Gina.

He sat on the stoop outside the hospital and thought about Gina.

Can I ever stop thinking about her, wondering who she's with, what's she's doing?

He looked up and noticed an old pickup sitting at the curb. There was a man in the driver's seat and it looked like he was sitting and staring in his direction. But it was dark, the hospital lights weren't hitting him.

Harry couldn't be sure. Still, it made him uneasy.

Just then, Abby walked out. "Hi, Harry. How did it feel to be back? I've got to say you're a glutton for punishment. If it were me, I wouldn't have agreed to sign in one minute before I was scheduled."

Abby looked at him shyly, but things seemed to be all right between them.

Harry pointed to the Porsche. "Want to hop over to that Mexican restaurant we went to last week?"

"Sure thing. I'm starving."

* * *

Voices drifted Dominick's way and he had to force his eyes open. There he was. Whoa! Gina's boyfriend was with another woman.

Ha! Ask me, she's cuter than Gina.

He watched the two of them walk over to the hottest car he'd seen in a long time. At least the man seemed to have good taste in both cars *and* women.

They drove off, top down.

He started the pickup, but it complained, as usual, and he watched that Lucke fellow zip away.

Man, that baby could really move. In the blink of an eye it was only tail lights in the distance.

Damn! By the time he hit the road, Dominick couldn't see the nurse's car at all.

He kept going, hoping to spot the Porsche, and sure enough, he was about to pass a small strip mall when he saw the fancy car parked in front of a Mexican restaurant. It had to be the nurse, there weren't too many of those foreign critters on the road down here.

He pulled into a sandy area of weeds alongside the building.

Thought you got away, didn't you!

Dominick reached into the glove box where he'd stashed the gun, shoved it into his back waistband, under his shirt. He stepped out of the truck and walked to the front of the restaurant. A small sign on the window said: "Takeouts our specialty."

He went through the door, took a quick look around, and spotted that Lucke nurse with the woman sitting at a table in the back. He couldn't see her face, but Harry Lucke looked wasted.

One of the waiters approached Dominick. "What can I get for you, *Señor*?"

He grabbed a copy of their menu from a table in a tiny, two-chair space where people who ordered take-out could wait.

"How about two chicken tacos to go. And put plenty of salsa packets in the bag."

216

"*Si, Señor.* You can sit here while you wait." The man pointed to the seats.

"Nah. Too hungry to just sit around."

He stood at the tiny reception spot and watched Gina's boyfriend.

Man, this is funny. The dude is cheating on Gina.

Hell, don't matter to me. He's going down.

Dominick turned away and decided to sit in one of the chairs. The only reason he's picked Arizona was to be close enough to hop back to Frisco and do Gina in. But right here in Arizona, second best was going to feel pretty damn good.

It took less than ten minutes before the waiter was back with his take-out bag of tacos. "For you, *Señor.*"

"Yeah." Dominick took the bag, checked the tab, and pulled some grubby bills from his jeans' pocket to pay the man.

"Come back again, señor."

Dominick nodded, went out the door, and stumbled his way next door to a package store and bought a couple of *Negra Modelo cervezas.*

Back in the cab of the uncomfortable truck, he settled in to eat his tacos, drink the beer, and wait for Gina's pretty boy to come out of the restaurant.

* * *

"I never thought she'd end it."

"Harry, you should have seen it coming." He watched Abby shift in her seat. "I'm sorry. I don't mean to be so blunt, but you must have known."

He looked at her, thought she'd been a godsend since coming to Tucson. Without her, he would have been all alone and all of this would have hit him even harder.

For the hundredth time, he wondered why he couldn't forget about Gina and love someone far less complicated.

"Gina is very independent, and I've tried to respect that. I admire her resilience and I hoped things would work out."

"Whatever it is you've done, or tried to do, it hasn't worked."

"I guess I was pretty naïve. I thought if I loved her enough, she would forget about her ex-husband. Forget his threats; forget the pain he caused her."

Abby nodded, remained silent.

"But she can't seem to walk away from her fears; and if she doesn't do it soon, it's never going to happen. Right now, she's not moving, one way or the other—"

"Not much of a secret about how I feel about you, Harry."

Abby took a forkful of her *enchilada*. She chewed slowly. "I need to know if there's a chance for us. A chance you might care for me."

Harry looked at her for a long moment. "You're a great gal, Abby, but I can't honestly promise you anything. Not even a maybe. I love Gina and I can't say when or if that will ever stop."

Abby put down her fork. "We can be friends ... maybe things will change."

"Maybe. But I hope you realize ... maybe they won't."

"I've been looking forward to eating Mexican all day," she said, ignoring his last comment. "Let's at least enjoy what's in front of us."

He could tell she was forcing a bright smile

* * *

When they walked out of the restaurant, Harry noticed the pickup at the side of the building.

"Didn't we see that same truck earlier?"

"I don't remember it," Abby said.

"I do. It was parked at the curb when we left the hospital. I'm going to check it out, talk to the guy who's driving. I don't like being followed."

"Leave it alone, Harry."

"Can't do that." He walked up to the truck and looked in the driver's window.

Bone Dust

The outside lights from the restaurant barely illuminated the interior of the truck. A man was asleep, a limp taco in one hand, the steering wheel gripped with the other.

Harry looked at the face for a long moment before turning around. He and Abby climbed back into the Porsche and took off.

Bette Golden Lamb & J. J. Lamb

Gina was caught up in the same vortex of nonstop flu treatments that she assumed was affecting every health professional in the city. It was an epidemic and it was exhausting.

The media was now questioning the CDC, especially now that they'd stepped forward and called it what it was: a guessing game that failed and failed badly. They chose the wrong vaccine mix for this virulent strain of influenza and were now faced with a severe public health crisis.

Poor Jenni.

She'd always been the first to point a finger at the CDC. She couldn't be dissuaded that they weren't in bed with Big Pharma, and that most viral infections were born out of efforts to create new biologics, not necessarily for the health of the public. And then there's the question of military germ warfare.

Those damn bugs get out of hand and escape, then innocent people around the globe pay the price.

Gina had laughed at Jenni's paranoia, but with everyone becoming ill, maybe her theory wasn't so far out.

Gina went down to the employee garage to meet Helen, who had brought her to work and had also put in several hours of overtime.

"How's Vinnie doing?" Gina asked.

"Thank God your brother is as strong as an ox."

"It's those Bronx microbes; they not only help you build character, they give you a potent immune system. Sink or swim for us."

"He's still not one hundred percent, but he's out of the woods." Helen laughed. "And my God, what a terrible patient he is."

They'd just gotten in Helen's Prius when Gina grabbed her arm. "Look, there's Russell Thorpe getting into his truck. Let's follow him."

"What, are you crazy? Didn't you tell me he's a nut?"

"He killed Jenni. I know it."

"And you want me to follow him? I must be totally demented to hang out with Vinnie and you."

"I think it just shows what good taste you have."

"Maybe good taste, but not a sound mind."

Gina pointed. "He's leaving. Follow him!"

Helen drove out of the garage, practically on Russell's tail. Gina scooted down in the seat so he wouldn't see her if he looked in his rear view mirror. Traffic near the hospital was terrible, but as they moved away, the streets were less crowded.

"Don't stay so close! He'll see us."

"This is crazy, Gina." Helen slowed a little.

"Maybe ... but I want to see where he's going."

They had been following him for about five minutes when he turned into a side street.

"Looks like the dear boy is going into the mortuary."

"How do you know?"

"I lost a friend last year. All the parking was taken for the memorial and someone told me about parking back here."

"Maybe we ought play it safe and pull up at the curb outside," Gina said. "That way we can get away if we have to without being trapped."

"Now that makes sense." Helen parked the car on the street near the alley entrance. They used a building for cover and watched Russell head for a large garbage bin. He was carrying a bundle in one hand and when he looked around they pulled their heads back before he spotted them.

"Let's get back to the car." Gina pulled on Helen's arm and they sprinted to the Prius, scooted down in their seats, and waited for Russell to drive out of the alley.

"Wonder what he stashed in that can?" Gina said. She peeked over the dash and watched until Russell's truck was out of sight. "Let's go look."

Bone Dust

"Are you kidding me? I don't like to get too close to those places." Helen gave her a squinched face look. "They might carry me inside and start draining all my vital fluids."

But Gina was out the door. "Come on."

They hurried down past a hearse with a flat tire. Gina got to the garbage can first, flung it open, and pulled out a bunched- up lab coat. "Now let's see what our lab rat has been up to."

Chapter 42

Russell circled his home work table, bones scattered across its smooth surface. He was trying to calm himself.

He went to the kitchen sink and gulped down a glass of water. He couldn't stop thinking about that damn Gina Mazzio, and that other nurse. He didn't know her name, but he'd seen her around the hospital.

They were following me in that red Prius.

Thought they were so smart; thought I wouldn't see them.

Well, I saw them all right.

When he'd put the soiled lab coat in the garbage bin at the back of the mortuary, he made sure it was thoroughly smeared with other trash. No way were they going to get any of his DNA from *that* coat.

Nice try you two, but try harder next time ... if I let you have a next time.

Need to focus. Think. Gotta be extra careful or I'm going to get nailed by that Inspector. He'll be back to question me again. Sure as shit.

Stupid! Should have left Jenni alone, or at least waited. Waiting would have been the smart thing to do.

Couldn't help it. Saw her going to that Fiat in the hospital garage and there was no stopping me.

Had to do it.

No one treats me that way, or calls me Russ and gets away with it.

Only his mother ever got away with using that nickname; called him Russie whenever she wanted him out of the way, or needed him to go to the store for her.

Always wanting me to do things for her ... things I never wanted to do. Had to leave the apartment when she had some sucker over... some shit who would buy her whiskey just to get into her pants.

That's when he started cutting himself. Seeing the blood made him feel like he was powerful ... in charge.

Dad Todd caught me and from then on I did it with him. It felt even better.

He walked into bathroom and took the jackknife from his pocket, the one he was never without. He stripped off his clothes and remembered how it felt to slash Jenni's throat. Still a perfect picture of it in his mind.

The look on her face as she tried to pull his fingers from her throat.

The slash.

Her trying to make it stop. Wild panic in her eyes when it kept flowing.

The thick smear of it all over her face and neck.

He soared as he watched the bitch's life dribble away.

"No"

The very last word she said to him, to anyone.

Anyone!

It was like a museum painting. A perfect picture in red.

He opened the razor-sharp knife, the same one he'd used on Jenni. He picked an uncut virgin spot on his upper arm.

Sliced.

A deep sigh held back a grunt of pain and he smiled at the beads of burgundy. He separated the skin and watched while it became a full stripe of blood.

A rush of pleasure filled his groin.

He could breathe again.

Chapter 43

"Shhhh!" Helen cautioned as she and Gina entered the apartment. "Vinnie may be napping."

While they were in the kitchen fixing a drink, Vinnie came in looking like the living dead, feet scuffling across the floor.

Gina looked at her baby brother and although he seemed better, he was still no poster child for the benefits of healthy living.

"Not feeling too great, yet, I see," she said.

"Just so you know," Vinnie said, "you look pretty run down yourself."

"I haven't really been feeling well, but I'm hoping it's just allergies and not this lousy flu bug that's dragging everyone down.

He collapsed onto a kitchen chair. "I can't remember ever being hit this hard by a bug."

Helen handed him a glass filled with V8 juice; he wrapped the fingers of one hand around the glass and took a few sips.

"So it's over with Harry, huh?" Vinnie said.

"I don't want to talk about Harry. I came to see you and how you're doing. I'm not here to get the third degree."

"Now both of you cut it out. No fighting," Helen said. "One of these days the two of you are going to have a grown-up conversation, maybe even more than one." She set a cup of tea in front of Gina.

Vinnie pushed himself out of the chair and sidled up to Gina, wrapped an arm around her shoulder. "You okay?"

Gina turned and looked into his red-rimmed eyes. "Not really. I miss him. A lot!"

"I think he'd come back if you asked." He squeezed her to him. "Why don't you?"

"I can't keep doing this to him, Vinnie. He needs to have a real life, not the one where he's in constant danger." Tears rolled over her cheeks. "It's not fair."

"Dear girl," Helen said, "don't you think he can make up his own mind? For heaven's sake, if you want to be with him, call him."

"Sorry, I'm going to go lay down on the sofa," Vinnie said. "Can't keep my eyes open."

Gina stood, took his arm and walked him back to the living room. She helped him down onto the sofa.

"Now you're spoiling him," Helen said. "Spoiled enough already. Nothing but a big baby." But when Helen smiled at him, there was nothing but love in her eyes.

When they were back in the kitchen, Helen said, "Do you want to stay for dinner?"

"No," Gina said. "I need you to give me a lift home, where I can take a long shower, then pack up Jenni's things. Her parents are coming out tomorrow and I want to have everything ready."

Those poor people," Helen whispered. "Bad enough to lose a child, but having her throat slashed open ... imagine finding out your daughter had her throat slit."

"I know that bastard was after me, not her."

"Gina! Stop that!"

"He was waiting at *my* car. That's how he got her."

* * *

Gina had just finished packing up Jenni's belongings when the Webbs arrived. The mother looked like an older rendition of her daughter and the father looked like he could be a brother to Colin Firth. He even had a slight English accent.

"Please come in," Gina said at the doorway.

"We can only stay a moment," Mrs. Webb said. "We have a plane to catch."

Bone Dust

Gina could tell they wanted to get all of the loose details over and done with, but the sadness in both of their faces made Gina's stomach clench.

"Please sit down. I've made some tea." Before they could turn her down, she brought in a tray filled with cups and a plate of chocolate cookies.

Jenni's parents looked at each other only a moment before moving to sit on the sofa.

Gina filled their cups from a ceramic pot. The father reached for the sugar, but didn't offer any to his wife. They sat holding their cups; each had propped a cookie on the edge of the saucer.

"I would like you to know how much I really liked Jenni. She was great nurse and a very good friend."

"How long did you work with our girl?" the mother asked.

"Mainly, in the last year since I began working in Internal Medicine," Gina took a sip from her cup. "She was a lot of fun to be with, but more than that, she was wonderful with patients."

"She must have known she was in danger," Mr. Webb blurted. "Otherwise, she wouldn't have been staying with you."

"It's true. Jenni was worried."

"Well, what are they doing to nab that killer?" Mrs. Webb said, her voice catching. "My God, someone slit her throat open." She slammed her cup and saucer down onto the coffee table, her hands shaking so hard she had to fold them into each other.

Her husband rubbed her back and tried to comfort her, but she was beyond consolation. He said, "I can't stop thinking about her last moments. What that must have been like for her."

Gina could barely catch her breath. She couldn't imagine losing a child, and with such violence.

"Inspector Mulzini is a really good investigator. If anyone can catch this killer, he can."

Jenni's mother reached out and took Gina's hand in hers.

"Promise me you will call us when they've put this monster in jail." She squeezed Gina's hand hard. "I want to look him in the eye."

* * *

"Oh, my God, Inspector, I'm so glad you called. I've just spent time with Jenni's parents this morning." Gina clutched her cell, wanting to scream. "They're in such pain."

"Parent shouldn't have to outlive their children."

"What about the lab coat? Tell me you found something. Anything at all that might help tell you who did this?"

"It was a nice try, Gina," Mulzini said softly. "But it looks like it may be too contaminated to give us useable information. There's also a problem with you bringing it in rather having someone official. All we have is circumstantial. Why did he dump it there? Why did he go there?"

"So there's nothing?" she said.

"'Fraid nothing that's going to help us."

"I can't stand the thought of that bastard getting away with killing Jenni.

230

Chapter 44

Helen placed a glass of orange juice on the side table next to the bed, then stood staring down at Vinnie as he slept.

Such a different person when he's at peace with the world.

His beautiful long lashes seemed to sweep across his upper cheekbones, making her wish for the thousandth time that they were hers.

Just like Gina's.

It was still strange how from the moment she saw him, there was no room in her heart for any other man. She'd asked herself many times, how that was even possible?

But she never doubted that Vinnie would always be the love of her life.

She sighed in relief. His hands were unclenched, and a small drop of drool was trailing down his chin, a testimony to his complete relaxation.

After a year of treatment following his return from Afghanistan, Vinnie was finally spending most nights at peace instead of waking her with shrieks of terror that made her heart race and her body shake in panic.

In those terrible moments, she wondered if PTSD ever really went away. Loud noises still made him jump and he never stopped talking about the men and women left in Afghanistan.

But he was slowly returning from a bottomless pit of despair.

Although guilt still plagued him, he told her most of the people in his recovery group suffered in the same way.

Sometimes in the middle of reading a book, one that had nothing to do with war, he would stop and cry. Anything could spark the memories of all the pain. And, yes, no matter how many times she asked the question, hoping for a different answer, she knew this would be with him forever.

His being alive came with a price.

In the past year, she'd grown to love him with all her heart. He might be damaged, but like his sister, he was kind and caring, wanting to make others feel safe, no matter how he felt.

"How many times have I told you to stop doing that?" Vinnie said, opening his eyes.

"What?"

He laughed. "You know exactly what I'm talking about. Watching me sleep."

She dived into the bed and cuddled up to him. "I could watch you any time or place ... and I'll never stop."

He opened the covers and pulled her underneath. "M-m-m, you're definitely feeling better," she said.

"I am. And having you home makes everything just right."

"How are you really feeling?" Helen sat up and tucked the covers tight up around his neck.

"Still very weak, but I've been getting up and wandering around the apartment on and off. I only fell on my head once."

"Ha, ha! Not funny." Helen reached for his juice on the bedside table.

"I'm so full of juice it's going to start leaking from my pores."

"That's not all you're full of, dear boy."

"Now who's being funny?"

Helen knew she had to tell Vinnie about Jenni, especially now that he was better. He would resent not knowing.

"Jenni Webb is dead."

The glass almost slipped through his fingers. Helen grabbed onto it and set it back on the table.

"What happened?"

She took hold of his hand and squeezed tight. "She was murdered."

"Murdered? In Gina's apartment?" He started to lift up out of the bed, but she held him back.

"No, no. In the hospital garage after work." Helen's throat was so tight she could barely speak.

"How did it happen?"

She grimaced and turned her face away. "Her throat was slit."

He was silent for a long time. He finally wrapped his arms around her and held her so tightly she could barely breathe.

He whispered in her ear. "How's my sister doing?"

"It's hard on her, but she's determined to prove it was Russell Thorpe who killed her."

"How does she know it was him?" he said.

"You know, Gina. It's something about her that I don't understand," she said. "She zeros in on what's wrong and that's that. There's no stopping her."

"Gina always sees the darkness in people," Vinnie said. "It gets her into all kinds of trouble."

Helen hesitated a beat, then said, "She even talked me into following Russell after work. See where he goes, what he does."

He raised up on one elbow, his eyes opened wide with alarm. "That's just crazy, Helen. The two of you could get into real trouble ... get hurt ... get killed."

"Would you rather she went by herself?"

"I'd rather you both let the police take care of that kind of thing." He pulled and tugged at the covers, then kicked them off. "Why do you have to interfere? That's just asking for it."

"Inspector Mulzini is involved. He's doing all he can, but they have nothing to go on."

He hoisted himself to a sitting position, but the sudden action wasted him. He sat at the edge of the bed. "Gina can't be alone now, especially with Harry gone." He fell back.

"Maybe I'll stay with her for awhile ... just so she won't be by herself."

"I wish I could go, too. But I'm not good for anything, yet." He took her hand. "But I think that's a good idea. Would you mind?"

"Silly boy, she may be your sister, but she's also my closest friend."

* * *

"I'm sorry, Gina," Mulzini said. "I wish I had better news. We still don't know who killed Jenni Webb. Whoever did it was very careful ... didn't leave behind any clues. Even the security cameras didn't pick up anything. There's simply not much to go on."

Gina was disappointed that the lab coat might not provide the police lab with any evidence. It was frustrating. She knew it was Russell, no matter what anyone else said. Why would he go to some out-of-the-way place like a morgue to get rid of his soiled lab coat if he didn't think it would be incriminating?

He was hiding something.

"There is a small piece of good news, though: you can pick up your car. I arranged to have it washed and thoroughly cleaned inside. You really wouldn't have wanted it back the way it was."

It all sounded so final. Yeah, Jenni was murdered next to my car, but everything is now fine again. We can all get on with our lives as though nothing ever happened.

"Listen, Gina, I've been digging into Jenni's past to see if we could find something to help us."

"Was there anything?"

The Inspector seemed hesitant, not at all like his normal outspoken self. "Yeah, well, I also spoke to her landlord. Seems Jenni's had a lot of roommates ... there's been a lot of men in her life, too. And one of them was Brad Rizzo." He paused, looked at her, and added, "Weren't you going out with him?"

Gina was floored. "Are you sure she dated Brad Rizzo? She never said anything to me. Not one word. Not even during the time I was going out with him. And she was staying with me then."

"Maybe she didn't want you to know."

Gina's temper was starting to kick in. "So what? This isn't a we-blame-the-victim kind of thing, is it? I mean, who cares if she had a million men in her life. That was her business."

"Maybe. But there's always the chance she might have pushed somebody other than Russell's button. Enough to want to kill her. I'm looking in every corner to find the creep who slashed her throat."

"The only buttons I saw her push was that lab rat's."

"All right, already. I get it. We both want the creep who took her life caged ... forever. Everyone deserves that justice."

Bette Golden Lamb & J. J. Lamb

Had that fuckin' nurse right in my sights. All I had to do was stay with it and shoot his ass off. Can't believe I fell asleep at the wheel.

Loser.

Those damn drugs kick in and I nod off like a fool. That damn Mex José has gotta be right. That's the end of it. I'm off the drugs.

But the fuckin' pain? What about the pain? How am I gonna work?

Shit!

He forced himself to smile at the old lady whose garden he was digging in. She lived in one of those big old adobe-style houses with another woman; just the two of them.

From the size of the place, Dominick guessed it had to have at least four bedrooms. He'd never had that much space in his life, but right now he'd give anything to be back in the Bronx, stuffed into a small pad with his mother and father yelling at him.

The thought brought tears to his eyes.

It had taken him long enough, but he almost had a hole deep enough to plant another damn, thorny cactus. He hefted the pickax to get through the *caliche*. Every time the ax bit into the ground he had to clench his teeth against the jolts of white-hot pain. Just two more hits and he'd have it done. He could do that.

He started fantasizing.

Gina's man with another woman? Bet she doesn't know about that other chick. Man, I'd love to tell her. Wouldn't that get her goat?

Dominick had been so intent on digging he hadn't noticed an unmarked police car that had coasted up and parked at the curb. One cop got out and started talking to José, asking for his papers.

Dominick's heart started racing.

Oh, shit, man. Good thing I left the gun in José's pickup or I'd be busted for sure.

He didn't know whether to bolt and run, or just keep working as though he had nothing to worry about. He wanted to run in the worst way.

Wet with sweat, he started dripping even more, he could feel it running like a river down his back.

He forced himself to pick up the cactus, close to its roots so he wouldn't get stabbed by the plant's long needles. They could go all the way to the bone.

When he looked up, the cop had his hand out waiting for the papers from the Mexican-American working next to him.

Dominick's heart was crawling up his throat. The only thing that kept him planted in one spot was the steadying look José gave him.

He tapped down the sandy mixture of dirt around the roots of the cactus. The cop walked up to him, looked him over from head to toe, and held out his hand. Never said a word.

Dominick pulled out his wallet and opened it to his driver's license. The cop just stood there waiting.

José signed for him to pull out the paperwork. Dominick's hands were wet and dirty, but he pulled out his counterfeit driver's license and handed it over.

He lowered his head like he'd watched the other Mexicans do around policemen and tightened his sphincter. It felt like he was going to pee his pants.

The cop turned the license over, fingered the paper, and looked at it carefully. Without a word, he gave it back to Dominick and moved onto the next worker in the crew.

José gave him a smile and went back to digging in the garden.

The old lady stood there as though cops coming onto her property and asking for papers was not only okay, but an everyday occurrence.

* * *

Bone Dust

"You should have seen your face, *hombre,*" José said at the end of the day when they were back in his truck

"Yeah, well, I don't like cops."

"Who does, man? But the worst they can do is toss you back over the border."

Dominick reached into the glove box for his pistol and shoved it into the wet waistband of his jeans. Fact was, every part of him was soaked with sweat.

"You don't know what you're talking about, man. I ain't no friggin' wetback."

José was about to turn the key in the ignition, but he pulled back, leaned into the seat, and looked at Dominick for a long moment.

"Well, now, that's no big surprise, *amigo.* Never did buy into your being *Mexicano.* Hell, you can barely understand Spanish, let alone speak it." He smiled when Dominick gave him a noncommittal shrug. "I always say, live and let live, man. Only maybe now you'll tell me your real story, and not some made up bullshit. *Comprende?*"

"I don't need to tell you squat."

José stared for several seconds without moving so much as an eyelid. Dominick began to feel trapped in his seat.

"Now you listen, man. And you listen hard." José turned the key in the ignition and the truck's engine came to life. "Fact is, no one likes you, Dominick. No one."

Dominick squirmed.

"I'm the only *amigo* you have," José said. "Reason I'm still here with you? Don't like to kick a dog when he's down. But you'll tell me the truth right here and now, *mi amigo,* or you're gonna hoof it home all by your lonesome." He waited a beat. "*Comprende, gringo?*"

"¡*Si, si! Yo comprendo, José.* First let's go get some *cervezas,* then do some talkin', and look for some pussy."

* * *

239

The bar stank from all the men who had come straight in from work; it made Dominick's stomach feel queasy. They found an empty booth and plopped down.

"I'll get the first round," José said, getting up from the table.

"Good ... sounds *bueno*. Maybe some tequila, too. Need to get out of this crummy mood I'm in."

José returned to the booth, set the brews on the table, went back for the shots of tequila. By the time he returned the second time, Dominick had tossed a few crumpled bills onto the greasy table.

"Put your money away, Dominick. Long as you're talkin', I'm buyin'."

They held their mugs up in a toast and Dominick gulped down half the beer before tossing down the shot.

"I broke parole."

"Uh, huh. Here, in Arizona?"

"No. New York."

José nodded. "I figured it was something like that," he said. "What happened?"

"Got drunk and I beat up my wife ... bad ... real bad. She almost died."

"Why'd you go and do that, *amigo*?"

"I've been doing a lot of thinking about that, José." He slugged down the rest of his beer. "I don't know why for sure. My head was fucked up, I guess. But it was *her* fault that they sent me away for three years in the slammer. Three long, stinkin' years."

"Pretty stupid to break parole, man. Hell, you were out. You were free."

Dominick tapped his fingers on the table to the rhythm of an old swing-era tune blasting from the jukebox. He picked up his mug again, tried to coax a few drops from the bottom of it.

"You know, I was almost a New York Yankee."

"The ball team? You gotta be kidding me, man."

"No shit, man," Dominick said. "I was pretty fucking fantastic, ya know?"

"What happened?"

Dominick looked away. He felt the bile rising in his throat. "It was my wife's fault I lost out."

"What'd she do?"

"You know women," Dominick said. "She kept after me to do this, do that. About drove me crazy."

"Like what?" José asked.

"She said I was drinking too much, that it was making me gamble our money away." Dominick gave up on the empty mug and shoved it aside. "Couldn't sleep nights ... my ballplaying got worse ... they finally threw me out."

Dominick lay his head down on the table and tears spilled onto his cheeks.

José reached across the table and squeezed his arm. "Hey, man, that's rough. I'm really sorry."

Dominick sat up. "Me, too. She's gonna pay for what she did, ya know?"

"Where is she?"

"In Frisco. Soon as I get a good cushion of cash I'm goin' back there and set things straight." He slammed his shot glass down on the table top.

The bar was crowding up. The stench was worse and there was a thickening haze of cigarette smoke despite the *No Smoking* signs tacked up here and there. The noise level made it almost impossible to carry on a conversation.

A couple of women breezed into the bar, stood in the doorway, and looked around. Dominick and José recognized the pair—waitresses from a diner where they ate dinner now and then. The women, one a dyed redhead and other a bleached blonde, spotted them and walked over to the booth.

"Hi, guys. How 'bout buying us a beer ... or two," the redhead said. "Might make up for those cheap tips you dish out."

"Cheap tips my ass," Dominick said, catching the bartender's eye. He held up two fingers.

Both men scooted over so the women could sit. The blonde, the prettier of the two, sat down next to José.

After a few rounds of beer, with some tequila thrown in, the four of them were laughing and in a good space when a guy with the build of a pro linebacker sidled up to the table. He was drunk and cruising for a fight.

He put his arm around the blonde's shoulders, bent down close to one ear, and said in a loud, fake whisper, "Hey, gal, what you doin' with this loser?"

"Get lost," José said.

Dominick had his hand buried in the redhead's crotch and wasn't paying too much attention until the big guy said, "Get your ass out of here before I reach over and break that stupid Mex neck of yours."

The blonde and redhead scooted. The drunken slob dragged José out of the booth by the neck and held him up in the air, ready to take a big swing and mess him up.

Dominick whipped out his gun, fired into the drunk's chest. A bright red burst of blood spread, soaking the man's shirt.

The big guy dropped José and staggered toward the bar, where the bartender fired off a double-barrel shotgun in their direction, and José's shoulder turned into a pulpy mess.

Dominick raised his pistol again, but couldn't pull the trigger ... he was falling head over heels into a deep, black hole.

Chapter 46

Idiot!

Harry had allowed Abby to pull him into a relationship that he knew wasn't going to be good for him. He knew that right from the start. He tried to discourage her, but not whole-heartedly—he was lonely and sad, needed someone to talk to. He allowed himself to succumb to that old-misery-loves-company crap.

Harry had always thought he was a better person than that.

Travel nursing had taught him that being alone wasn't necessarily the same thing as being lonely. But now, he *was* lonely, and conflicted, and so down in the dumps about Gina that he couldn't think straight most of the time.

So, yes, he'd been a selfish fool to give Abby *any* hope that their dating was going to turn into a long-term relationship. It just wasn't going to happen.

He pulled out his cell and punched in Vinnie's cell number.

"Hello."

"Vinnie?"

"Yeah, it's me, Harry."

"You still sound pretty sick."

"No, no. I'm a helleva lot better. Stronger every day." Vinnie started coughing. Took him a moment to stop. "What's up with you, man?

"I'm thinking of coming back to San Francisco. I can't live this way ... I have to see Gina."

"Maybe you ought to cool it a while longer." Vinnie coughed again. "She's in a bad place over Jenni and I don't think she can handle one more crisis. And believe me, man, you're one big crisis."

"What's with Jenni?"

"She's dead. Gina's positive it was that guy who'd been stalking her. Nothing definite, though."

"Damn! How's she taking it?"

"You can imagine."

"Yeah. But I do need to talk to her ... try to get her to understand ... understand things can be different."

"It's your neck, but I'd give it more time if I were you."

"I'm in a bad place, too, Vinnie. I've become friends with a woman out here, and she wants to work toward something permanent, if you know what I mean."

"And I thought you were only into Gina." An edge of irritation laced his words.

"Hey, don't get the wrong idea. For me, it's strictly friendship. She's the one trying to take it a step further."

"Can't come and you can't go, so to speak."

"Not funny, Vinnie. I need to see Gina."

"Give it a few more days. Try to get your shit together before you come back."

* * *

Harry'd gone to the hospital administrator and that hadn't gone so well.

"I know I signed up for some extra time over and above my original agreement, Mr. Simms, but that needs to be changed."

"If you weren't going to be able to stick to your contract, why did you sign up again? I could have had someone else, someone who was up and ready to go."

Harry looked at the man's pinched lips and stony eyes, knew he was in for it.

"I feel bad about this, Mr. Simms. I really do. But my future brother-in-law is very ill. You might have heard about how influenza is going wild in the San Francisco Bay Area. He needs help."

"And there's no one to take care of him?"

"Look, I don't want to get into this. I have to go home." Harry was already agitated, this was making things worse. "I've put in plenty of overtime, have done my best for the hospital, but I have to go."

Bone Dust

"When?"

"Within the week."

"It's going to cost you, Harry. I can't have my nurses just up and going ... not fulfilling their contracts. You'll have to pay a heavy fine for leaving in the middle of an assignment. It's right there in your contract." Simms shifted in his desk chair. "And forget about working at this hospital ever again."

Harry was up and out of the chair. "If that's the way it has to be, so be it ... it doesn't change a thing."

* * *

Harry ended his swing shift with a complicated emergency. At 9:00 P.M. there'd been some kind of shootout at El Peso bar.

Harry had never been in the place, but he'd heard it was a hangout for a rough bunch of people; people who were known to tote guns and knew how use them.

The EMTs brought the three men straight to ICU, bleeding out. All of them were critical, with head, chest, and shoulder wounds.

The attending was all over the unit. Of the three, the really big guy had taken a bullet in the chest; it shredded his lung. Not only was he covered in blood, he was spitting up blood and gasping for air. Watching him had Harry hyperventilating, like someone was sitting on *his* chest.

Another victim had a shattered shoulder and was screaming in agony. It wasn't until they flooded him with morphine that he quieted down enough so they could work on him.

The x-rays could have been read by an idiot with complete accuracy—the man would be in the OR as soon as the on-call ortho could line up a surgical team.

The third man had a nicked carotid. Someone had been smart enough to put pressure on the wound, but by the time the EMTs got to him, it was all but over. He was immediately put on life support.

Harry guessed that the EEG wouldn't show much of anything going on past basic survival function, if that. He probably would have been gone already without the ventilator breathing for him.

He was one dead man.

Harry checked the vented man's hospital ID—Dominick Machado. The name had a familiar ring to it. He scanned the computer, read his history. He'd been in a recent car accident.

Yeah, Harry thought the name was familiar. He saw his nurses' notes and remembered taking care of him during his hospitalization. It wasn't all that long ago.

What a mess.

By the time Harry left the ICU, his only thought was to dive into his bed and conk out. But he couldn't help remembering what Vinnie said—if he ever wanted to be with Gina again, he'd have to first straighten out his messed-up life in Tucson.

* * *

Each time he tried to plan his necessary conversation with Abby, he would fall into reminiscing about Gina.

He usually loved his travel assignments, which took him to all parts of the country—an education in itself. Not too long ago, his and Gina's schedules were in unusual harmony so they were able to accept travel assignments at the same facility.

It had been Gina's first outing on the travel nurse network—an Alzheimer's research facility located in remote gold mining country near Virginia City, Nevada.

It was unlike anything he'd ever gotten involved in, and not in a pleasant way. He had a feeling it might have scared off Gina from ever trying a travel assignment again.

On the plus side, he found it amazing how medicine and nursing were practiced so differently from state to state, region to region. Sometimes, it was like being in a totally different world.

It was difficult for smaller towns and less affluent areas to compete with world-class urban hospitals that had state of the art technology.

Bone Dust

New and developing technology was a wonder to work with, but Harry liked the challenge of having to think outside the box; it was how he liked to practice nursing. And it was that kind of thinking that often allowed so many small hospitals to give good care.

On this assignment, his whole attitude had changed. All he could think about was how it was keeping him from Gina. He needed to be with her. Needed her. And nothing was going to stop him from going back to San Francisco, going back before he lost her forever.

He stepped outside and took in several deep breaths. His shoulder muscles were bunched into knots and his feet were on fire; it was difficult to appreciate the bright moon and the raucous chirping of crickets.

When he got close to where he was parked, he saw Abby waiting for him, leaning against the driver's door of the Porsche. Her face lit up as he approached.

"I was beginning to wonder if you were ever coming out." She reached out as he drew near, winding an arm through one of his.

He walked her around to the passenger side and opened the door for her. When they hit the highway, the fresh air started to revive him. After about ten minutes of his pushing the car up to 100 mph, she rested a hand on his thigh.

He immediately pulled off the highway onto a long, quiet stretch of roadside desert. The glow from the moon made everything eerie and silent.

"Abby, I'm going back to San Francisco ... and I'm leaving very soon."

She shifted in her seat and even in the shadows he could see the frown on her face. "But why? I thought you extended your contract for another two weeks."

"That was a terrible mistake."

"I don't understand."

247

"You and I have become really good friends over the last six weeks." Harry's heart was pounding in his ears. "But I can't give you what you want."

He let the words fly. "I don't love you Abby ... and I know that's what you've been hoping for ... but it's not going to happen."

"But why? Tell me why?"

"Abby—"

"Haven't I been here for you? What do you want? What do you want from me. I'm a good nurse ... I'm a good person." She reached over and pounded on his chest and he didn't try to stop her. "What do you want?"

He screamed out into the night, "I want ... I need ... Gina!" He turned back to Abby and said, "Do you understand? She's who I want! If I can't have her, I don't want anyone."

Chapter 47

Gina had to get up—it was time to go to work. But she was in stasis. Her arms and legs didn't want to move, her head was pounding with the same unbearable headache she'd had since she turned Harry down, pushed him out of her life. Since Jenni's murder.

Jenni's gone.

That thought made her stomach turn.

She'd always trusted her instincts, which had saved her butt too many times to ignore, even saved her life a couple of times. Yet she'd never picked up on what Mulzini had dumped in her lap.

All that talk about Jenni having other roommates, that she'd had some kind of fling with Brad.

Why didn't Jenni tell her about it? And the even bigger question, why didn't Brad?

She finally dragged herself out of bed. At first her body was so heavy she just hung over the edge of the bed, trying to pull herself together. It took twice as long as usual, but she did manage to get dressed for work and was out the door.

Helen was waiting for her in front of the apartment complex. Gina could see her in the red Prius through the heavy glass entrance door.

She stopped and looked at the mail box—both Harry's and her name were still posted together. Several times she'd tried to get up the nerve to tear out the old label and replace it with only her name. She had yet to accomplish the small task.

She pushed out the door, made it to the car, and plopped into the passenger seat. "Hurrah, hurrah! I can get the Fiat today. Mulzini called, said he'd had it cleaned up."

"I didn't know the police provided that kind of service."

"They don't," Gina said snapping on her seat belt. "They'll bill me for it, but I don't care. I couldn't deal with it any other way."

Gina knew Helen was studying her. "You don't look up to snuff, dear girl."

"I still have this awful headache and I'm not sleeping too well. It's not only Jenni ... I ... can't stop thinking about Harry ... sending him away the way I did."

Helen took for her hand. "You know he loves you, would do anything for you."

"I know. But I need to be strong enough to do the same for him."

"What on earth are you blathering about, Gina?"

"I can't let this Dominick threat hang over his head, too."

Helen pounded on the wheel. "For pity's sake, will you stop with this Dominick stuff? I'm sick and tired of it. Just the mention of his name makes me want to vomit all over the car."

Gina didn't know whether to be angry or sad. "I used to be like you, Helen. I thought if I could survive growing up in the Bronx, I could survive anything."

Gina's head kept throbbing. "But after Dominick almost killed me ... something changed inside my head."

They were silent for a few minutes, then Helen said, "My poor Vinnie, and my poor friend. You both deserve some kind of break."

"Well, at least we're both still alive," Gina said, pulling a tissue from her purse.

Helen burst out laughing. "I swear you carry everything in that huge purse. Doesn't it ever get too heavy?"

"Nope. And for the thousandth time, all the teasing in the world is not going to get me to give it up."

"Mmmm, stubborn, like your brother."

* * *

Before Russell came to work, he'd spent an hour sanding and trying to polish the flawed bones he'd gotten from the morgue tech. But no matter how hard he worked on them, the bones remained porous and crumbly. If anything, they were getting worse.

His foster dad would have told him to throw them away a long time ago, get new bones, just like they did with the deer remains when they would fall apart.

Todd would have dragged Russell out into the forest and made him kill another animal. That way they could also watch it bleed out before they carved out the bones.

For some reason, he didn't want to throw them away. He sanded and sanded, but knew they would never make solid handles for his knives. Still, he kept sanding and sanding and sanding them, knowing that they would eventually turn into nothing but bone dust.

* * *

The morning Ridgewood on-line bulletin news warned of the continuing reduction in staff. The virulent strain of influenza had cut into the medical staff and all other employee departments.

More and more untrained volunteers were being brought in to take care of patients that had been admitted before the hospital had been forced to divert all new cases.

The ER was only taking care of the most acute problems: bleeders had the highest priority. There were rumors of using the school gyms to care for all the sick people.

The unit was just as busy as it had been for the past week. People running around, nursing techs taking morning vital signs while the nurses huddled together in the station.

Russell slipped down the corridor while the nurses were crowded together taking morning report. He planned on drawing blood for the lab and had to be careful, stay above suspicion, no matter what.

He was restless but everything had to quiet down before he could drain anyone.

He'd cut himself twice before coming into to work, making long stripes on his thigh. That usually kept him calm, at least for a short time. But it wasn't working. His stomach was filled with hot coals of frustration. He had to get back into control.

He looked at the last order sheet and recognized one name—Aaron Dobbs.

That was the patient he'd planned on draining when the daughter interfered. He dreaded going into that room again. The daughter might kick up a fuss when she saw him.

He edged his way around a cot in the hallway outside of the Dobbses' room and walked into the dimly lighted area.

He sucked in a gasp of surprise. The daughter was gone. He could barely make out the form of the father. There were IVs with an antibiotic piggyback up and running.

He looked at his watch.

Should leave it alone.

But the man was moaning softly in his sleep and the smell of sickness and suffering was bouncing off the walls.

Blood was relief. Blood was compassion. Blood meant comfort. Blood meant peace.

Russell set his tray on the bed stand and took out the tubes for lab test specimens.

He placed a needle in the patient's arm, filled all the tubes very quickly. Then he pulled out a huge syringe from his tray and set the urinal right next to the bed.

He was quickly back into the rhythm of drawing and tossing it into the container. The aroma of blood made Russell dizzy.

In a trance, he filled the syringe over and over, emptying it each time into the urinal. He finally snapped out of it. It was like he'd been sleeping. The urinal was filled almost to the top with Aaron Dobbs's blood.

He jolted into action: Pulled out the needle, fixed a dressing for his arm and took the container into the bathroom. He carefully emptied it into the toilet and flushed the blood away.

Bone Dust

Dobbs was very still when he returned to his side. Russell knew if he didn't get out of the room right away, he would be trapped.

He grabbed his equipment, his collection tubes, and hurried out of the room.

Chapter 48

Brad Rizzo was grabbing a quick breakfast when he heard his name over the hospital intercom; his pager went off at the same time.

Shit, can't I even have something to eat?

It had been that way for the past week. All of his patients were sick or dying from a bug that seemed to have infected all of San Francisco.

For years, he'd educated, pushed, and tried to encourage all of his patients to get the annual flu shot to protect themselves and others in the community from severe illness, or even death.

He'd been very successful—ninety percent of the people in his practice were inoculated and it seemed that was the exact percentage of his patients who were now sick.

What kind of justice is that?

A wrong turn by the CDC and the pharmaceutical companies had put the populace in a whirlwind of physical destruction. He was let down, cheated, and it didn't seem fair.

He picked up his cell and checked his page. Without any preliminaries, he started in on the person who answered.

"This is Dr. Rizzo. What's going on and why won't you allow me a moment to have a bite to eat?"

"I sorry to bother you, doctor," the floor clerk said, "but Aaron Dobbs is critical. They're coding him now."

Brad almost choked on his toast. He dropped it to his plate. "I'll be right there."

* * *

The Code team engulfed Aaron Dobbs' bed. Gina was the one who had found him nonresponsive when she brought his breakfast tray into the room.

She'd called a Code Blue from his bedside as soon as she saw what had to be done, then immediately began CPR. The

255

team arrived within minutes, but it seemed like hours that she was pumping the patient's chest. She was exhausted.

They all but shoved her aside as they took over. By the time Brad Rizzo raced into the room, they'd shocked Dobbs three times and were inundating him with the medications.

The teamwork brought Dobbs back. Everyone watched the rapid sinus rhythm displayed on the telemetry over the head of the bed. They looked relieved, breathing sighs of relief. But Aaron Dobbs was still unconscious and he looked like he was in shock.

After the team left, Brad said, "Last time I checked him, he looked like he was doing much better. He'd all but beat the pneumonia. I thought we were winning. What the hell happened?"

"I have no idea. When I walked in he was already in respiratory arrest. It was pure luck I popped in when I did."

"I'd say he caught a damn lucky break with you calling a Code."

Brad walked up to the computer near the bed. Gina could see he was bringing up Aaron Dobbs' lab work. "Everything looks normal here." He reached over and gently pulled down on the patient's lower eyelid. "This can't be right; he's anemic. Let's get a stat crit on him."

She pulled her cell from her pocket, punched in the number. "Yeah, Rod, we need a stat crit on a patient. Can you do it?"

Brad was agitated. He held out his hand and Gina gave him the phone.

"Rod, this is Brad Rizzo. We need that blood value ... and I mean right now." He handed the phone back to Gina. "Thanks."

It was awkward when Russell walked in to get the blood for the test. Gina couldn't stand to look at him. She left the patient's room to Brad and the lab rat and went back to the station, where she collapsed into a chair.

Her chest was tight, her muscles wasted. Worst of all, she couldn't get away from the rank smell in the unit.

It smelled like death.

She was so shaken, she barely noticed Brad sit down next to her.

"I've got to say it again, he's lucky you walked in when you did."

"How is he," Gina asked.

"You know, I would expect him to be much worse. His crit is low, but his B/P is back to normal, breathing's good, his chest is clear. The guy's a high-powered lawyer. Maybe it's a bleeding ulcer."

"Could be," Gina said.

"We'll do all the tests. He's alive ... that's what counts." He paused, tilted his head to one side, and said, "So, how you doing, Gina Mazzio from the Bronx?"

If he really wanted to know, she couldn't resist the opportunity to tell him. "Why didn't you tell me you dated Jenni Webb?"

He turned pale. "There wasn't much to tell. We went out on a few dates ... that's all it was."

"But to say nothing. Why were you both so quiet about it ... telling me would have been the honest thing to do."

He tapped into the computer and started to write his notes for Aaron Dobbs. He stopped, fingers poised over the keyboard. "That was my fault—I asked Jenni not to say anything."

Gina could feel her face turning red. "And your reason?"

He took her hand. "I didn't want to lose you and I knew telling you would complicate things between us." He gave her a humorless laugh. "See how well that worked out."

Gina carefully removed her hand from his.

A wave of exhaustion swept over every part of her. She looked at Brad and his handsome face, dimpled smile, and once again realized how good looks were unimportant. What really mattered was being completely honest. How else could you show true respect for another human being?

* * *

Russell forced himself to remain in the lab, do his job, complete his shift, not run away from the department. He would find out soon enough if anyone suspected what he did to the Dobbs patient.

No one came. No one questioned him.

He'd pulled it off again. Everything had worked out perfectly.

With his refined technique, he could go on draining patients forever without anyone suspecting. The relief never lasted—his gut was already tightening up again. Tightening in frustration.

Never enough blood.

He left the department around four-thirty. First he went to his locker to pick up his backpack and the rest of his belongings.

He fought the urge to run; he walked with a deliberate, slow pace, his lab coat over his arm. When he got to his truck, he threw everything onto the back seat.

Rod gave him a lot of shit for not leaving the coat in his locker again, but Russell made a point of ignoring any of his manager's comments about the coat. Today was no exception.

Once he was in the vehicle, he took several deep breaths, which did nothing for his jitters. He headed for the highway, taking off into a few side streets to see if anyone was following him.

There was no one.

When he was out of the city, he headed for his foster dad's cabin in the woods—it was about an hour away.

It was a big surprise when Todd left it to him in his will. The idiot told his foster sister what he was going to do. It must have really messed her up even more than she already was, because it wasn't long after that that she killed him.

The satisfaction she got from that perfectly placed arrow in his eye would have to last for the rest of her life—in jail. Her hatred had done in both her and Todd.

Bone Dust

Russell did a lot of thinking as he drove. He should have left that bitch Jenni alone; first when he tried to rape her years ago and now when he killed her.

It had put him right where he didn't need to be—in the spotlight. Until then, he'd mostly been smart. Being very careful with the draining had kept him in the shadows.

Jenni had ruined everything, and so had Gina.

Someday his luck would run out. If he wasn't careful, his hunger for blood and revenge was going to do the same to him that it did to his foster sister.

He stopped in the little village about ten miles from the cabin and bought food supplies. When he reached the place, there was still plenty of daylight.

He pulled his backpack from the car, along with the bow and arrow he kept in the trunk and lugged them to the cabin door and pushed inside. He never locked up the place. What for? You could blow the whole thing down with half a breath.

In a few minutes, the smell of the woods and the old fireplace, packed with kindling, calmed him, as it did when his foster dad used to bring him here to hunt and drain blood together.

Russell picked up his bow and arrow and walked quietly into the woods. He was keyed up, looking for a kill.

As he walked, his ears picked up every animal sound, but he finally settled into one of his favorite spots to wait. If he was patient, everything would come to him.

He began to sweat under his jeans and his flannel shirt was plastered to his back.

He turned his head slowly, sensing something live was nearby.

A large fourteen-point buck was about 20 feet away.

Russell barely shifted, readied his arrow without making a sound. He eyed the buck, pulled back on the bowstring, aimed for the neck, took a breath, and let loose.

At first, the only sound was the buck falling. Then there was the thrashing and gasps.

Russell ran as fast as he could. He had to get there while the animal's heart was still beating.

Sliding to his knees, he spread his body on top of the deer. Its struggles to breathe past a torn throat blasted the quiet around them.

Russell pulled out his knife, cleaned the mud away from the deer's neck, and made a surgical cut into the carotid. It was like a fountain spraying blood into the air.

He leaned over and watched the blood drain.

Chapter 49

Harry spent the morning driving the Porsche, tearing up the roads around Tucson. His insides were hot, dry, and scorched like the desert all around him.

He didn't care if he got tagged for speeding; some part of him even hoped the cops would nail him. He deserved it.

This separation from Gina, with little prospect of getting back together, had left his nerves exposed. And he'd passed that on to Abby.

Yeah, he deserved to be punished.

Without a word, Abby had changed her work hours to the graveyard shift. When he left work after 11:30 P.M., she would already be on the unit. He'd tried to talk to her when he spotted her around the apartment complex, tried to apologize. But she looked right through him.

And he deserved that.

He'd used her as a surrogate without telling her there were strings, strings that were unraveling but not yet broken.

He'd allowed her to take him partway down a road he never wanted to be on. He'd given her false hope that sometime in the near future they would have an intimate relationship.

If he'd been thinking about someone other than himself, he would have realized that relationship was doomed from the start. What had happened was the only possible ending for Abby and him.

Harry's attention span was drifting when he signed in and took report; he was only half listening to the team leader.

The ICU, after all the excitement surrounding the gunshot-wounded men, had quieted down dramatically. Two of the men were still critical, but it looked like they were going to make it after extensive surgery. The other beds were taken up by a pair of kids who had OD'd at a teenage party. Only four patients was about as good as it gets.

"Lordy, what a day," the dayshift team leader said. "The kids are doing okay. Probably out of here on your time. But maybe someone ought to do something extreme to the parents."

"It's hard when you almost lose your kids to dope," he said.

"You're a pushover, Harry," she said. "The kids are okay but I'll be a lot happier when I come to work tomorrow and the bunch of them are outta here."

I'm out of here, too, and if I never see this place again, it will be too soon.

"You know the guy who bled out ... that Dommi Machado?"

Harry nodded.

I'll hang in for a couple of days and then I'm gone. Maybe I'll even start sleeping again.

"You know my boyfriend's a cop, don't you?"

"Huh uh."

"Well, Jorge told me that 'cause it involved firearms, they ran prints on all those guys to see if any of them were in the system."

"In the system?" She finally had his attention.

"Harry, you're not listening to me, you jerk."

"I am. I mean, now I am. Tell me."

"It seems the one guy, Machado, had broken parole in New York. He was pretending to be a Mexican. You can bet Jorge was pretty pissed off about that."

Harry was getting one of those moments that Gina got all the time. He could swear his eye was going to twitch.

"Go on!"

"So, I really do have your attention," she said, her voice laced with sarcasm.

Now she took her time. Played it up for all it was worth.

"Anyway, they've been looking for this guy for over a year."

She laughed. "Just another loser, the kind Arizona attracts like flies to dog shit. Too bad he had to get into an old-time shootout. My boyfriend said they might not have ever picked up on the dude, if he'd only kept a low profile, if he hadn't been so stupid."

"Where is he?"

"How do I know? Probably in the morgue."

"A New York parole buster?"

"That's what I said, Harry."

"Do they know his real name?"

"How would I know?" the team leader said.

"How about doing an old friend a favor?" Harry said, sidling up to her. "Maybe your boyfriend can get us the real name of the dead guy."

"Maybe he could, if I asked him." She picked up her purse and hung the strap on her shoulder. "But you're not an old friend, buddy," she said, smiling at him. "*But* you *are* a good guy, so-o-o-o..."

She pulled her cell out of a side pocket of her scrubs and punched in a number. "I'll ask him for you."

Chapter 50

Gina stepped up to her Fiat, which she'd retrieved from the police impound. She'd heard that blood was the hardest evidence to get rid of, but if any of it was still there, she couldn't see it.

It just looked like her little old lady sitting there patiently, waiting for her to hop in.

Gina wasn't hopping anywhere. She could barely find the energy to walk. All the excuses she'd given herself about her headache were bogus. She was used to ignoring aches and pains when she had to go to work. The past week was no exception.

She stared at the car. Her Fiat was the last thing Jenni had seen, other than the killer.

Maybe Russell wasn't the killer.

Maybe I'm wrong.

Gina's mind kept wandering, she couldn't focus on anything except that she knew for sure she had the damn flu. She was going home to bed and collapse.

She unlocked the car door, ducked under the canvas top, and slid into the driver's seat. Every muscle and joint in her body was screaming for relief.

The inside of the car still had a strange odor, probably from the detergents they'd used to clean it, but otherwise everything was the same.

Her head was so heavy, she laid it down on the steering wheel, tried to pull herself together so she could go home. She reached into her purse and found an aspirin bottle and dry swallowed two of them. Her throat was so raw, she choked before she could get the pills down.

What an awful day with Aaron Dobbs almost dying. After they pumped him up with fluids, Brad decided Dobbs could probably pull through without a blood transfusion.

Something Harry often said flipped through her head.

"Blood is dangerous. Think twice before infusing."

Gina smiled. She remembered listening to Harry, his soothing voice telling about his ICU experiences.

Chills swept up and down her body. He'd always taken such good care of her.

But she was alone now.

It's not that far. You can drive home and crawl into bed. You can do that. One step at a time. First thing, put the key into the ignition.

She turned the key.

Click.

And what did she expect after virtually sitting around for days? So much for step number one.

She picked up her cell and punched in Helen's number and was immediately put onto voice mail. Helen was probably driving—she would never answer the phone at the wheel.

Gina punched the direct dial for a local cab company.

"Lady, I don't like our drivers picking up passengers in an underground garage," the dispatcher said in a disgruntled voice. "Not only that, it's a damn madhouse around that hospital."

"Please! You won't have trouble finding me. I'm in a red Fiat in the employee parking lot, in the very last section. You'll spot me right away."

The line went silent.

"Listen, I always call your company when I need a cab. Doesn't that count for something?"

"Yeah, well." There was a really long pause. "Okay."

"I'm really beat. I'll wait in the car."

She described the car again and gave him the license plate number. He promised to send someone right away.

She put her head on the steering wheel again and must have gone out because the next thing she heard was someone tapping on the window. Her head jerked up.

"Hey, lady. Did you call for a cab?"

She looked into the kindest eyes she'd ever seen. "Oh, yes. Thanks so much for coming for me."

Bone Dust

She grabbed her purse. It felt like she'd stowed a block of concrete inside. Up and out, she locked the Fiat, and walked to the back of the taxi.

* * *

Helen had just fed Vinnie, who was sitting up in the living room and smiling at her when she came in.

"Well, aren't you the chipper one." Helen walked over and kissed his cheek.

"Now watch it! You'll end up as sick as I was."

"You are a silly lad. Never thought about that when we were in bed together, did you?"

"I have my priorities." He laughed. "Sick or not, my woman sleeps in my bed."

She sat down on the couch next to him, looked into his soft brown eyes. "Am I your woman, Vinnie? Are you my man?"

"Why do women always need to hear the words," he said, looking at her. He lowered his voice and grumbled, "I'm here, aren't I?"

"Tell me, Vinnie." She wrapped an arm around his waist and cuddled into him. "Tell me."

He bent over and kissed her neck. "Helen Trent, I'll love you forever ... I'm the luckiest man on earth that you would even consider being with such a broken-down schlub."

* * *

Mulzini had no solid leads on who murdered Jenni Webb.

He questioned the men she'd hung out with ... the ones he could find. They all said she was a fun kind of girl who changed partners frequently.

Mulzini took it all in, not sure what to believe and what not to follow up on.

It wasn't until he cornered Brad Rizzo in the ER that he got a real handle on the dead nurse.

"Jenni was running away from her roots," the doctor said. "That's why she came to San Francisco in the first place."

"So how did you happen to date her, Doc?"

"I'd just gotten out of a long-term relationship and I saw Jenni all the time in the hospital. We sort of fell into going out after work. It wasn't anything serious. We liked each other."

"I've talked to some of the men she dated," Mulzini said. "They seem to think she was a party girl."

"Seems to be a label many men use when they can't make a gal do what they want." The doctor seemed sad talking about the dead woman. "Jenni was just trying to find out who she really was. She was questioning what she wanted out of life."

Mulzini felt sad for her, too. "Had she finally decided?"

"It makes me happy to think she did. She'd stopped dating altogether by the time she moved in with Gina. Wanted more time to think. I do know she was spooked by one of the phlebotomists at Ridgewood—Russell Thorpe. They seemed to really hate each other. I saw them interact a few times in her unit."

"What do you think was going on?"

"I don't know, Inspector," the doctor said. "Why does anyone hate another person? The smallest slight can cause a lifetime feud."

Brad looked thoughtful. His gaze held Mulzini's. "I've been dealing with people for a long time, Inspector. To tell the truth, I don't really understand them any better today than when I first went into medicine."

Mulzini liked talking to the man. Time had made him more humble instead of arrogant like so many in his profession.

* * *

Digging into some of Russell's connections, Mulzini found one high school buddy who still lived in the area and seemed to keep in touch.

He went out to Carlin's Mortuary, where Eddy Tyson worked. Mulzini was a little spooked having to go to a funeral home to question a suspect. But that was the job.

They talked in one of the body reception areas with a fancy coffin in the room.

Mulzini thought it was a creepy place to question the guy, but Eddy seemed even more uncomfortable.

"So you went to school with Russell?"

"What's this about, sir?"

"I'm only questioning everyone who knew our victim."

"You told me her name before. I didn't know her." The guy kept shifting his weight from one foot to the other.

"But you know Russell Thorpe."

"Yeah. So what?"

Mulzini held a palm out. "Hey, nothing to worry about. Just checking out everything and everyone."

"Okay."

"What can you tell me about Russell?" Mulzini saw the guy start to relax.

"We used to hang out in high school. Sometimes I'd go to his foster dad's cabin with him."

"Uh-huh. That must have been fun. What did you guys do out there." Mulzini watched Eddy shift from foot to foot again.

"Oh, we mostly did some hunting. You know ... hung out."

Mulzini nodded like it was something he did every day. "Is it far from here?"

"Nah, it's about an hour north of San Francisco."

Chapter 51

It was late. Mulzini thought he should just call it a day. He wasn't on call anymore and going home to a nice dinner with Marcia, maybe a tall beer with a little television, might be a good way to end the day.

He got into his car, checked the GPS for the address Eddy had given him, and knew how warped he really was.

He convinced himself that it was a pretty straight shot to that cabin of Russell's, and it shouldn't take too long to make the roundtrip.

Also, it was either go now or let thinking about it ruin his evening and probably keep him from getting any sleep.

By the time he'd finished with Eddy Tyson, he had a pretty good handle on Russell's background—no known father and an alcoholic mom who died when he was fourteen. He'd ended up in a foster home.

At least he wasn't shoved back into the system—his placement couldn't have been all that bad.

Russell had finished high school and had taken some college before becoming a phlebotomist, Tyson had told him.

Never really been in trouble before. Or had he just been crawling under the radar?

It was after eight when he found the run-down cabin that was more of a shed. A deserted shed?

He left his headlights on, grabbed his Maglite, and headed for the cabin door, which was partially open. He reached for his gun and walked inside.

The first thing he noticed were glowing embers in the dilapidated stone fireplace. Then the rank smell of sweat washed over him, along with something else.

Blood!

He shone his flashlight on a work table near a utility sink. A few steps brought him to a wooden board that was covered with bread crumbs, discarded food wrappers, and a tin cup half filled with ... blood.

Jesus!

From whom? From where?

A shiver ran down his spine.

And all of it was fresh. If Russell did this, Mulzini must have just missed him.

There was nothing else inside worth looking at.

He went outside, started to circle to the rear of the shed when the light picked up wet footprints coming from the woods.

Better call the locals for some backup.

He got into his car, tapped into his computer, searched for a wifi connection.

Shit ... nothing to hook into.

He got on the radio and connected with the Sonoma County Sheriff's office. He explained to dispatch what was going on and was told they'd send out a deputy. It was going to be twenty to thirty minutes.

He turned off the headlights. Sat with his window down and listened. Nothing.

Better call Marcia.

But his cell phone couldn't pick up a signal.

"Screw it!" he mumbled.

He flipped the car lights on, shone the Maglite on the footprints, and started into the woods. It wasn't long before his light picked up the bony rack of a dead deer.

The closer he got, the metallic smell of blood burned his nostrils. There was blood everywhere. It had sprayed and covered piled-up pine needles and the buck's coat. Mulzini fought the nausea that was tickling his throat as he leaned over the dead animal.

There were two wounds—an arrow protruded from the neck and the carotid had been sliced open.

Why was the artery cut?

Bone Dust

The cup in the cabin! If it was Russell, all he wanted was the blood.

Wasted a life, left it to rot ... just for the blood.

Mulzini had seen a lot, but this scene was ugly. It made him shiver.

Chapter 52

The cabbie had to wake Gina when they arrived at the apartment complex. She'd spread out on the back seat the moment she crawled into the cab and had gone right to sleep.

Instead of driving away, he helped her inside and up the steps.

"Thank you. I would have had to crawl up without you."

"Listen, lady, you nurses saved my life too many times to count. The least I can do is give you a hand."

When she paid him, he refused a tip.

Inside, there was a brief moment of relief to be home, but her eyes were heavy and she was burning up. All she wanted to do was lie down.

"Must have a temp," she muttered as she pulled off her clothes, letting them drop onto the floor. She automatically walked to the shower and got the water adjusted and stepped inside the stall. Holding onto the wall with one hand, she ran soap over her body.

When she stepped out, the room started spinning and she sat on the toilet seat to steady herself. She zigzagged the towel over her body, only partially drying. Her eyes kept closing and her chest felt like it was collapsing.

Finally, she took her temperature. When she looked at the readout, she was too sick to care. All she wanted to do was go to sleep. She staggered into her bedroom and crawled under the covers. "One zero four ... too high."

* * *

Harry should have been in a good mood. Dommi Machado, born Dominick Colletti, was dead. But Harry wasn't used to celebrating anyone's death, even that miserable bastard's.

Maybe Dominick *had* tried to kill Gina a year ago.

He'd broken parole in New York and was probably hiding out right here in Arizona, waiting for an opportunity to return to San Francisco.

Gina was right all along. He had been there and tried to kill her.

That thought gave him a weird feeling.

How many times had he told Gina she was imagining things? You'd think by now he would have more faith in her intuition.

But he felt a real spark of hope. Maybe with Dominick out of the picture they could find their way back to each other.

At least he was going to try. The last two months without her had been unreal. He'd only gone through the motions of living when all he was doing was surviving.

He'd been lost without her.

Harry tried her phone again; it seemed like he'd been trying to reach her for hours. She still wasn't answering.

Things didn't feel right.

It was 10 P.M. when he finally gave in and called Helen and Vinnie. He had to know for sure.

Helen sounded sleepy when she answered.

"Hello?"

"All right, Helen, please don't hate me for calling so late."

"You have a way of calling at the worst times, and I don't mean the hour."

"Oh, I'm sorry. I'm really sorry. But I'm worried about Gina. She's not answering her cell, and that's just not like her."

"When have you not worried about that girl? Maybe she doesn't want to talk to you, dear boy."

"That's not it. There's something wrong. I know it in my gut."

"Mm-m-m, I just got my cell out while we were talking. Hold on. Let's see if there's a message from her."

Harry waited, holding his breath.

"Well, it seems she did try to call. Looking at the time, it must have been after she went off shift. Strange for her not to leave a message. I'll give you that, Harry."

"I can't shake this horrible feeling. Do you think you can go to her apartment and check on her?"

"Well, yes, now that you have me worried, too. I have a key to her place, so if she's sleeping I can pop in and out."

"I'll really owe you a big one for this."

"You bet your sweet ass you will, especially since you interrupted Vinnie and me getting reacquainted for the first time since he's been ill."

"Too much information, woman," Harry said, laughing. "Meanwhile, I'm catching a flight out of here. I've got some really good news for Gina."

"Like what?"

"Oh, no. You'll find out when I get to San Francisco."

"You listen to me, Harry boy, you don't get any favors if you don't give me those little tidbits."

There was a long pause before Harry answered.

"Dominick Colletti is dead."

"What!"

"That's it until I get there. And don't tell Gina. I want her to hear it from me."

"My lips are sealed."

* * *

Helen had been naked when she answered the telephone. Vinnie watched her put on underwear, jeans and a tee shirt.

"It's almost as much fun watching you put them on."

"Dirty boy," she said and blew him kisses.

"You weren't saying that five minutes ago."

"I wasn't worried about your sister then."

"I heard ... that must have been Harry?"

Helen was putting her belt through the loops of her jeans. "The good news: Dominick is dead!"

"Son-of-a-bitch!" he said, sitting up. "Does Gina know?"

"No, and you can't tell her. Harry made me promise and I can't breathe a word."

"How did it happen? I'll bet they probably caught the bastard doing something stupid. It would be just like him."

"I don't know all of the details. I was lucky to get that much out of Harry." She stopped to look in the dresser mirror and run a comb through her hair.

"Yeah. I'm sure Harry wants to tell her himself." Vinnie smiled. "Things are going to be a lot better for my sister, and probably Harry, too."

"I'm kind of worried about Gina," she said, stepping over next to the bed. "She's been under the weather and not herself since she and Harry broke up. But in the last few days, well, I think she's coming down with this rotten flu."

"I've been worried, too. She's been looking worn out. I try to be there for her without interfering, but I gotta tell you, she is one independent gal. I don't see how Harry puts up with her."

"You take that back, Vinnie Mazzio." She bent over to kiss him goodbye. "Or I'll never take these clothes off again."

"Okay, okay. How about, I don't know how *I* put up with her."

He pulled her down on the bed.

"You be careful out there, woman."

Chapter 53

Russell was speeding back to San Francisco. He was high.

High!

Out in space, in the universe, looking back at everything. This is what the Presence tried to teach him. He could be a super being now.

Drugs never gave him this; he'd never felt like this in his whole life.

Perception and awareness were exquisite. He sensed every nuance of living. So acute. Almost unbearable.

He, Russell, had drained the vitality from a living beast. All its blood had drained away.

Warm.

Thick.

Rhythmic, with its burst of energy.

Dad Todd had tried to tell him, but Russell never really understood until today.

He could still see his foster dad lying on top of an animal, covering it with his body after taking it down. A buck. A bear.

He would cut its neck and watch it drain.

Strip the skin and meat, then cut up the bones.

Dad Todd threatened, connived, and punished in the beginning when Russell wouldn't watch the draining.

But Russell had learned.

Now he wanted to drain again and again and again.

Chapter 54

Helen tried Gina's phone again.

No answer.

"You still can't get her?"

Helen tucked her shirt into her jeans as she answered Vinnie. "No. I'm going over there. I promised Harry. And I think something's wrong."

"Hey, she's my sister. I should be the one."

"Silly boy, I don't think you're ready to be up and about. Today was the first decent day that your lungs were clear and you didn't have a temp." She bent over the bed and gave him a kiss on the forehead. "I'll call you when I find out what's up."

"Thanks, Helen."

She gave him a bright smile and was out the door.

* * *

The streets were deserted when Helen eyed her surroundings and unlocked the Prius. Once seated, she immediately pressed the button to lock the doors, forgetting that they would lock automatically once she started the car.

She hated giving up her once-in-a-lifetime parking place right in front of her building. But it was for Gina.

You're going to owe me big time, Ms. Mazzio, RN.

Gina's apartment was only about ten minutes away and there was barely any traffic. She zipped there even a couple of minutes faster than her previous best time.

She looked up at Gina's windows on the third floor. Lights were blazing in every window but one, where the tree that Gina called her garden covered any interior light.

Well, she's definitely home.

Helen circled the block and finally squeezed into a parking spot a half a block away. She stepped out of the car, grabbed her purse, and hurried down the street.

Helen was a little jittery remembering some of the stories Gina told about walking alone at night in the Bronx. But there wasn't a soul anywhere.

She had the keys out and ready so she could slip into the building. She felt better once she was inside, hurrying up the three flights.

She opened the apartment door and shut it, set the chain in place. Helen never did that at her own apartment—she couldn't remember the last time she was so spooked.

Helen set her purse down on the kitchen table, tossed her jacket across a chair, and tiptoed toward Gina's room. She bit her tongue to keep from crying out.

Even at the doorway to the bedroom, she could see Gina was feverish and sick.

She rushed to the beside and pulled the comforter up around Gina's nakedness. Gina was out cold, shaking and moaning in her sleep.

Helen hurried back to the kitchen, pulled the cell from her purse. It rang only once before Vinnie picked up.

"How is she," Vinnie asked before she could speak.

"The girl's in bad shape."

"Is it the flu?"

"That's what it looks like. I'm going to have to wake her and get some meds down her throat, along with gallons of fluid."

"Maybe it would be better if you just let her rest." Vinnie's voice had dropped to a murmur.

"You go back to sleep and let me worry about Gina. I'm just going to make her comfortable and help her get what she needs."

Silence.

"Vinnie. She'll be all right, but I'm going to stay here tonight. I can't leave her alone."

"Call me."

"I will. In the morning. Promise."

* * *

Gina was drenched with sweat and the sheets were as wet as she was. Helen got fresh sheets, turned Gina on her side, and started changing everything.

After turning her again, she finished making the bed and slipped Gina into a pajama top.

Helen only had to look around to see what had happened. Gina's scrub clothes were scattered everywhere, the bathroom was covered with water, and a wet towel was flung on the toilet. She must have barely made it to the bed.

Her friend moaned, opened her eyes once, and Helen could tell Gina wasn't really seeing anything.

"It's okay, little one. I'm here."

She propped Gina up with pillows and covered her chest with a towel. "I want you to take these pills and with lots and lots of water. Can you do that?"

She said something that Helen couldn't understand, but when she put the meds in her hand, Gina tossed them into her mouth and reached for the bottle of water.

"Good girl. What a pro. Now drink some more."

After what seemed like hours of forcing fluids, she tucked Gina under the covers. Helen scrutinized her. She looked a little better. Her breathing was good, her pulse was a little rapid, but she was definitely better.

Helen shucked her own clothes and pulled out one of Gina's PJ tops and went to take a shower. Soaking under the hot water felt wonderful, but she was pretty well done in.

She turned out all the lights and crawled under the covers in Gina's spare room. All she had to do was close her eyes and she was gone.

Bette Golden Lamb & J. J. Lamb

Chapter 55

Harry grabbed all of his clothes from the rickety wooden dresser and crammed them into his suitcase. When that was settled, he sent a formal e-mail resignation letter to the hospital administrator. There'd be no glowing recommendation for his work this time.

He was also going to be out a big chunk of money.

Yeah, so what?

Dominick was gone from Gina's life, from everyone's life. Forever.

It was finally sinking into his head—Gina was free. Really free.

He left a note under Abby's door, apologizing again, but it was more for his benefit than hers. She'd wanted nothing less than having him as a lover, a mate. Friendship alone had never really been her goal.

She was a bright, pretty woman. She should have seen this coming. He'd warned her, but she'd refused to understand no matter how clear he tried to make it. She never believed him, never understood that Gina was the only one he wanted, the only one he needed in his life.

Without Gina, he'd stopped living. He needed to breathe again. He hadn't really been alive since they broke up.

He wanted to call Helen or Vinnie to find out what was happening with Gina, but he would have to wait for Helen to call him. That's what he'd promised.

As Harry boarded the plane for San Francisco, all he could think about was getting back to Gina.

He was never keen on flying and he made a deal with the powers of the universe. If they could just keep the plane from crashing, he'd do anything just so he could hold Gina in his arms one more time.

He was filled with hope. Hope for the two of them to be together again, hope that their love for each other would mend all wounds.

* * *

Inspector Mulzini was conflicted. Most of the time he went by the book, but this was one of those other times when things weren't black and white.

He had no legit reason to drag Russell Thorpe down to the precinct. He might qualify as a person of interest in Jenni's murder, but Mulzini really had nothing concrete to go on.

Someone had been out to Russell's cabin recently, but was it him or some other woodsy nutcase?

No way to prove it either way. Anyone could have walked into that disintegrating cabin. It was unlocked and deep in the boonies. Not even a *No Trespassing* sign posted anywhere that he could see.

It had been dark and he was working with a flashlight. It could have been anyone who left the fresh bloody animal carnage.

Even if Russell *was* the one to cause the mess out there, deer hunting was not a crime. Mulzini thought of that stag lying out there in the woods. What a travesty to kill a beautiful creature and just leave it there to rot.

He knew there were plenty of cults that used blood, both their own and that of animals, as part of their rituals, but it was disgusting as far as Mulzini was concerned.

By the time he got home, it was after ten; he sat in his driveway thinking, making no attempt to get out of the car and go inside.

After a while, Marcia came out with a tray of food and a Coke. "If you're going to spend your time out here working something out, have a bite to eat, big guy."

"How'd you know I was here?"

Marcia laughed. "You've been doing this for years. Think about it. How many trays have I brought to you while you worked out some problem?"

"Maybe once ... or twice—"

"A week ... or a month?"

The glow from a full moon shone on her face; they looked at each other for a long moment. Sly grins turned to laughs and Mulzini took the tray from his wife.

"I'm going in now," she said. "I'll see you when I see you."

Mulzini took a big bite of the healthy tuna fish salad sandwich. While he chewed, he wished, as he often did, that his wife would stop trying to keep him alive forever. All he really wanted was a triple grilled cheese sandwich packed with bacon.

He sipped the Coke and thought about Gina and Harry.

It had caught him off guard when Gina told him that she and Harry had split. If he were a betting man, he would have put a C-note on them to be one couple that would make it.

Yet, something always seemed to go wrong for his nurse friend. Smooth sailing was never part of her crystal-ball vision.

As they say, life is shit ... and then you die.

Chapter 56

Russell's high bottomed out, was gone by the time he walked into his apartment.

His mind was full of confusion; his thoughts jumped from one to another in no particular sequence. He paced around the work table, moving faster and faster until he almost slipped and fell.

Everything hurt inside.

Pain! More pain.

He flung open a drawer, pulled out a straight razor with one of his best bone handles. He looked at one arm, shifted to the other, then back and forth until he found the right spot.

He cut deeper than he ever had before, watched the blood race from the wound, spill onto the table until it formed a growing puddle.

Pain.

Nothing stopped the pain.

He drained, but there was still the pain.

He pressed a hand over the wound, thought of Jenni. Her blood had sprayed everywhere.

He should have left her alone, should have ignored her.

But she laughed. Laughed at me.

His mother had laughed when she caught him watching her having sex with a man. His foster sister laughed at him, too.

Jenni laughed and called him Russ ... wouldn't stop. Russ ... Russ ... Russ.

The nurses laughed. Women laughed. Gina laughed.

But no more.

* * *

Russell stood outside Gina's apartment house. It was after midnight and everything was quiet except for the terrible static that filled his head.

Bette Golden Lamb & J. J. Lamb

He looked at the window where he'd seen Gina the last time he followed Jenni to the apartment house. He stared at the window for a long time. He was waiting.

Waiting.

He noticed a tree growing up next to one of the outside windows.

He'd seen that tree in the daylight. It was a rich green, thick with leaves, leaves that he could hide in, like he hid from his sister in the surrounding woods at Dad Todd's cabin.

He would hide while she stalked him with her bow and arrow; she wanted to use him for target practice, wanted to kill him. She would keep him treed for hours sometimes, or until Todd came looking for him and chased her away.

His head was pounding as he crossed the street, walked up to the tree, reached up for the lowest limb, grabbed it, and pulled himself up.

Up. Up.

He sat on one of the highest limbs and tried to see through the glass, see if Gina was in the room, but it was dark inside.

The window was cracked open enough so he could wedge fingertips under the frame. Stuck. He tried again and again, harder and harder until he threw himself off balance and almost fell.

He gave it one more shot; it started moving up bit by bit, inch by inch. He avoided pushing too hard, fearful of a telltale squeak. Static filled his head, growing louder and louder with each push.

Quietquietquietquiet!

* * *

Gina could hear a hear a faint voice from deep within: "Get up! It's a work day. Get up!"

Her head was heavy, almost made her tumble forward as she struggled out of bed. She shuffled to the bathroom in the dark, sat on the toilet, started to doze.

290

Bone Dust

Trying to shake off the drowsiness, she stood, filled the washstand glass with water. Drank. Filled the glass again and again. It wasn't working. Her eyes fixed on the glass. It was dirty ... needed washing.

Gina headed back to her bed, thought she wasn't going to make it, had to swim through the heavy, thick air. She was so hot, and her head was pounding.

Not the flu ... just sleepy ... need a little more rest ... a few more minutes.

Curling back under the covers, she drifted off, thinking she was still sitting on the toilet staring at the dirty glass.

* * *

Russell finally lifted the window all the way and eased into the room. His eyes adjusted to the darkness; he could make out a bed, someone was in it.

Gina. Sleeping.

He wrapped his hand around the human bone-handled razor in his pocket.

Jenni would never laugh at him again.

Now Gina would never laugh at him again.

He stumbled in the dark and fell.

* * *

Helen jumped at a sound. Reached for the bedside light.

A hand grabbed her wrist and squeezed.

She screamed.

The attacker flung himself onto the bed, straddled her hips.

* * *

Gina heard a scream ... from far, far away.

Helen! Someone was hurting Helen.

She stood, almost fell over, grabbed the nightstand. She moved on wobbly legs to the hallway, then went hand over hand along the wall until she reached Helen's room.

"Get off me, you bastard!" Helen screamed.

Gina could see the shapes of two people struggling violently on the bed, the one on the bottom twisting and kicking viciously.

Gina tried to rush to the bed, but her legs moved in slow motion. She reached out through a sea of goo to grab the bedside lamp, held it high, and brought it down hard against the attacker's head. As the intruder started to tumble over, she struck again.

Helen jumped out of the bed, flipped on the overhead light. They both stared down.

Russell Thorpe was on his back, out cold. A straight-edge razor was splayed out on the floor, just beyond the fingertips of one hand.

Gina pointed to Helen's chest.

A spread of blood was blossoming across the PJs, where Russell had slashed her.

* * *

Mulzini, still sitting in his car in his own driveway, was on the last bite of the tuna sandwich when he heard the radio call. He recognized the address—Gina's apartment building.

He backed out of the driveway, planted the mobile police light on top of the car, and sped off.

When he arrived, three police cars and an EMT vehicle were parked haphazardly outside Gina's apartment house. Red, blue, yellow lights flashed out of synch with each other.

Every window in the building was flooded with light that framed the tenants looking down on the scene.

Russell was cuffed and a pair of SFPD cops were escorting him to a squad car.

Jeez!

Mulzini flipped open his wallet to show his badge and hurried up the steps to Gina's apartment. The door was open. Gina's friend Helen, her ashen face contradicting her wise-cracking at the EMTs, sat with a pressure dressing plastered against her chest.

"You should come with us," one of the EMTs said. "That's a nasty gash. Could use some stitches."

"I'll steri-strip it and it'll never leave a scar. Besides, I can't leave my friend. She's pretty sick and I'm her nurse."

Mulzini looked closer at Gina, who was sitting in a chair, staring glassy eyed.

That's one sick duck.

Gina was covered in a robe and looked as though someone had pulled her plug. Blood-less face, totally stunned.

Mulzini nodded at Gina, who didn't respond, then turned to Helen and said, "Remember me?"

"Who could forget the great Mulzini?"

"Listen, you go with these guys. Really. I'll stay with Gina. Don't have to be a medic to see she's got the flu bug real bad."

"Yeah, she's pretty damn sick," Helen said.

"I'll take care of her until you get back."

Helen looked closely at him for a moment. "Okay, boys. Let's get this over with. Take me, I'm yours."

The EMTs laughed. "Yeah, sure," one of them said.

Chapter 57

Mulzini finally got Gina to drink a glass of juice, then tucked her into bed. He thought everything was nice and calm now until she started crying.

"Hey, hey. It's all right, Gina. That Russell guy is going away, and for a long, long time." He pulled a tissue from a bedside box and handed it to her. "And I'll bet when it's all said and done, we'll get what we need to hang Jenni's murder on him, too."

"I know. It's not that."

"What is it?"

"Harry ... he's still gone."

"Listen, forget about Harry for now. You need to rest. I'll be sitting in the living room until Helen gets back. Take a little nap and don't worry."

* * *

Harry used his key to get into Gina's building and hurried up the stairs. When he opened the door, Inspector Mulzini was sitting on the sofa staring back at him.

"Heck of a way to spend my day off, wouldn't you say?"

"Where's Gina? I thought Helen would be here."

"Gina's resting; asleep, I hope."

Mulzini stood and they shook hands. "It's been a while."

"Has something happened to Gina?"

"She has the damn flu ... like everyone else."

"Well, what happened to Helen? Why isn't she here?"

"Don't worry, she's okay. I just checked in with the Ridgewood ER. They're about to release her. Seems that lab tech, Russell Thorpe, came here to kill Gina and got into the wrong room. Helen got slashed trying to fend him off, but Gina came in just in time to clobber the creep." Mulzini smiled. "That's the short version."

Gina's shaky voice called from the bedroom, "Harry? Harry, is that you?"

"Thanks for everything, Inspector. I think you can go now. I'll take care of her."

Mulzini laughed. "You nurses are all so bossy."

* * *

Harry wrapped his arms around Gina; they kissed, then kissed again and held onto each other for dear life.

"I've got some news for you," Harry whispered in her ear.

"Mmmmm, what?"

"Your ex is gone."

"Oh, Harry, I know that. But the bastard will be back."

He held her at arms' length. "When I say gone, I mean *really* gone. Like dead and gone."

Her eyes widened. "Dead? How? Are you sure?"

"He was killed in a saloon shootout in Tucson."

"Oh, my God, Harry."

He pulled her hard against him again. "It may take a while for it to sink in, but you're finally free of that scumbag."

"Are you really, really sure?"

He squeezed her tighter. "Without a doubt."

Her voice turned to a whisper. "I'm so glad you're here."

"Baby, I hate to say this, but you look like hell."

"And I always thought you were so romantic."

He buried his face in her neck, kissed her several times. "I missed you, doll. Oh, God, how I missed you!"

"I don't know why you love me, Harry ... I'm such an idiot."

He eased her back down onto the pillow, pulled the comforter up around her shoulders, and kissed her lips.

"Yeah, but you're *my* idiot."

The End

About the Authors

Bette Golden Lamb, a feisty ex-Bronxite, writes crime novels and plays with clay. Her sculptures and other artistic creations appear in exhibitions, galleries, and stores. She also hangs out with her 50+ rose bushes, or sneaks out to movies when she should be writing. Being an RN is a huge clue as to why she writes medical thrillers and Sci-Fi novels. Award-winning *The Organ Harvesters-Book II* is her latest, a dystopian medical thriller.

J. J. Lamb intended to become an aeronautical engineer/pilot, but was seduced by journalism. An AP career was interrupted by the Army, which gave him a *Top Secret* clearance; a locked room with table, chair, and typewriter; and the time to write short stories. A paperback PI series followed, the most recent of which, *No Pat Hands,* a 2014 Shamus Award nominee from Private Eye Writers of America.

The Lambs live in Northern California.
www.twoblacksheep.us

About the Author

www.ingramcontent.com/pod-product-compliance
Lightning Source LLC
Chambersburg PA
CBHW062125170626
46813CB00002B/569